The End of Spring

The End of Spring

by Sahar Khalifeh
translated from the Arabic by Paula Haydar

Interlink Books

An imprint of Interlink Publishing Group, Inc.
Northampton, Massachusetts

4-08 Amazon 15⁰⁰

First published in 2008 by

INTERLINK BOOKS
An imprint of Interlink Publishing Group, Inc.
46 Crosby Street, Northampton, MA 01060
www.interlinkbooks.com

Copyright © by Sahar Khalifeh, 2008
Translation copyright © Interlink Publishing, 2008

Library of Congress Cataloging-in-Publication Data
Khalifah, Sahar.
[Rabi' harr. English]
The end of spring / by Sahar Khalifeh ; translated by Paula Haydar.
p. cm.
ISBN-13: 978-1-56656-681-0 (pbk.)
I. Haydar, Paula, 1965– II. Title.
PJ7842.H2938R3313 2007
892.7'36—dc22
2007029682

Cover painting: "The Wall" by 'Abed 'Abdi
Reproduced by permission of Resistance Art: www.resistanceart.com

Printed and bound in the United States of America

To request our complete 40-page full-color catalog, please call us toll free at 1-800-238-LINK, visit our website at www.interlinkbooks.com, or write to Interlink Publishing, 46 Crosby Street, Northampton, MA 01060
email: info@interlink books.com

Contents

Part One   1
Part Two   163

Notes   277
Acknowledgments   281

PART ONE

1

He was an artist by nature. Everything he saw caught his eye. Every scene was a painting: a woman hanging laundry, a child playing, a cat napping, a kite flying in the sky, a butterfly flitting over a flower, over meadows in the spring.

"That's beautiful," the art teacher said to him. "But is that what you see? Why don't you draw what is really around you?"

A muscle in his temple twitched and he cast a glance somewhere off to the right. His eyelids remained half closed as if he were about to fall asleep, but his sideways glance betrayed his secret: he was a delicate boy, sensitive, gentle. And that was exactly what the art teacher explained to his father the bookseller. But his father just stood there blinking and scratching his head.

"Okay, fine—but what about it?"

"Your son is great," the art teacher said. "The best in his class."

The father blinked and scratched his head some more. "But the boy is always daydreaming."

"Because he is talented," the teacher said. "Because he is a dreamer. He is the best student in my class."

That was what sent the father home that evening with a brand new watch in his hand. He had seen it at the shop near the mosque, the shop where his neighbor sold watches and sunglasses. But the boy seemed bewildered.

"A w.. w.. w.. watch?"

He picked it up and turned it over and over, examined it out of the corner of his eye with the strange look that made his face seem almost deformed.

"It's a very valuable Swiss watch. It's digital."

"I.. I.. ha.. ha.. have a w.. w.. w.. watch," the boy stuttered.

"That watch is old," the father rushed to say. "This one, though—this one is digital. Never one minute too fast or too slow."

The boy didn't respond. He kept fiddling with the watch and muttering something inaudible. At last the father got fed up. "So what is it you want, then?"

The boy's eyelids drooped as though he was about to fall asleep, and the muscle in his temple twitched. "Sunglasses," he whispered.

His father looked at him in astonishment, unable to comprehend why the boy would refuse a valuable Swiss watch and instead ask for a ten-shekel pair of sunglasses made in China. The boy had seen them two days earlier and had stood there gazing at them like someone possessed. Was it because the boy was...? No, not true. As the teacher said, he was the best student in his class. That meant the boy was not stupid, not semi-retarded. He was doing well in school. That meant he might graduate one day and get a scholarship to study abroad. This boy, really? He was hardly suited for staying in the country, never mind leaving. He was always dreaming, always absentminded. Always half asleep and stuttering. But no, the teacher said he was a productive boy, talented, the best in his class. Okay, then, the glasses and the watch.

And so his father bought him the digital watch and the sunglasses, too. But the boy's demeanor didn't change. He continued moping and stuttering and looking out of the corner of his eye from behind the sunglasses, sometimes to the right, sometimes to the left, and sometimes as though he were asleep or partially blind. He continued to work behind the counter at the Galilee Bookshop, reading magazines and newspapers and selling books and notebooks without making a sound.

His father owned the shop. He'd begun his career just after the Nakba. He started out delivering papers on bicycle. Then after the Naksa, when the rest of Palestine was occupied, his career advanced in a big way, because the town of Ayn al-Mirjan suddenly expanded with a new influx of displaced people that was heavier even than the time before. The mosque and its number of worshippers grew and so did the *waqf*, which funded the construction of a string of little shops. He chose the smallest one and the one right under the stairs, and got it for practically nothing. In that way he became well known in the town for being intelligent and educated, because he sold printed material and because his name appeared in *Al-Quds* as a correspondent. Sometimes we would read with great interest about our unknown little town whose name had become a household word thanks to our very own courageous correspondent Fadel al-Qassam. We would read, for example:

> Our correspondent Fadel al-Qassam reports that the municipality of Ayn al-Mirjan has decided to relocate the town dump outside the borders of the municipality at the insistence of the town's inhabitants and summer vacationers due to the mosquitoes, the flies, the disgusting stench, and crawling pests that abound in summertime.

Or:

> Our correspondent Fadel al-Qassam reports that the inhabitants of Ayn al-Mirjan refugee camp attacked the settlement of Kiryat Shayba, smashing the sewer pipes and causing waste to flow into the streets and almond groves. A skirmish with settlers and the armed forces ensued.

That is how we came to know that our correspondent Fadel al-Qassam was a man of principles who was not afraid of the army or the occupation and who spoke the truth without a care. And that explained his disappointment in his son Ahmad, who did not care about speaking the truth or telling a lie or saying anything else. He usually did not say much at all, always daydreaming and stuttering, and casting strange glances that gave the impression he was hiding some secret or some strange impediment, God forbid. But no, that was not the case. He was a nice boy, very polite. He was always saying "thank you" over and over again, and then swallowing the rest of his words by muttering and making obscure sounds before withdrawing behind the counter to read or draw or scribble. Whenever anyone came in asking for a newspaper or drawing pad, he would fetch it without speaking, take the money and count it from the corner of his eye before putting it into the drawer and resuming whatever he had been doing before: reading or drawing or scribbling.

When his father gave him the sunglasses, Ahmad smiled cautiously, took the glasses into his hands as though they were a priceless work of art and polished them several times, fogging them first with his breath. Then he put them on with utmost care. And from that moment forward, he never took them off except to go to bed or take a shower.

One day, his father took him up into the hills to take a picture of the town dump, because the new dump had become the cause of a new conflict between the municipality and Ayn al-Mirjan refugee camp. The municipality had moved Ayn al-Mirjan's town dump outside the town's borders, right near the camp, and the smoke and odors from the burning garbage reached the camp with every little breeze and gust of wind. The inhabitants of the camp complained, but the municipality didn't heed their complaints, so they decided to publish them. And that is what brought our correspondent on that particular afternoon, with his camera and his son Ahmad, to that place to take pictures.

2

Ahmad looked at his watch and then at the numbers on the camera and noticed the discrepancy. His father explained that the numbers on the camera were counting the pictures whereas his Swiss watch was counting time. He pointed to the opening and spoke slowly so his son could understand.

"See this? These numbers are for counting the pictures, and this thing in the middle is the lens. If we press on this button the zoom goes out and if we press it again the zoom comes in. Look through here."

The boy pushed the camera away from his face in alarm.

"What's the matter? What's wrong?"

The father looked through the viewer and saw a dog, huge and close, in the zoom lens. The boy had been frightened by the dog. That meant that the boy was very soft, very delicate. He needed to be toughened up and hardened. How could such a boy live in this environment? It was a very difficult town to be in with the occupation and tribunals. There were men underground and aboveground and military operations and funeral processions. There was Ayn al-Mirjan refugee camp, where he and his family had taken refuge more than fifty years ago, when he was still a young boy. There he had begun his life like everyone else in the camp—down in the dirt. Then came the boxes of Chiclets, then the trays of *halawa*, then the newspapers. He would hop from one sidewalk to another, onto the streets, in front of the pedestrians and the cars, shouting tirelessly, "News! News! Fresh and hot off the press! Read all about it!" A few cents here and a few cents there until he was able to afford his first sidewalk stand, then the little kiosk near the mosque, and then the shop. But all through those steps and phases he hungered and thirsted and suffered in the cold and faced the neighborhood dogs and cats, and had it not been for his thick alligator skin he would be like so many others still waiting behind their sidewalk stands. That's what it took to survive in this town: thick alligator skin and a hard heart and alert, unblinking eyes. How was this son of his going to make it with his soft heart like a girl's and his tied tongue that stuttered and his eyes hiding behind those sunglasses?

"Take off those glasses and come here," he shouted.

The father was standing on a big rock that overlooked the garbage dump and the almond groves and the settlement of Kiryat Shayba just at the edge of the horizon. The boy looked up, bewildered and nervous, and didn't respond. Again his father shouted. "I said come here!" Ahmad started walking sluggishly, looking beneath his feet and choosing where to place each foot with amazing slowness. His father grew furious and lost his patience. "Come on. Move it!" He kept staring at him until the boy got close enough for him to grab. He pulled the boy so hard he nearly fell on top of him. But he regained his balance, held his son to his chest, and turned the boy's face toward the horizon and the almond groves.

"Look and see," he said, panting, as he looked over the boy's head. The father yanked the sunglasses off of his son's face, causing the boy to tremble with fear. The father sensed his son's fear, which made him even angrier and more impatient. But when he felt his son's heart pounding under the palm of his hand, he melted with compassion. His voice quavered and cracked and he was filled with sadness. He said again, "Look and see." He pointed to the dump down below them, then to the settlement of Kiryat Shayba, and then to the sprawling refugee camp, and he pushed the camera into his son's hands, pressing hard on the boy and on the camera.

"Look through the camera. Look and take a picture. Taking a picture with a camera is like making a drawing. Look and take a picture."

The boy looked and saw the trees and the faraway horizon and the wide open space and the birds. He saw the flowering almond trees and apricot trees and under them the meadows of red anemones and rose mallow and snapdragons. The dog was there, too, amid the greenery, moving away from him toward Kiryat Shayba, toward a green backyard behind the fence. In the middle of the yard a little girl was swinging. She was blond, like a doll. Her hair was in a ponytail, and the ponytail was flying in the wind. Up it would go and then come back down and fall onto her shoulders only to fly back up again like the tail of a kite. The girl was like a butterfly, or a little bird with two wings.

His father noticed the camera was directed to the west, so he turned his son's shoulders to the east.

"The picture is over there," he said angrily.

That evening the father said to his wife, Umm Ahmad, a plump, fair-skinned woman who loved to eat and who worshipped her son, "Umm Ahmad, I think you and I might have spoiled the boy."

She didn't look up. She went on chewing and knitting. She took her time before saying, "What do you mean we spoiled him? Your son, God protect him, is neat and well-behaved and smart in school and his shirts are always as clean as can be."

"But the boy is like a little girl. He's so tender and skittish. His whole life he's never opened his mouth to say yes or to say no."

She looked at him without getting excited and quietly said, "He can learn from your son." She was referring to his other son, Majid. He didn't respond, just kept playing with the remote control and flipping from one channel to another until he landed on *Ghazl-il-Banat*, an old film starring Naguib al-Rihani singing with Layla Murad. He smiled and sighed and asked God to have mercy on Umm Majid and thought nostalgically about the old days. Umm Majid had been dark-skinned, the color of wheat bread. Her eyes were small, like Japanese eyes. But when she laughed and showed her pearly teeth, her eyes shined like diamonds. She had the hearty laugh of a hashish smoker, the kind of laugh that issued from the bottom of her belly. She would suck in a deep breath and slap his thigh and make him feel that fire consume his body. And she would sing to him in her captivating voice, "When will time be kind to us, O handsome one?"

"Allah! Allah!" he would shout with excitement and joy. He had set up his first sidewalk stand with her. He had his first son with her. And with her he also suffered the bitterness of life in the refugee camp, in a tiny room the size of a chicken coop, amid the clamor of people and their secrets and their junk all over the street. Despite their meager means, he had been happy, because Shahira and her mother used to sing at weddings and parties and play the tambourine and the tabla like gypsies. Later on Shahira got even better when she began to sing and play the oud. That was why he married her, against his father's wishes, his father who said that anyone who would sing in people's houses was a gypsy and a tramp, a lowlife that did not deserve their family name.

"What family name?" he said to his father. "Dad. We're living in a refugee camp!" But his father was from Haifa, from Wadi Nisnas. He still had the key to their house and a picture of the Haifa carpet gallery that had displayed the most expensive and most beautiful Persian carpets.

As he watched al-Rihani, he shook his head and laughed, thinking about those old days and comparing them to now. He looked over at his wife sitting knitting, looked at her tires of fat and flesh and remembered his first wife and how she danced and sang and laughed and shone with smiles, her eyes sparkling, her hips undulating. Majid had taken after her. Majid inherited her lightness of spirit and sweet voice and movement. This other one's son, on the other hand, was heavy just like his mother—a heavy presence and a thick tongue and heavy steps and movements. How was he going to succeed in the world? Was there any place he would fit? But the teacher said he was the best in his class.

3

When Majid came home from the university Thursday evening, his father encouraged him to take his brother to the athletic club to lift weights and play billiards. The boy was in need of some firming up, so that he'd be more like him, more like his brother, the son of Shahira, who knew how to joke around and hang out with the guys and get into trouble.

"You've got to be a man in this world, hard as granite, and this boy is like a girl. His muscles are like yogurt. He needs some tightening up! Take him and firm him up!"

So as not to disappoint his father, the older brother did exactly that. He took his brother to the athletic club and stood him there against the wall to watch him work out and watch him examine his muscles in the mirror.

The boy stood there five minutes, ten minutes, and then crouched in a corner and began reading a copy of *Al-Quds* he found on a chair. He read his father's name and saw the picture he had taken under his father's supervision of Ayn al-Mirjan dump and a long column about the dump and the people's complaints. He hadn't read the column or seen the picture, because his father had stopped bringing the newspaper home or taking him to the store. Instead he encouraged him to play with the kids from the neighborhood or from school. He told him that books and reading were nice and worthwhile, but life required *gusto*. When he saw that his son's expression was grave, as usual, and that he was considering the meaning of those words, the father explained: "To make a living, you've got to have *gusto*. To have a life like all these people, you've got to have *gusto*. To survive in a difficult and harsh town like this one, you've got to have *gusto*. When you go to demonstrations and throw stones, can you flee without jumping and running away with *gusto*?"

Ahmad didn't answer the question, because he didn't take part in demonstrations and he didn't throw stones and he didn't jump or run. He only fled. Every time things flared up and the kids went out into the streets to protest—at first shouting and pandemonium, then stone throwing, then tear gas—he would sneak away without making a sound and hide in some faraway place: in the bathroom, under the stairs, behind a garbage bin, in the Ayn al-Mirjan cemetery. There he would stay, not daring to breathe, until the day's little battle was over, and then he would go home without anyone noticing. When his mother would see him soiled with dirt from the cemetery or grime from the garbage bin, or cobwebs and gunk from underneath the stairway, she would hit her face in despair and call to his father. "Look at your son," she would shout. "Look!" The father would pretend not to hear and let her go on squealing. "I don't understand," she would yell. "If they shoot your son, or arrest him, then what will you do?" The man would stay right where he was without moving, reading his paper and smoking. Then he would give his son that meaningful look as if to say, "You're such a con artist!" And the boy would withdraw to the bathroom and let his mother go on squealing and begging God to take her away, and along with her take the demonstrations and the *tanzims* and the schools, because all they did was lead children to this. The man would jump out of his seat on hearing that and utter the sura, "*La hawla wa la quwwata illa bil-llaah.*"

Majid looked over at his brother and saw he was reading the newspaper, not watching him or looking at the equipment or the machines or his muscles, not learning anything. He shook his head with disappointment and disgust and muttered, "What a blob." He focused on how white his brother was and how red, how heavy his eyelids and how puffy his cheeks. And he remembered his father's fears. His brother really was a weakling, a fat bear like his mother. But he wasn't really fat, not as fat as he used to be. Maybe the way he'd shot up recently made him seem not as fat as Majid remembered. During previous vacations he had seemed a lot fatter. Had the boy grown? Had he reached puberty? A fourteen-year-old? He himself had reached puberty much later, but maybe because of his weight and height and width and because of his mother, who stuffed him like a pig, maybe Ahmad was maturing earlier. His voice was raspy and his features were more like a young man's despite his father's complaining and griping. "You're like a girl. Come on! Move it!" But he wouldn't move. He just sat there in front of the television watching movies or Michael Jackson dancing on MTV.

Majid thought of himself at that age. Had he watched MTV? In his day there was no MTV or CNN. Of course there was dancing and singing and music. But he had lost his mother and was left in the custody of a sad and lonely widower. His house had been like a stable. Every once in a while his grandmother would pity him and take him for a few days. Then she would bring him back home, huffing and puffing, and tell his father, "Thank God I'm too old to have any more children!" She was "an old lady" now, as she used to say, barely able to get around without crutches. On the other hand, when it came to parties and weddings, by God she was able to summon strength! She ran to those parties like a spry young goat, taking with her a young dancing girl in a sparkling dress and castanets. At the end of the night she would return to the camp with wedding favors in her pouch and pay for the dancer and lots of food and *knafeh*. She had taken him to those celebrations many times. He carried the tabla and followed as she rushed around. And when the dancing girl pointed to the lights and pinched his cheeks and said, "See all the electricity, honey?" he'd run with excitement toward the lights, his grandmother shouting, "Be careful with that drum!" "Don't worry," he would yell, without looking back. "I've got a good grip on it." And he would rush to stand in the doorway to get wedding favors and Jordan almonds.

That was the way it was for the son of Shahira. An orphaned child with disheveled hair and long fingernails like a chicken's claws, playing in the neighborhood with the other children, attending demonstrations—or else not attending demonstrations, but instead playing Arabs and Jews in the streets. When protests erupted and demonstrators headed off in some direction, he would follow with lots of enthusiasm, as though he were following a wedding procession. The only difference was that at wedding receptions they got favors and sweets, whereas at the demonstrations they got tear gas and beatings and bullets and arrests. That was the difference between his childhood and his brother's, and between his grandmother and his brother's grandmother, who'd left her daughter a house and olive groves and a piece of land. And his father complained and griped because the boy didn't have muscles? With all due respect, what was his father thinking? After all, does a person build muscles by eating honey and butter and drinking milk? Muscles came to boys like him who grew up in the streets. As for butter boy, let him enjoy his yogurt muscles and glasses of milk.

4

When he got back from his trip to the club with his brother, his father asked him, "Well, what did you learn?"

Ahmad looked to the right and then to the left, remaining silent and watching the TV news.

"Sit up straight and tell me what you did!" his father scolded.

His mother came into the room carrying a plate of *fattoosh* and pleaded, "Okay. Okay. Take it easy on him!"

"Be quiet, woman! Let me deal with the boy."

To the boy, he continued: "Tell me what you did. For God's sake, move!"

"I r.. r.. r.. read the article," the boy stuttered.

The man opened his eyes and ears wide. "What article?"

"The d.. d..," the boy said.

"Speak! Move!"

"The d.. d.. dump."

The father became furious and yelled, "Majid! Come here!" When Majid did not respond, the father yelled a second time. "Majid! Come here right now! Get a move on!" Majid came running with a towel in his hand and dripping hair.

"Yes, Dad?" He stood there, looking from one to the other and getting the feeling that something was uneasy in the atmosphere. "Is everything all right?"

His father stared at him with a look of anger and disappointment. "I told you to take him and firm him up. Not read newspapers and magazines."

Majid tried to say something, but his father continued. "This boy is your responsibility. Take him to the club. Take him to the café. Take him to hell if you want! Just make sure he stops sitting around here like a girl doing nothing. You get it?"

"Yes, sir."

"Wherever you go, he goes."

"Yes, sir."

"And during the summer, you take him everywhere you go."

Majid stared straight ahead and didn't try to argue, because arguing in this loaded atmosphere would make it very difficult for him to go out in the evenings.

"Should I take him along at night with the band, too?" he tried to joke lightly.

His father grumbled as he took a bite of food. "Stop being stupid!" He swallowed the bite and said in disgust, "He needs some muscles. He needs some firming up."

He turned to the boy and said angrily, "And you. Hand over that watch." When Ahmad didn't respond, the father shouted, "Hand over the watch and the sunglasses too. Move!" When the boy returned from his bedroom with the sunglasses and the watch, he found his father holding the camera. His father took the sunglasses and the watch and handed him the camera. "Tomorrow," he said to the brother, "You take him to the town dump and let him take another picture. Understand?"

"Yes, sir."

"Okay, then. Sit down. What are you doing standing up?" He pointed to the dinner table. Everyone sat down, and no one moved.

Later in the evening, the two brothers went to Ayn al-Mirjan dump. Ahmad led his older brother to the rock his father taught him to stand on to take pictures. Silently, he began taking pictures while Majid looked around, bored.

"Hurry up. Let's go."

Majid knew the refugee camp like the back of his hand. His grandmother still lived there, and most of his childhood had been spent there. He had friends and relatives there. That was why he didn't find anything of interest in the view, including the settlement a few miles off that had been there for several years and was still there. When it first went up, there had been a big uproar. Fighting and bullets and arrests. Then people quieted down when they gave up hope and got tired of it and got used to it and pretended to forget about it. Some of the guys worked there, in construction or sanitation or in the fields. Even Majid had worked there two summers ago, and made a little money without his father knowing. There were a lot of things he did without his father knowing: dancing, singing, and performing at parties and restaurants and festivals with his band. His band was a group of his college friends—one played keyboard, another flute, and a third the drums to Majid's singing and guitar-playing. He had a beautiful voice, and an even more beautiful build, and his *dabke* steps were famous among the students at his university and in Bethlehem and Ramallah.

But when his father asked him about the band, he downplayed it. "It's a student band. We sing patriotic songs at festivals."

"Wow. That's great," his father answered, with some mockery. But he didn't bicker with him about it, or scold him, or deter him. True, some people winked slyly and said, "Did he inherit the profession?" By which they meant his grandmother's profession. And the father would reply, "The boy is a very smart student at the university, and besides, it's not shameful for boys to sing and dance."

"He sure gets around," they would say.

"Gets around with whom? The ladies? So what? Would it be better if he sat around at home like a housewife?"

Majid heard his father's remarks and was delighted. He started thinking about becoming a professional singer and going to Egypt to make a recording. After all, was Hani Shakir any better? Was Mustapha Qamar any more handsome? Was

Kazem al-Saher taller? Majid had become quite famous in his own circle, but it was a small circle. The entire population of the West Bank was equal to the population of just one street in the Heliopolis section of Cairo, and all of Bir Zeit University, big as it was, would fit into a little corner of Haram Street or Muhammad Ali Avenue.

He said to his brother, "Take a picture of me."

The younger brother turned and asked why—with his eyes, not his tongue, which made the elder brother laugh.

"If I win the talent contest and my picture gets into the newspaper, I'll have a big present for you."

Ahmad smiled and gestured for him to move out of view of the dump, so Majid stood with his back to the west. Ahmad zoomed in and zoomed out until the settlement appeared behind his brother as if it were right there surrounding him. There was a tree and a red rooftop and a swing and a girl, a blond girl with a ponytail, sweet and pretty as a doll or a picture. Did she speak Arabic or Hebrew? Would she understand him if he spoke to her? No, she wouldn't understand him, and neither would she know how he stumbled over his own tongue. Was she shy, too, like him? She seemed to be his age or a little younger. What grade was she in? Did she have a Swiss watch? A digital watch? Would she speak to him if he spoke to her? She was a Jewish settler and her father was a Jewish settler and that meant her father owned a machine gun and had forelocks and was the scum of the earth. Ahmad's father called them that. The settlers were the dirtiest people. So her father was scum. Her, too. But she wasn't dirty. She didn't seem dirty or ugly at all. She was pretty. When she flew up in the swing, she laughed and bit her lip, her cheeks like two white apricots tinged with red. Was this scum? Was this ugliness?

His brother called to him. "What's the matter? Go ahead." Ahmad took the picture and then walked with Majid to the club. He stood there admiring his brother's muscles and watching him work out, but all the while his mind was on the swing, and the two white apricots tinged with red, and the ponytail.

5

The picture of the dump turned out to be expressive and clear, full of life. When you looked at it you could feel the sunlight and hear the rustle of the trees and smell the flowers as if you were standing right there in the heart of that place via the lens and the zoom. His father rewarded him by buying him a new camera and giving back his digital watch and sunglasses.

And Majid's picture was superb! Like Omar Sharif in his prime—or even better. The father examined the picture and wondered where Majid got those flashing eyes, despite his mother. Two big eyes, with long jet-black lashes. The boy really was as handsome as the picture. He belonged in the movies or on television, but he was here in the West Bank, in Ayn al-Mirjan. If he were in Cairo or Beirut, he would have become as famous as Abd al-Halim. Abd al-Halim was dead, though. So he could be like Marcel Khalifeh, singing for his homeland and his nation and his people, well known in the West Bank and everywhere from Cairo to Amman. But he was here, in the West Bank. And his beauty—was it real? He'd never seen his son as that handsome until he saw the picture. Was the secret the camera? The expressive, lively eyes—was that the camera or the person behind the camera? He smiled sorrowfully, because he knew that his slow, sluggish son, the one with the heavy presence and heavy steps, was not so lively. And he knew that photographing the real world was merely making a direct copy. But then again, when he took pictures, they did not come out with such beauty, such control, such movement. So perhaps the boy really was talented. From now on Ahmad would be in charge of taking pictures. Majid boasted that his picture was going to be enlarged and made into concert posters. He patted Ahmad on the head and tousled his hair and asked gleefully, "Happy, Champ?"

Ahmad smiled bashfully. He hesitated and thought about it. "S.. s.. so this m.. m.. m.. means I take pictures?"

"Yes, you take pictures!" the father replied. "Take pictures all you want!"

"W.. w.. what of?" he asked curiously.

"People, your mother, our house," the father rushed in. "The neighborhood kids, the traffic circle. Think of them as paintings. The teacher said you were good at that."

"P.. p.. pictures of the tr.. tr.. traffic circle?" he asked.

The idea had come to the father in connection with Majid's poster: an enlarged picture of Jerusalem hung everywhere, along with ads for singers and musicians.

"Shoot pictures of the town and the traffic circle near the mosque. Take a picture from the hill and widen the zoom. Make it come out like Jerusalem. Get my idea? If it comes out really good, we'll have it enlarged and make a poster, just like the poster of Jerusalem. Go ahead, son. You can do it."

From that day on, Ahmad took trips up the hill nearly every day to photograph the town. From the west, from the east, from high up. Then he climbed up onto the rock and shot pictures of the wild flowers and the almond blossoms and the peach and apricot blossoms and the native mountain stones and rocks and the swing and the doll-like girl with the ponytail.

6

Spring flowers filled his heart with delight. Red crown anemones, chamomile, bird's foot trefoil, fennel, and thyme. He walked on a carpet whose fibers were grasses and lilies and wild wheat stalks, yellow and red and blue flowers, and above the sun shone, a daffodil amid the white clouds. Her hair glinted like gold and silver embroidery, like waves of silk. When Ahmad's mother used to comb his hair, she would sing sweetly, "O what strands of lovely thread, threads of silken hair, O what lovely threads of silk, how lovely Ahmad's hair." And he cried whenever he heard that tune. Or any tune for that matter. So she stopped combing his hair. At first she thought she was pulling on his hair, so she stopped singing and took her time carefully combing through the knots. But when she went back to singing about the silken hair, he again cried so sadly it tore her heart. It was so strange. "Watch your son. Watch this," she said to his father. She turned on the radio and the child's face would wrinkle, right between his eyes, his lips would quiver, and then he would start crying. When the singing stopped, he stopped crying. When the singing started, he would start crying and trembling and sobbing with pain. His father shook his head and mumbled in amazement, "Praise God!" And so his mother started putting the amazing child who cried to music on display for all their friends and relatives. And they, too, were amazed by a child who cried to music.

Then the boy grew up and no longer cried to music. Instead, he stuttered and daydreamed and withdrew. Deep inside, he continued to cry to music, or upon seeing small things with feelings. A bird, a kitten, a setting sun, a girl. A blond girl with silken hair like golden threads shining in the light. He remembered the song his mother sang when she combed his hair, and he started humming as he took pictures and walked amid the flowers and the grass. "O what strands of lovely thread, threads of silken hair, O what lovely threads of silk, how lovely—How lovely whose hair? Whose hair? He enlarged the lens and widened it and brought her face in, right up to his own. The beautiful face was pale and delicate, the nose small like a peanut, her mouth red as the anemones. Why were her lips so red? Was it because she was so pale and her hair so blond?

He heard his name from behind the fence, over the bleating of the sheep and the shepherd's wooden flute. He heard it, deep and distant, so he turned his lens toward the sound and saw Issa, his brother's cousin from the camp, who was working in the field behind the fence where the girl and the swing were.

Issa waved to him with his dark hand and yelled loudly. An echo bounced off the hill and disappeared into the sun. He cupped his hands around his mouth and yelled again, a long, drawn-out "Ahmaaaaaad." The girl turned and saw him there with the camera, and he could see her eyes through the lens. Like the sky. Like windows open onto the western horizon where the flowers and the breezes and the wispy summer clouds were. He felt as though he himself were on the swing and his body swaying and fluttering like a bird. She came and went before the lens like a pendulum, and his heart rang out like a clock, like his brother's guitar. "Tick, tick, boom, boom. Tick, tick, boom, boom." Her eyes opened onto him like summer windows without curtains. How beautiful she was! A lock of hair flew up in the wind, and then wafted down.

"Hey, Ahmad. What are you doing here?"

Ahmad turned toward him. Now the voice was very near. Issa had climbed the steps toward the upper levels and came very close to the fence until he was within the camera's range. But he was still some distance behind the fence and the barbed wire that separated the settlement from the hill.

Ahmad was startled. When his father had found out that Majid was working in the Kiryat Shayba settlement, he had made a big fuss. He'd threatened to beat him and disown him. "I'll tell everyone you are not my son, and deny that I know you at all. I'll run it in the newspaper for an entire week so everyone will know you are cast out. Do you understand what I am saying?" That was two years ago. Ahmad had listened and recorded it all in his memory as he trembled with fear. But Majid had picked up his guitar, left the house, and gone to his grandmother in the refugee camp. When his father went to retrieve him, Issa had been sitting with him on the doorstep, smoking a cigarette and drinking tea and tapping his fingernails on the side of his cup. Issa's fingernails were black and his face was sunburned. His clothes were filthy and falling apart and the smell of sweat under his armpits was like cumin. Ahmad hated cumin and eating cumin, and every food that had cumin in it, because cumin was like Issa and the smell of sweat.

His father had said, "Okay, I can understand you working in their factories, but on the land? In Ayn al-Mirjan? Just great!"

Majid didn't reply. He kept his head down and looked at the ground. Issa, on the other hand, looked up insolently and said, "What's the difference?"

The grandmother came out and stood in the doorway. "It's okay. Don't worry," she said trying to calm things down. "They're just kids!"

The father clapped his son on the back of the neck and said vehemently, "Kids? Each one is the size of a bull. Kids! Get up, you son of a... Hand over that guitar. Damn you and damn that guitar. Go on. Get moving, right now. And if I ever catch you doing that again, I'll break your skull!" He turned toward the younger boy and repeated himself in order to drive the lesson home. "Working for the Jews on our own land. Isn't that wonderful! Sons of bitches!"

Then he addressed Majid again, who was walking with his head down, guitarless. "Do you hear what I am telling you?" Then he turned to the younger one, who was tripping over his brother's guitar. "And you, too. Do you hear what I am telling you?" When neither one answered, he shouted furiously, "And Issa, that son of a bitch, if I ever see you talking to him, I'll smash your head! Do you hear me?"

And here Issa was, looking at him through the sun's rays with his brown hand on his forehead. "Hey, Ahmad. What are you doing here?"

He had come very close to the fence, and Ahmad, too, had gotten very close without realizing. Ahmad's feet and a strange tingling all over his body, and his heart sounding out like a clock or his brother's guitar, had led him to the swing.

He stuttered shyly and timidly, "T.. t.. t.. "

"Wow! Nice camera!" Issa said, his eyes moving back and forth between Ahmad and his camera. "Let me see it."

Ahmad took a step back, even though there was a fence separating them and Issa's fingers were caught in the little openings in the wires of the fence.

"What's the matter? What are you afraid of?"

Issa turned and glanced behind him in the girl's direction then turned back with a nasty smile on his face. "You're afraid of her?" He waved his hand abruptly. "Don't worry," he whispered. "I know them. Are you scared of them?"

Ahmad didn't answer. He stood there with the camera in his hand and that strange feeling of confusion and excitement and tingling all over his body and his heart flip-flopping. He wanted to speak, to talk to him and get nearer to him, nearer to her. He wanted to cross over to where he was, to where she was, across the barbed wire. He wanted to ask about her. Her name, what grade she was in, her father's name. And that father of hers, did he have a machine gun slung over his shoulder? Did he have forelocks and a skullcap? Did he pray like a lizard in front of the wall like they did on television? Did he hate Arabs and shoot Arabs, or was he nice like his daughter? And this daughter of his, did she talk to Issa and call to him? How did she call him? Was she afraid of him because he was an Arab? What did she call him, and how did she call him? In what language? Did she pronounce the letter *'ayn* like an alef? And her name— what was her name?

Ahmad went a little closer to the fence and looked at Issa sideways and said, terrified, "W.. w.. w.. "

Issa laughed and yelled, "Stop stuttering. What's wrong with you? Are you scared?"

Of course he was scared—but he was scared of Issa and of his father, not of the girl. He was compelled by the girl on the swing. He moved closer. "W.. what's her name?"

Issa looked toward the girl and asked mockingly, "Afraid of her? She's just a little girl. A puff of air could blow her away…" He pressed his index finger to his thumb as if to squash something and said, "Like a louse."

He rubbed his two fingers together again and blew at them and then went back to looking at the camera enviously. "Let me see. Come closer. Closer. Lift it up."

Ahmad did not. He stood there motionless. He wanted to run away from Issa, but the girl—he wanted to know the girl's name at any price, even if the price was talking to Issa and disobeying his father and having his skull broken. And there was Issa saying the girl was like a louse and rubbing his fingers together as if he was squishing her. Ahmad hated Issa and was disgusted by him, but he came closer again and whispered, "W.. w.. what's her name?"

"What is it with you and her? Lift it up, I'm telling you. Let me see."

Ahmad backed up very slowly, then widened his steps. Then he turned around and started running. He ran and ran as if Issa were right behind him, following in his tracks, reaching for him, rubbing his fingers together and saying, "Like a louse."

7

Ahmad was intent on picking up the pictures himself.

"Good for you!" his father said. "I want you to be smart and energetic and take on some responsibility." He gave him the money to develop the pictures.

Unlike usual, Ahmad walked quickly to the studio, went right in, and immediately said, panting, "P.. p.. p.. p.. " The guy behind the counter smiled and repeated after him, "P.. p.. p.. p.. ?"

Ahmad's face turned beet red, his eyes squinted, his hands balled up into fists, and he swallowed his saliva. The photographer came out from behind the curtain and asked, "Are you Abu Majid's son? Welcome. How's your father?" Ahmad managed a smile, with some difficulty, and tried to look natural. "He's f.. f.. fine." The photographer turned and looked over at the curtain, because a customer back there was calling, "Let's go. I'm ready." The photographer turned. "Say hello to him for me, and tell him to stop by for coffee."

Ahmad shook his head without answering, looked at the guy behind the counter, and reached out his hand. The guy nodded his head and whispered, "P.. p.. p.. p.. ?" Ahmad felt his blood rising to his head. It was tingling and his ears were tingling and starting to itch. He scratched one ear and left the other in hopes of scratching it on the way out, pictures in hand. But the guy was mean and wanted to play around a little with the boy who had the tender face of a girl. He picked up the envelope and started shaking it and whispering, "P.. p.. p.. p.. " Ahmad could feel the tears darkening his eyes, so he did not look at him. He stayed there with his lids half-closed and his hand held out like a beggar. The guy leaned over the counter and came so close to him he was nearly touching his face.

"P.. p.. p.. p.. pictures of who? Who's the blonde?" he whispered. The boy didn't answer, so he went on whispering wickedly and laughing, "Who's the blonde?" A wave of bawling welled up into Ahmad's chest, then into his throat, then into his eyes. He pounced on the pictures, snatched them up, and took off running, running, running. Then he stopped and wiped his eyes and scratched his ears and blew his nose and slipped the pictures inside his sweater and held them tight with both his hands as if he were hiding something stolen. He rushed through the entranceway to the house, to the garden, and hid behind the olive tree. He sat on the ground and took out the pictures. He flipped through them, searching until he found it. A face surrounded by a halo of hair like the moon and sun. The small profile of a beautiful face of a big girl. She wasn't a little girl and she wasn't a woman, either. She was in between, like him. Was she embarrassed about her age too? Did she lie about it sometimes and add a year or two when someone asked, "How old are you?" Was she embarrassed about the changes in her body and her voice and the hair under her arms and there in that other spot? Did she allow her mother to bathe her? Did she get embarrassed and yell, "No!" if someone tried to come into the bathroom when she was undressed? Did people make fun of her voice the way his brother made fun of his voice? But girls only have one voice that doesn't change. It changes a little, but it doesn't crack and turn into two voices. Did she have things to hide? But Jews don't hide their things like Arabs. They put everything they have out on display for people to see, for the sun to see, until their skin gets as brown as a baked potato with strange freckles on it. Did she have freckles? He looked at the pictures, examining her. He saw a few freckles around her little peanut of a nose, and he saw a red mouth like an anemone and big white teeth, bigger than the little jawbone could handle. But once the jawbone grew and the face grew, the teeth would fit right, as his father said. He hadn't said it about her, but about him, and she was like him, the same age.

Ahmad touched his teeth and his molars and said to himself, "For sure she hasn't lost her 12-year-old molars yet." Then he felt his neck where his Adam's apple would be and grinned at himself, because he didn't even have an Adam's apple. And girls didn't have Adam's apples either. They had apples somewhere else, two of them, and later they would grow into watermelons like his mother's. He laughed at the analogy and the comparison. Where was this one's chest compared to that! He looked through the pictures trying to find the apples, but found only a flowery dress over a flat chest. But tomorrow he would make certain.

And the next day he climbed the hill to try to make certain. He saw two little apples the size of olives that stirred his emotions and sympathy. Still her hair was like golden thread, and her cheeks were burning from the spring sun and fatigue. She was playing hopscotch by herself, without a playmate. She hopped on one foot, and her flowery dress jumped and her ponytail fell softly onto her chest and then onto her back, as she hopped and counted the squares. "*Achat, shtayim, shalosh, arba.*" He repeated after her silently, "*Wahid, ithnayn, thalatha, arba'a.*" He went up very close to the fence while she repeated, *Achat,* hop, *shtayim,* hop, *shalosh,* hop, *arba,* hop. Then she turned around and continued counting. This time, at each hop, he repeated in a loud voice so she could hear, "*Achat, shtayim, shalosh, arba.*" She turned toward him and stood there for a moment, looking him up and down. Her eyes paused on the camera, but then she went back to hopping without counting. So he raised his voice. "*Achat, shtayim, shalosh, arba*" He saw that she was smiling secretly, so he raised his voice further. "*Achat, shtayim, shalosh, arba*" She pretended not to hear him and kept jumping with her head down. So he took hold of the camera and aimed it in her direction and acted like he was taking a picture. She hid her face in the palms of her hands, shook her head and said, "*Lo, lo.*" He started laughing. "*Lo, lo, la, la?*" He came even closer to the fence until his fingers were up against the openings in the wire. She peeked at him through her hands and saw the camera hanging around his neck. She stared at it and whispered, "Digital camera!" With pride, holding the camera and pointing to it he said, "Digital camera!" She didn't say anything further, just stared. He extended his wrist and pulled up his sleeve and pointed to the watch and said proudly, "*Saa'a digital.*" "*Shaa'a digital,*" she whispered back, looking at the watch with great interest.

"*Saa'a,*" he corrected.

"*Shaa'a,*" she insisted.

Quickly he pulled his sunglasses out from his pocket and put them on and said, laughing, "And digital sunglasses." She hesitated for a moment, then whispered, "Digital?" She burst out laughing and laughing and laughing, and the ponytail swayed, now to the right, now to the left, now to the back, while she covered her big teeth with her hand and said, "Digital." And he said, "Digital, digital." And every time he took the sunglasses off and put them back on and repeated, "Digital," they would burst out laughing harder and harder until suddenly they heard Issa's voice. "Hey, Ahmad," he was shouting, "What are you doing here?" She turned astonished toward the voice, then back to Ahmad and the camera, but he had backed away some, then more, then some more, until he headed for the hill, running.

8

When he took off the sunglasses, she pointed to his eyes and said, "*'Aynayim.*"

"*'Aynaan,*" he corrected.

She pointed to her ears, smiling, and very clearly, as if she was teaching him, she said, "*Udhnayim.*"

"*Udhnan,*" he insisted.

She stretched her hand out toward the fence and the camera and said, "*Yadayim.*"

He pressed on the camera, emphasizing the words, and spoke very confidently, as if he had discovered the similarity between the two languages, and also discovered that he didn't stutter when he spoke to her, because she did not understand him. Or possibly because he was pronouncing the words so slowly. He was very pleased and his confidence grew. He put his palm over his chest and said slowly, "*Ana* Ahmad."

She pondered him and smiled. "*Akhmed?*"

"*Ahmad. Ahmad,*" he repeated, and her smile widened and she repeated, "*Akhmed. Akhmed.*" He shook his head no and placed his hand over his chest and said clearly, "*Ana…*" He wanted to continue with the word "Ahmad" but he heard her say, "*Ani* Mira." He nodded and smiled and pointed to his chest. "*Ana* Ahmad. *Anti* Mira." She repeated after him, "*Ani* Mira. *Ata* Akhmed."

And just like that, they became friends. Or at least it was the start of a friendship, a secret friendship. A secret he did not dare reveal even to his brother or his mother. Who was this friend of his? The daughter of a settler with a skullcap and a heavy machine gun, whom his father called the scum of the earth. Scum of the earth. He was certain that Mira was not dirty and was not ugly. Indeed she was the most beautiful creature he had ever seen. And she was nice and playful and lively. She liked hopscotch and jump rope, the opposite of him. He didn't like anything except the camera and art lessons and reading and watching MTV. And he didn't like dogs, either, unlike her. She had a little white dog named Bobo that she played with and fed bread and cans of tuna fish. She would bring him a little can with tuna in it that was dark colored and covered with a waxy substance. Was it tuna? Tuna was light colored and expensive. His mother served it for dinner when Majid came home from the university or when an unexpected guest showed up, and he would gobble it up, competing with his brother for each morsel. Majid would win by scooping up bigger and bigger bites until his father would shout, "Why are you being such a glutton?" Majid would steal a glance at his brother and find him smiling and eating, his head in his dish, so he would pinch him under the table and call him a "bear." He would whisper it, but his father would hear him and yell, "When are you going to grow up?" Majid wouldn't grow up. In fact, sometimes Ahmad felt Majid was younger than him, or was still a child like him, a little kid. Or rather, a big kid who shaved. And Ahmad would shave, too, one day. But when? His face was still like a girl's face. Like Mira's. And his voice still cracked as though he were hoarse, and he had little ugly pimples on his chin and forehead. "Those are teenager spots," his mother would say. And that would fill him with optimism—they meant he was growing up. He really had started growing. His pants were too short, his sleeves were too short, and his dress shoes were too small, despite the fact that 'Eid hadn't been that long ago, just a few months, and the shoes had fit just right then. "The boy's got big feet. He's really filling out," his father said. And Majid whispered sarcastically, "He's the size of a bear." So Ahmad kicked him and said angrily, "Y.. y.. you are."

"Stop it, both of you!" their father shouted, chewing his food. "Be quiet and eat."

The size of a bear? No, that was not true. Ahmad had seen his own waist and how it was becoming leaner, and how his stomach was shrinking, and how he was now taller than he was last month. And likewise he had started understanding the meaning of love. When he saw people kissing on television, he wondered if kissing like that was reserved for foreigners or if Arabs did it too. Did his father do that? His brother? Did his mother? He removed his mother from his imagination, because his mother was not like other people. She was the one who sang "O what strands of lovely thread, threads of silken hair." She would sing that to Mira, too, if she saw her. "O what strands of lovely thread." But his mother would never sing to Mira, because Mira was one of them. His mother had said spitefully and angrily that the Jews were not nice, and of course Mira was a Jew. And even if she didn't know or care or if she was outside the issue completely, she was still one of them, even if she didn't pay attention to anything other than hopscotch and her swing and her little dog Bobo. He noticed, too, that he was not afraid of her dog Bobo. Maybe because it was so small, the size of a cat, and it had long hair like feathers and its tail sprawled out like a palm tree and stood up straight and wagged whenever he called it. It even licked Ahmad's hand. He had stuck his fingers through the fence and the dog licked his fingers and looked at him strangely, like a human being. Were dogs like human beings? And was that dog one of them? If that dog were to come across an Arab dog, would it attack him and bite him? But that dog in the camera near the dump had been very scary, even though he was an Arab dog. Whereas this dog, this Bobo, was like Mira. The most beautiful creature in the world.

9

He remained preoccupied for some time, constantly looking in the mirror, fiddling with his "teenager spots" and running his fingers through his hair, inspecting his Adam's apple and his teeth. He tried to imitate his brother's hairstyle by using lots of gel so his hair would stand up straight like a porcupine's. When his brother came home from the university and noticed his tub of gel had been dipped into, he grabbed a lock of his brother's hair as if it were a rat's tail, and said, disgusted, "Is that gel or lard? Are you pretending to be Michael Jackson, fatso?"

He began to stutter even more than before and said, "Y.. y.. you are." Majid waved his hand impatiently, took the tub of gel, and hid it. But then a few hours later, smiling affectionately, he said, "You have nice soft hair. It's nicer without gel." Ahmad didn't look up, just kept watching Michael Jackson and pretending he didn't hear. So Majid said, "Michael Jackson dreams of having soft hair like yours."

"Y.. y.. yeah, okay, but what about you?" he said, disgruntled.

Majid smiled sympathetically, kind of proud that his little brother was trying to imitate him. That meant he saw him as a role model. And later on, when he won the talent contest and made a recording and became a star, there would be even more for this fatso bear to try to imitate.

"My hair is curly," Majid said. "Gel is made for my kind of hair." But when he saw his brother's sad and bewildered look, he consoled him, saying, "Your hair is nicer." His love of bright lights and stardom made him add in earnest, "Nicer without gel."

10

Bobo licked Ahmad's fingers and crawled under the fence to get to him. Bobo's belly had made an opening, a small hole between the fence and the ground, so Mira raised the edge of the fence with her fingers, but the fence was too sturdy to bend. She looked to Ahmad for help, but he looked around, then at the fence, and said, "*Lo. Lo.*" Ahmad repeated reassuringly to himself, "*La. La. Lo. Lo.*" She reached beneath the fence with her hand and said, "*Keen. Keen.*" Then she got up, backed away from him, and ran over to a little stake that was supporting a young tree and guiding its growth. She pulled it out of the ground and came back with it. She stuck the stake into the hole and started pushing up on the fence. The wire came up a few inches and stopped. She pushed and pushed, and her face turned rosy, and she bit her lip as she tried, all the while her bangs fluttering over her face and her ponytail swaying and flowing and her forehead reddening. She looked up at him as she was bent over with her head at his knee level, and his fear was overpowered by a feeling of embarrassment, so he knelt down to her level and said, "*Haati.*" She repeated like a parrot, without understanding, "*Haati. Haati.*" She handed him the stake and kept saying "*haati, haati,*" while he lifted on the fence. The fence came up and there was an opening large enough for a child, so she started to crawl through. He stood up, took a step back, and signaled with his hands for her to go back, "*Lo. Lo. La. La.*" But she crawled toward him and suddenly there she was in front of him. She reached out and he reached out spontaneously and pulled her to him. Bobo jumped on them and started barking and licking her legs with his palm-tree tail wagging back and forth. She picked up Bobo and started running over the grass and on top of the rocks and between the olive trees and the plum trees and he ran too. She looked at Ahmad as she shouted, "Bobo. Bobo." The dog jumped our of her arms and slithered like a chameleon on its belly. When she tried to pick the dog up, he ran away. The boy looked on, amazed. She finally caught the dog and looked at him. "Camera," she said, but Ahmad didn't follow. She pointed to him and put her fist to her eye and said again, "camera." He was very proud that he owned such a valuable camera and the girl was requesting it. He began taking pictures and started counting, the girl repeating after him. *Achat, shtayim, shalosh, arba.*" She counted and he took pictures until she reached ten and shouted with glee, "'*Aysar!*" But then he suddenly remembered his father and the photographer and the mean man behind the counter and how he had leaned over and said wickedly, "P.. p.. p.. picture of who?"

11

Majid came home from the university and made an important announcement: Thursday was the talent contest and for that reason he needed a new pair of jeans, a leather jacket, and fancy new Italian boots.

"God help us. Why Italian?" his father said.

"There were these amazing Italian boots in the store," Majid answered. He wanted to dazzle everyone. Good singing was not enough. The judges were going to notice every detail.   "They're going to notice the Italian boots?" his father asked.

Majid didn't answer. He just kept staring at the various heaps of food in front of him without touching any of them. His father took note, as this was a signal that the boy was going to go on a hunger strike. He shook his head with restrained anger. Look at that! He's refusing to eat? In my day it was the father who forbade his children from eating if they made the slightest mistake. In my day, food was a reward, not something to bargain with. Was it because he raised his children properly and taught them to be nice to people that now he had to pay the price? Was it because there was always plenty of food in the house and his refrigerator was always stocked with meat and eggs and butter, that food was now a means for blackmail? Was it because his son had never gone hungry, never made the rounds selling chewing gum on the sidewalk, never lived in a refugee camp, that he acted like a big shot and turned his nose up at food and refused to eat? That son of a gun!

"Dinner's ready," his father grumbled. "Go ahead and eat."

"I'm not hungry," Majid said.

To hell with you! Don't ever eat! His father wanted to shout and threaten. He wanted to fly into a rage. He wanted to remind them of the misery of the past, of the bitter cold he suffered while carrying his tray of chewing gum and slipping in the muddy streets, and his father's tears when he recalled the good old days in Haifa where he sold Persian carpets and had a showroom like a museum, and now here he was selling bushels of spearmint on the sidewalk! The good old days. The days of security and dignity were over. The human being had become worthless. His father had wept, wept quietly, because the mint did not bring in enough for the family, because the family needed to eat, and food had become a rarity, because the children had become laborers, one selling chewing gum and another fixing tires and a third grinding chickpeas and fava beans, and all of them marrying maids and gypsies. He himself had married Shahira and his father had cut him off. A lowlife gypsy who sang in people's houses didn't deserve the family name. The family name! Was there still a family that had a name to speak of? "Wake up, Dad!" he said to his father. "We are in a refugee camp. Mount Carmel and Wadi Nisnas are gone. Haifa is gone!"

"Come on, Dad," Majid argued. "Students stretch themselves thin. I've never asked for much. My requests have always been reasonable."

Reasonable? He looked at him furiously. He thought about Majid's hair spiked up with gel, and his American tee shirt. And he remembered the sneakers he'd bought him for 20 dinars, or was it 25—or 30? A pair of sneakers for 30 dinars! They had the name Benetton on them, or Carlton, or Washington, he didn't know. All he knew was that sneakers had names now. What kind of generation was this? So pampered. What kind of people were they? He really wanted to give Majid a stern lecture that would shake him up and remind him that their country was gone, had sunken into the ground, that three quarters of the people had sold chewing gum and stood in line in front of the UNRWA and took relief provisions like beggars and lived like junkyard dogs. He wanted to say this and many other things, but he was afraid to say anything, because he had said it all a hundred times before and his speech had become boring. He looked at the two boys and noticed they were exchanging looks that said, "Here we go again." The tragic story of his childhood and selling gum and living in the refugee camp and the provisions for the refugees had become something for the two of them to scoff at. For dozens of them, for hundreds of this new generation. This yo-yo generation, this Western music generation, this MTV generation. Brats! Was this the generation of hope, the generation of the future? This generation was what they called *maayi', saayi', daayi'*. Raised on pampering and chocolate. They didn't read or write. Instead of listening to Umm Kulthoum, they listened to Mimi and Madonna. What kind of voices were they? Those aren't even voices—they're meat and broth and chunks of fat. Where did they get all these disgusting things from? Wow. Hello, hello, to the satellite-dish generation.

He said to Majid, "Wherever you go, he goes."

"Okay," Majid bargained. "And the boots?"

"No boots, no nonsense, no idiotic talk!" the father shouted at the top of his lungs. "Be a man. Don't melt into a fool. That's all we need. You wanted the guitar, okay, we understand the guitar. A leather jacket, okay, we put up with that. And now the boots, too?"

He looked at his son and saw his sad, sullen expression as if the whole world had suddenly collapsed. "So all this time your singing was missing the right boots?"

Majid turned his head away. "The judges judge your voice by your shoes?" his father continued. "Oh-ho! What a great judging system! What great judges! When you sing, your voice emanates from your boots? So what if someone is barefoot? Where does their voice come from?"

Majid jumped up from the table and kicked his chair back. "Come back here," his father yelled. "Come here."

But Majid did not come back. Instead he went to his room and slammed the door.

Brats! What a disaster! What was he going to do with these kids? What would he say and what would he write? He had written a lot about this generation and their wishy-washiness. He had written about their lack of awareness, the spread of corruption among the student body, and about Israel's manipulation of this generation, these students, by marketing prostitution and collaboration and AIDS and drugs and cheap weapons. And as if our market was not enough for them they exported it into all the Arab markets. And here we are, one generation after another, reaping nothing but shame and defeat. How can we rid ourselves of them? How can we find rest? How can we live and raise our heads among people when we are trash? Trash, trash!

He glared at his younger son angrily and suddenly yelled, "Where are the pictures?" Ahmad didn't know what to say and turned red and turned yellow and started to stutter, "P.. p.. p.. p..?" His father raised his voice, "The pictures of the town. The pictures of the garbage!" A wave of bitterness came over him. He burst out laughing and said dryly, "Pictures of the town, pictures of the garbage, is there a difference?" His son didn't answer, and instead began fidgeting nervously and looked back and forth from the food to his mother's face.

The mother looked at her son, her only child and the light of her eyes, squirming in fear and alarm. "Take it easy on him," she said.

The father shook his hand at his wife, and without looking at her he rebuked, "Be quiet, woman! Let me deal with my son!"

"Okay. Okay," she said. "But take it easy. Take it easy on him."

He didn't answer her, satisfied to shake his head bitterly. That boy was his mother's darling, and all her spoiling and pampering had turned him into a kind of doormat. And the other one had gone soft from all that music and guitar business and dreaming of being like Mustapha Qamar and Amr Diab. He was one of the Nakba generation, raised in poverty and revolution and the Vietnam War. That is, to him the catastrophe caused the revolution. And the revolution was nationalistic. And the Vietnam War was the light and the lighthouse for all downtrodden peoples like his people. It was an example and a motto for every revolution. And now here his sons were with no light and no revolution and no lighthouse, with no Vietnam either. How were they supposed to get out of this mess, this worry, this degradation? What a difficult mess they'd fallen into, up to their ears. A mess they'd made with their own hands and swallowed off the edge of a knife. What had they done? What had they conceived and given birth to? What had he fathered, he, the child of Ayn al-Mirjan refugee camp? A retarded boy who looks sideways and talks sideways and stutters, and another who sings out of his boots, Italian boots at such and such a price. Some revolution! Some price!

The mother said with measured tenderness, "Please. Don't break his spirit. Don't degrade him."

He turned to her and shouted, "I'm breaking his spirit and degrading him? Me?"

She said, "I mean, the poor guy. In front of the other students, at the contest, let him enjoy himself. Let him have fun."

He looked at her and contemplated what kind of woman she was. She was the kind of woman with whom a man could live very peacefully. She truly was a feather pillow he could plunge into, sleep upon. He could grab hold of her and she would submit to his grasp, and he could feel her tenderness below him and above him and on top of him. A pleasant face, a pleasant voice, soft skin, and flesh like a feather pillow. And she had a heart of gold, as pure as milk. She had embraced his son Majid after his mother's death and made him forget he was an orphan. And despite his calling her "auntie," she always addressed him tenderly, calling him mom. And likewise, her son, when he speaks to Majid, says "Majid, Majid, Majid," as if his older brother were the master of the universe or Shater Hasan or the genie of the magic lamp. And that satisfies the father. Yes, it satisfies him; it even softens him and turns his heart into a swing or a feather pillow. He himself had turned into feathers. He, too, had become doughy, like pudding. Why say something firm only to forget it the next day? Why was he so shaken by this woman and her son's tears? Why did he forget everything he had written in the newspaper whenever she got upset? Even with his other wife he had been doughy. That devilish one with the hashish-smoker's laugh and the castanets. He thought the cause of his laxness and kindheartedness was love. But the secret was not in Shahira or Latifa or his children or his father's tears, but within himself. His heart was not like his pen. His heart was very, very tender, very sensitive, very weak, and he loved his home and his family. He loved to be alone with them.

"Please. I beg you!" she said sweetly and reached to him with that soft, moist hand, and he felt the vapor of his emotions rising up out of him. He forgot his anger over this generation and Israel and his frustration as a small-time journalist bookseller in an impoverished country. He thought to himself, the revolution is going to come out of a pair of boots?

He looked at her and said, "Okay, okay—we'll buy him the boots."

12

Ramallah looked like something out of a movie. The Ramallah girls were like movie actresses, wearing tight jeans and tank tops. Their hair was ruffled and dyed and they drove Jeeps and cars and went out at night to restaurants and drank beer and smoked and strutted around like hotshot boys. True the lighthouse and the downtown area were not very different from Ayn al-Mirjan in terms of the level of cleanliness, the commotion, and the urbanized village atmosphere through which women traversed in long gowns and robes and prayer garments. But the regular passing of groups of young men and women from Bir Zeit University and other colleges, all carrying books and notebooks and magazines and wearing jeans and tee shirts with their stylish haircuts, made the atmosphere feel more like something on television or on an Amr Diab video. And all those huge buildings that sprouted up after Oslo set Ahmad's eyes moving up and down without stopping and his hand squeezing his brother's arm for fear of getting lost in that strange, winding marketplace. A country boy in the city, or a semi-city, at any rate a place bigger and stranger than anything he had ever seen. Ayn al-Mirjan was a village that had turned into a town not too long ago. Instead of a mukhtar now it had a *baladiyyeh*, and beside its one main street with the mosque and public water fountain, now it had a traffic circle with a little garden and a fountain. Ramallah, on the other hand, had streets lined with restaurants and coffee shops and bars and parks and store windows that caught one's attention with their stylishness and uniqueness. In addition, since Oslo, the traffic circle was decorated with awe-inspiring statues of lions, erected for protection and to refute once and for all any allegations or complaints from those who doubted self-rule or that the Jews had been defeated.

As his eyes followed a girl in tight jeans and a tank top, Ahmad's brother said to him, "So, what do you think of Ramallah?"

Ahmad peered out from under his glasses and said in amazement, "P.. p.. pretty." He exchanged a quick look with his brother and smiled in fear. He was afraid because of his tongue and his clothes and what might happen to him and cause him embarrassment in the dorm, in front of the students at Bir Zeit. But his brother did not take him to Bir Zeit and the dorm, but rather to a room on the ground floor of a fancy villa in a rich neighborhood with trees and gardens and villas with red-tiled roofs and verandas and fountains and green grass like a carpet. "Don't you dare tell him," he ordered.

Ahmad peered out from behind his glasses and shook his head to show he understood and agreed to conspire with him. But Majid insisted, "Don't you dare tell him, or I swear I'll..." Ahmad understood. He still remembered the uproar over Issa and working in the settlement of Kiryat Shayba and singing at parties and similar things. Those uproars had been marked by insults and accusations and an explosive atmosphere, followed by short periods of quiet fraught with caution and anticipation. Majid was moody and reckless. He liked clamor and he liked girls and he squandered his money on cassettes and hair gels and cigarettes. His father had said once when he was yelling at him, "And cigarettes, too?"

"I bought them with my own money," Majid had replied.

"Your own money? You mean from the sweat of your brow and the work of your hands? No, that's my sweat, my fatigue, my suffering, you son of a ... But what can I say? It's my own fault. I raised you. I deserve a million lashes for it."

"Here we go again," Majid mumbled and fled to his room before having to listen to that story, that same old story, that broken record, followed by the inevitable and well-known finale, "this yo-yo generation, the sons of bitches."

13

He suddenly became aware of a sweet voice calling, "Lucky." He looked out the window and saw a girl in jeans and a tight cotton tank top. She was pretty and light-skinned with short black ringlets and a long neck. "The daughter," Majid whispered. "Of the owners of the house." Here was the daughter with her dog, out in the garden picking cherries and strawberries.

Majid went outside to flirt with her while his younger brother stayed inside, looking out the window and eavesdropping. He heard laughter, and the trees rustling, and the dog making sounds that came from his throat and his feet and the collar around his neck. And then footsteps. Heavy footsteps, a car door, and lots of commotion. Then the sound of the daughter running past the metal shutters of the window. Majid rushed into the room, whispering, "Her father, her father!" He locked the door, panting.

Her father came from a clan of gypsies who had set up camp at the turn of the last century in Ramallah and bought land in exchange for some goats and some fire tongs and meat skewers and braziers, as well as some dancing and fortune-telling and tattooing. They progressed and in time became a family, then a tribe, then an established name with a weighty reputation among the locals. The Washmis, they said, were nasty folk with no morals who did certain things secretly, and then eventually openly—things that people were terrified to mention. They would obtain permits from the Jews for trucks and taxis and ID cards and building permits, in exchange for dinner parties and partnerships and commissions. And so with the army officers eating and drinking the night away in the garden beneath the cherry trees and in the gazebo, the head Washmi—the girl's grandfather, her father's father—would spend the day raking in revenue and strengthening his fortress and his privileges. In time, the Washmis became important people, practically an entire government in themselves. But despite all the fortifications and all the power, al-Washmi was murdered. A bullet of betrayal, they said publicly. A bullet of the revolution, it was held secretly. The revolution had been well known at that time for being efficient and earnest and trustworthy and for protecting people. His beautiful young widow with the mysterious origins fled to Canada and lived there with the children until Oslo. Then, with the transfer of the revolution to the seat of power and the nationalization of the issuance of permits and ID cards in return for services and compensation, the Washmis were no longer outlaws, but rather right smack within the law itself. So the widow returned from Canada and though she was not young anymore, nor beautiful, she reopened the house that had been abandoned since the 1970s. She rented out a room to a polite university student in return for pruning the garden and watering the flowers. Then she heard him playing his guitar and singing, so she kept him on and increased his pay and started inviting him to parties for the well-to-do at the gazebo, where he performed for the highly esteemed, prominent guests. In the gazebo, forgiveness for the past caught up with the present and even went beyond it. Her son became a government adviser and was on his way to becoming a cabinet minister.

So the pretty girl was of questionable origins, surrounded by rumors, and her fancy house was veiled in suspicion. And her powerful father was practically a cabinet of his own. Her grandfather was the head Washmi who had been found murdered by a bullet in the back. People on the street said things that included the father and the mother and the son and consequently the girl. But the girl was pretty and flirtatious and liked music like her grandmother, and dancing and lights and singing. But she did not have very good voice, so she liked Majid for his beautiful voice and the way he played his guitar and lifted her into the world of Amr Diab. As for al-Washmi the cabinet minister-to-be, he had begun to have suspicions that his daughter was becoming enamored of a gardener with no background or status. He did not leave any stone unturned in his attempts to quietly get rid of the boy. But the grandmother was not convinced by the arguments of her son the "Minister." She argued that Israelis had lured away all the laborers so they had to rely on students to be watchmen and gardeners. And this student was very nice and clean and polite and worked without making a sound. But his voice at the parties around the pool opened the hearts and delighted the ears of the guests, creating a friendly atmosphere. And here was her son now—thanks to that friendly atmosphere—a government adviser on his way to becoming a cabinet minister. So what was he complaining about? Al-Washmi reluctantly quieted down, letting go of the subject for the time being, but not giving up entirely.

That night, another party sprang to life. Without any preparations or fuss, groups of prominent people streamed into the garden and the gazebo. An extravagant spread was set out on the dinner table—the most expensive *meze* of spleen and sheep testicles and tabbouleh—and to go with it, of course, whiskey and Ramallah arak and beer. A chef from a fine restaurant appeared, carrying a serviette and wearing a bow tie and going around whispering to each important guest, head bowed. Every glass was filled and the night was filled with a friendly and tranquil atmosphere, the kind of quiet that only the presence of an occupier brings about.

The singing began with the *muwashshah*: "O Night, when will the young lover set off? Will his promised rendezvous ever come?" A high-ranking minister smiled and began nodding his head to the music. "Who's that young man?" he whispered to another guest. "What does he do?" They told him he was a student at Bir Zeit—what did he think of him? "Superb!" he said. "He has talent. We have to develop such talent." The grandmother caught what he'd said and quickly agreed. "Truly. He has talent. He deserves to be sent to Italy." Al-Washmi heard that sentence and jumped up and grabbed her and exclaimed, "Exactly! To Italy."

The daughter, though, became very upset. As far as she could tell, whatever the minister said, the minister did. So she decided to discuss the situation with Majid. Either he would refuse to go or she would run away with him to Italy. But Majid was not the least bit interested in the idea—in either idea. He did not want to go to Italy to learn opera and sonatas and concertos and Beethoven—he wanted to wear jeans and sing with his guitar strapped onto him as he danced with girls who shook their breasts and rolled their hips at him. And the other idea—well, the girl, whose name was Laura, had taken his song literally when he sang to her one night when her father was in New York and her Canadian mother was in Canada and her grandmother was deep in a valium-induced sleep. "O Laura, your love has tortured my heart." Laura became teary-eyed and said, "I love you," and urged him to sing "I Love You." So he sang "I Love You," changing the words "I wish I could forget you" to "I will never forget you." Laura laughed and sang along with him and dreamed of undying, heroic love, like something out of a Charlotte Brontë or Sir Walter Scott novel. Unfortunately, Majid was not a big reader. Affected by the moment and by what he had inherited naturally from his grandmother the gypsy, Majid dreamed of making a recording and a video and taking it to Cairo, then Beirut and the LBC, and all the other Arab international broadcasting stations.

Laura could not wait for the guests to leave and the night to quiet down. She stole over to the room where Ahmad was hiding and eavesdropping behind the shuttered window, and called out to him in a whisper, "Ahmad, Ahmad." Ahmad was startled. He hesitated at first and then amassed some courage and dared an answer. "Y.. y.. yes?" She told him he had to come out to the party and call his brother to come right away for something very urgent. It was dark outside and she was not visible in the shadows of the trees. He could barely see the outline of her face. But her voice was close, very close, because his brother's room was low to the ground and so were its windows. And since he could not see her face and she could not see his, it was very easy for him to delay and keep quiet and back away a little bit from the window so she could not hear his breathing.

"Ahmad, Ahmad," she urged. "Go out and call to him. It's urgent!" He didn't answer. He backed away from the window a little more. She took a few steps around outside. He heard her turn the knob and open the door. She came in quickly and locked the door. She hurried toward the lantern beside the bed and lit it. Light poured into the room and she could see Ahmad, glued to the wall, gripped with fear and astonishment. She had entered the room without warning and lit the lantern with the expert touch of someone who knew exactly where everything was and exactly what to do. That was strange, strange indeed. If something like that had happened in his town of Ayn al-Mirjan, you would never hear the end of it, but not here in Ramallah! How strange!

She plopped onto the bed and reached over to a pack of cigarettes lying on the night table. She put a cigarette into her mouth and started looking for some matches. Here in the drawer? On the table? The sofa—the only sofa in the room? When she didn't find any, she looked up at the boy, who was still staring with fright and shock, and smiled at him. "Why are you standing there like that?" she whispered. "Do you have any matches?"

He went quickly to the table and came back with some matches. He handed them to her and she lit her cigarette, puffed out some smoke and looked around the room. Then she returned her gaze to him. Smiling, she whispered, "Why are you standing? Sit and relax. Who are you afraid of?"

He didn't reply, but he did move closer to the sofa and sat down on it. He continued to scrutinize her and her movements and the smoke coming out of her mouth and her leg swinging, crossed over the other.

She was wearing a sandal that exposed her small foot with its painted white toenails. Her leg was slender in her tight pants, which were cropped in a revealing way that matched the rest of her curvaceous body. Everything about her was round. Her face was round. Her hair was round. Her mouth, her eyes, her breasts, even her lap when she sat down. Despite her relative slenderness, she had curves and turns and fullness. And what was even stranger than all that was her little upturned nose like a foreigner's.

She smiled at him and said in a motherly fashion as if she were speaking to a child, "How do you like Ramallah? Is this your first time here?" She kept looking him over as he sat cowering on the couch and watching her out of the corner of his eye. She asked again, "Is this your first time?" He didn't answer, just kept staring at her sandal. First time in Ramallah? First time to stay in a house like a castle? First time to see this kind of place? Hear this kind of place? Smell arak and cigarettes, hear laughter that rings out with a melody, hear his brother sing in front of strangers, sit by himself in an isolated, locked room with a girl as beautiful as this, pretty and fair as vanilla pudding and with fingers like Turkish delight and Jordan almonds. First time? First time for everything. This was the first time he'd left his hometown and traveled away from his parents and seen the big, wide world, which was more fragrant, more beautiful, and more appetizing than he had ever imagined. Not in his dreams, not in the movies, not in the settlement of Kiryat Shayba, not with little Mira and Bobo. Mira seemed so far away now, so small, so innocent, like a cartoon or a character from a children's story. Her fine image grew distant in his imagination because here in the present reality, the most exciting and unusual things were happening.

She kept prodding him as she smoked. "Are you enjoying yourself in Ramallah, Ahmad?"

He shook his head without elaborating, without saying anything. "Why are you so quiet?" she asked sweetly. "Don't you have a tongue?" He smiled shyly and whispered with his cracked voice, "Y.. y.. yes I do."

"You'll get used to it," she said to encourage and console him.

Would he get used to it? No—impossible. This was an environment that didn't suit him at all. It suited his brother Majid with his courage, adventurous spirit, and rebelliousness, his beautiful voice, good looks, and his band. The evening parties, the girls of Jerusalem and Ramallah, the talent contest, Marina, and Cairo were all very well for Majid, with his dreams of stardom. Ahmad would never get used to it. He wouldn't dare.

The door opened and Majid burst in and said, "Are you crazy?" He reached over to help Laura up but she backed away. He looked all around and paced like a lunatic, whispering frantically, "You want to get us killed? What a scandal!" He started pulling her to get up, while she uttered a series of sentence fragments. "No Italy." "I go with you." "No. Impossible." Finally she yielded to his persistence and went out into the darkness. Majid remained tight-faced, his hair disheveled, and his chest pounding. He looked at his brother, who was wide-eyed with alarm, so he stroked his face and patted his hair. He looked right and left and said, in apology and explanation, "Her father is al-Washmi. A murderer!" When his brother did not reply, he shook his finger and warned, "Don't open the door." Majid went out quickly, then came back with the key and locked the door from the outside.

14

He woke up to a rattling sound and the nighttime Ramallah breeze, which was as cold as ice. A very dim lightbulb shone into his sleepy eyes. The lightbulb was outside, on the walkway in the garden behind the house. That meant the door was open, which was why he felt so cold and could see the light and hear movement. He looked over at his brother's bed. In the dim glow he could see that his brother's bed was empty and unmade. So his brother must have opened the door and left it partly open like that. But what about the sound, the soft, hushed weeping out in the garden? Was that his brother weeping that way? But it sounded like a woman, a young woman. It had to be that girl, Laura al-Washmi, al-Washmi's daughter. What on earth was his crazy brother doing with the daughter of a murderous criminal? Was it a continuation of the scene he had witnessed earlier? What was his crazy brother doing?

He felt a powerful desire to go out to his brother and drag him by the arms—just as Majid had done to the Washmi girl—and say to him, "What are you, crazy? For God's sake, let's get out of here!" But he knew ahead of time that Majid would not heed him. He would probably scold and make fun of him. And anyway, he wouldn't dare do it. He was a scaredy cat, as they said—he was shy and stuttered all the time. And what if words were to stumble off his tongue? What if the girl's father came and accused him? But he was not involved; why should he be accused? But the girl was not crying now. Now the sound was of hushed laughter. A hoarse voice. What was she doing? And his crazy brother, what was he doing? He imagined a love scene like something on television. He felt his genitals swelling and his heart pounding. A storm blew up within him. The memory of Mira returned to him, her freckled face and her flowery dress. Mira was small and pretty and delicate. She aroused in him a feeling of compassion and pity for her innocence and her teeth that were too big for her mouth and the two blossoming apples and her dog Bobo. Laura, on the other hand, was like Turkish delight, like whipped cream. Everything about her drew his eyes and aroused his appetite and his desire to touch her white cheek that was like a wheel of cheese and her toenails that were like Turkish delight or Jordan almonds.

He lunged out the door like a sleepwalker, barefoot, and walked in the dark, in the shadows, near the grapevines and the jasmine. The laughter increased, and there were snorting sounds that aroused him further—surely he would find a hot scene.

He was disappointed when he saw his brother there in the gazebo holding his guitar and pressing with his fingers without strumming the strings. "This, my lady, is the key of C, and this, my darling, is the key of D, and this, my soul, is the key of G. C'mon now, you tell me, what key is this?" She touched her finger to her cheek and put on an air of deep thought and repeated after him, tapping on her temple. "This is the key of 'my sir,' and this is the key of 'my darling,' and this is the key of 'my soul.' What do you think of that?" She didn't wait for an answer to her question. She placed her hands over her mouth and began laughing and squirming and snickering in a hushed voice, while he watched her, smiling, not getting excited. When she finished her laughing episode, he put his guitar aside and said with unbecoming seriousness, "This is a waste of time. You have no talent, no desire, and no voice."

She stared at him. The smile and laughter on her face slowly dissipated and reshaped itself into something new. Her mouth clenched and her brow furrowed and her eyes fell. She no longer looked at him or spoke. Majid watched her, not knowing how to reconcile the contradictions. The girl was very pretty, very nice, and her grandmother was nice and sweet, but her father was awful: very powerful, very rich, influential, and if he said one word against him it would shut all doors and ruin everything. The pretty girl's only use was as a stepping stone. It was through her that he had found the room, and through her grandmother that he found a job— sort of a job. He made enough each month to make ends meet. Singing was not an easy hobby, and leading a band and satisfying all its demands required money and a steady income. Without planning and direction and budgeting, those guys would not be reined in. And he needed to have a small band so that he would stand out and have a chance to make it big. Up to this point, he was only known among university circles and festivals and conferences, none of which bought even a meal. Working in hotels and concerts and weddings lowered the artistic level of the group, forcing them to sing Mustapha Qamar songs and Ihab Tawfiq songs rather than Marcel Khalifeh and Sheikh Imam. This elicited derision from the other students. Instead of the incredible poetry of Tawfiq Ziyad and Mahmoud Darwish and the roar of the crowds of young people singing along with the band for freedom and dignity and human rights, they found themselves surrounded by old, traditional folk dances and shrill ululations and a stifling atmosphere with nothing special about it, no dignity, and not the least bit of art. So they abandoned weddings and went back to singing only at festivals and formal gatherings. But that choice came at a hefty price, which he paid out of his pocket, from his work in the Washmi family garden and appeasing their spoiled, bothersome daughter. What did this idiot know about the fundamentals of singing? Or its appreciation? What did she know about poetry? Did she know Marcel Khalifeh or Mahmoud Darwish? Did she understand their words? She was half foreign and the daughter of al-Washmi, so she didn't understand. She didn't understand the meaning of the cause or the meaning of poverty or living in a refugee camp and doing humiliating jobs like his grandmother the gypsy and poor Issa in the settlement of Kiryat Shayba. Or even himself, hadn't he worked in Kiryat Shayba and gotten slapped by his father for it so hard that his nose bled and he'd ended up sleeping several nights in the camp? Did she know what it felt like to get slapped that hard or to taste life in a refugee camp? And what if she found out about his mother and his grandmother and the wedding parties and their scraping to get by? If her father found out what was going on in his own house, the lowest level of his house, how would he treat him? But this spoiled girl was not going to leave him alone. She would disgrace him in a second if she got upset. He had a lot to lose if she got upset.

She said, "I should be in the band. Suad is not better than me. I'm a thousand times better."

He didn't answer. He kept quiet, thinking about how to get out of this bind. He wanted the girl, and he didn't want her either. He wanted the room and the income and a way into her world, a world of people who could get him places, people who had made themselves. Made it. He would make it, too, to Rome, through the girl, through the minister. There was no way out of playing the game. It was either make it to a higher place or plummet to failure.

She repeated, disgusted, "Suad is not better than me."

He didn't answer. He remained silent, frowning, confused, unsure of how to get rid of her without ruining everything. He said anxiously in a soft voice, "Your father, your father. I hear something."

"Dad's sleeping," she snapped. "He's the drinking sort."

"I hear something," he warned her, trying to make his voice sound nervous and afraid. "I hear something moving."

Ahmad backed up, thinking his brother had sensed his presence, and bumped his head against a vine. The leaves shook, making a quiet sound, and the branch also shook. He hid behind the vine, behind the leaves.

"Do you hear it?" he whispered. "Hear it?"

She stood up slowly and looked down at him sitting there. "I'm in the band," she said coldly.

"Okay, but what about your father?" he warned.

"Grandma's on my side."

"Okay, but what about your mother?"

"Mom's in Canada."

She took a few steps and turned around. "I'm in the band," she whispered. "Do you hear me?"

He opened his mouth to say something, but she had slipped away into the dark behind the wall. He sat where he was, weighing the matter and mulling it over, trying to find a way out and avoid problems. Out of nowhere a hand appeared on his shoulder and his brother was saying, "Please, Majid, my brother. Please. For God's sake."

He looked at him, startled. Ahmad went on, without stuttering or stammering, "For God's sake, let's go. Let's get out of here!"

15

Majid didn't run away. Before noon a Filipino maid came to him and said that the Mister wanted to see him. She didn't know what he wanted, but it appeared to be something good, because the Mister seemed excited and happy. How did she know he was excited and happy? She didn't answer, but gave him a sly, smart look from her small eyes and smiled. He smiled back at her and winked, and then she turned without showing any concern or surprise over his gestures. Everyone knew Majid was a jokester and a show-off who liked to play around. The grandmother knew it and found it charming, and the servants knew it and found it entertaining. The girl knew it and was skeptical and jealous. But the father did not know. The father was always busy and rarely saw his servants. But because of the parties, he had noticed the talented young man and noticed the way his daughter looked at him. He belittled the matter, though—it was an insignificance, a joke, a desire that would melt away just as all desires do when they are realized. And who knew what would come of the young man, especially if he were to drown him in worldly pleasures, wouldn't he win him over to his own ranks? He was merely a student at a university, which—to say the least—was a hotbed of activism, organizations, festivals and gatherings, journalists, television cameras, and many large delegations. The notorious visit of the French foreign minister still hung in the air, evoking derision from the world and sparking the interest of the West. The campus was a hotbed of activism. The campus was the driving force of the revolution and demonstrations and sit-ins and problems. That was what was on the surface; its depths had not been fathomed yet. What were its depths? Al-Washmi was not going to make the same mistake many others made, the way his father got lost and shot by a stray bullet. He was not going to swim against the tide or walk in an opposite direction. Rather he would plunge into it headlong and sail along from within. The game was on the inside, should be played from the inside; from there he would plow into its depths. He was not his father, raised like a gypsy and roaming from camp to camp like a Bedouin. He had been brought up by Princeton and CNN. His wife had a degree in Middle East Studies from Washington and was a researcher specializing in the economics of developing countries and OPEC nations and water resources and oil. And as for him, even if he had inherited that ill-omened title from his family and his father's scandal, he remained an educated and cultured man who knew many languages and cultures and civilizations. He played piano, too, and tennis and squash, and his daughter wore revealing clothes and drove a Range Rover and an Audi through downtown Ramallah and no one dared say a word, because he was up and everyone else was down. The world was always on the side of the one on top. That was his motto. That was his philosophy deep down. People always got behind whoever stood on top. Whoever stood on top wielded power, and power in this world, this world of globalization and open trade and corporations spanning continents and oceans and ideologies was no longer as it used to be—a game of capital and influence and position—now it required the highest level of technical skill and the knowledge of ions and microchips. Tiny microchips mere millimeters in size, but they contained secrets and ideas and electrodes, and the electrodes were connected to wires that branched out in every direction and changed colors to every color and every nationality. And that's what the world was all about.

And so whether they called him al-Washsham or al-Washmi, he was no longer a gypsy son of a gypsy. Now he was prominent and tough and had muscles and owned real estate. His mother in particular was not just anybody. She was a highly regarded woman by any measure. In her youth she had been a lovely and fashionable widow who was well-spoken in several languages and sought after in social salons, because she had been raised in Jerusalem and had a slight accent of strange origin that made her mispronounce her r's.

Majid and Ahmad entered the parlor. The room opened onto the courtyard with its white marble tiles like mirrors that reflected things on their surface and also reflected light and the shiny flowerpots and dangling palms, giving off the purest green and blue tones. The windows were open, the sky was summery blue, and there was the shade of the pine trees in the background and the fragrance of roses.

Ahmad's brother poked him on the shoulder and joked, "Take a picture of this." There was no need to remind him, because everything there was meant to be a picture. A picture of the reflected flower pots. A picture of a window opening onto the hills of al-Tiri and the olive trees and the red-tiled rooftops of the old houses and the masses of cypress trees. A picture of his feet reflected beneath his shadow. And a picture of a picture—there was an oil painting on the wall of a pretty, youthful woman with fair skin and black hair who looked like Laura, but it wasn't Laura, nor was it the mother as they said, because the mother's hair was reddish-blonde. It was her grandmother in her youth in a wine-colored taffeta dress with an open neckline. She had a half-open fan in her hand and her fingers were laden with diamonds.

The Filipino maid let them in to a large parlor that overlooked a dazzling hillside. From there the mountains and valleys looked like a painting or a picture in a geography magazine. The man was sitting at the table, on which there were papers and a pitcher of juice and a plate of grapes and tender wild cucumbers. He caught sight of them in the light, so he squinted and waved for them to come in. The maid approached with the two brothers and he ordered her in English to bring glasses for the juice. He motioned for the two brothers to sit down. He gestured toward the grapes and cucumbers, so Majid thanked him as he remained standing, patting his chest with his hand in a well-known gesture of gratitude. But the man insisted. Majid plucked a grape and handed his brother a cucumber. The two sat down.

Al-Washmi began by praising the roses and the garden and the green grass in the courtyard. Then came the juice, and then a cluster of grapes for this one and one for the other, then tell about your brother, where does he study? What does he study? What does he want to be? And the older brother would answer for him while the younger brother fiddled with the cucumber and counted the grapes between his fingers and glanced out of the corner of his eye. Then, "Majid, you are very talented and have a beautiful voice, and you play well, too, but you need some pruning. You know, some trimming, like a tree. Do you know what I mean? Of course you do. But Majid, the training here is not very strong. You know that. I'm talking specifically about music. And now we are concerned with building and discovering talents and abilities so we can grow and climb and be like the rest of the world. All of that depends on the leadership and the new generation. The new generation is the target. Our generation lived through two wars—no, three—and all of them bitter. All defeats. What can we do? What will this generation and the next do? We have built what we could, but you, you are the new generation. Do you understand me? Of course you do. What if we were to teach you, prune you, trim you? Would you come back like a professional, highly regarded, someone who understands art and music better than Omar Khayrat and Salim Sihab? Not Omar Khayrat and Salim Sihab? Then what about Kazem al-Saher? See how that rascal made it big and imposed himself? He went to Cairo and pounded in his tent pegs and became a star, despite Saddam. Do you think politics don't play a role? They do. But art has its market. Art sinks into the ground, across generations. Kazem al-Saher made it—imagine that!—despite Saddam, and you will, too, despite Arafat. The West sees us in a very ugly and negative light. One minute Saddam, the next Arafat, and the next some Bedouin with a dirty lice-infested beard holding a knife behind his back. Do you know our image in Canada and Washington and London and Paris and even Oslo? Do you know what it's like? You don't. I do. Ask me about it and all the times I lived through the bitterness of being an Arab in the marketplaces of the West. The West does not respect material things. It respects ideas. It respects art. It respects power and ingenuity. Don't be confused. I know. I know that the West is inclined toward material things. The West works for material things, kneels and prays to material things, but the West also knows that material things come and go and do not last forever. Like the Arabs' oil. What will we have when it runs dry? The West knows our crisis. We own the oil, but they have the knowledge. And what is the value of owning something you know nothing about, nothing at all, nothing about its origins, its depth, its weight, its extent, or its history? Do we even know what it is composed of? Or where it is formed? Do we know how to find it? Do we know how to tap it and where to tap it and how to filter it and sell it for the highest price? Why is OPEC Third World while they're First World? Why is OPEC, despite the oil, impoverished and backward? Because OPEC possesses a resource it knows nothing about except to export it. When it comes to refining it and circulating it and gambling with the price of the yen and exploiting the dollar and the euro and the NASDAQ and the Nikkei, we are ignorant about it the way we are ignorant about people and women. You laugh and your brother is shy, but truly, tell me, young educated man, what do we know about the opposite sex except as wives and mistresses and eyes peering through veils? Is it reasonable that we should interact with heads hidden behind veils and layers of cloth? Is it reasonable that we should enter the marketplace, the global marketplace, with the women of Pashtun and Khomeini? Do you see their pictures? Sacks of rice and potatoes are better looking than they are. Is that what we want? Is that what we are satisfied with? And if they come into power, will they let us live in peace? Eat in peace and drink in peace and sing and dance and treat women like human beings and pray to God in our own way and according to our own beliefs? What will happen to the Christians? What will happen to the Alawites? What will happen to the Baha'is? What happened to Buddha under the Taliban? They blew Buddha up, blew up the stone statues with all that history and civilization and glorious artwork. Touristic treasures, and they blew them up. They blew up history. They blew up the principle and freedom to worship each according to his own belief. Is that what we want? Is that what we will allow to come into being? If they reach us, it's all over. Art and civilization are over. But art is the pivot, the mover. Do you understand the role of the artist?"

Majid shook his head a number of times, his heart pounding. He had been swept away by the words. He felt his soul rising up and flying away with him above a garden the size of the whole world. He was a bird passing from branch to branch across distances and civilizations, and an ancient tree, strong and deep-rooted, planted in the ground, from whose location energy and rays of light emanated. And he was the artist, the bird of the earth, on the highest branch in the tree, looking at the earth and seeing the world as a huge open space and people as very small.

The man reached out to pick up his glass of juice and began drinking. Majid watched him and studied him as if he were looking at a ghost embellished with golden thread and crystal. Was this Badr al-Washsham? Was he the same one whose reputation Majid had heard all about? Was this the agent, son of an agent, son of the rootless bastard? Was this the one they called vile? How strange! How baffling!

He felt his brother's hand against his elbow and his voice whispering, "The c.. c.. contest." The man looked up and smiled at the boy. With an affectionate tone he asked Majid what his brother wanted. Majid stammered and said, still moved by what he had seen and heard and felt, "He's reminding me of the party and the contest." He looked at his watch and said, "The contest. We're late!" He looked right and left and said, "But I am totally confused! I don't understand! Believe me, you are great!"

The words fell heavily on the younger brother's ear, like a bolt of lightning and a clap of thunder. He had heard about al-Washmi what he would never forget: about commissions and smuggling and selling ID cards and trafficking goods and drugs, and Jews coming and going and houses under suspicion of corruption and cheating. That was what he had heard his father saying, and his father was someone who knew the matters of the town and people's secret affairs. That was what he read in the papers and publications. But Majid didn't read and rarely looked ahead. Occasionally his fog and his artistic spirit would lift and he would fight, and then he would retreat and back off just as quickly. And now here he was filling with a passing puff of air, feeling the summit approaching him and a hand reaching out to raise him up and push him toward Rome and Marina and Cairo of the East. He was filled with exuberant praise and said sincerely, "I am very grateful. I will always cherish your kindness and your favor."

Ahmad nudged him and nervously whispered, "Come on! The show!"

Al-Washmi quieted him with a wave of his hand, bringing the visit to an end. "We need your grades and diplomas and recommendations, and above all else, your father's signed consent."

He called out in excitement, "Of course, of course. It's all there."

He took leave of the man, shouting boisterously, "Rome! Rome!" He looked at his brother and jumped for joy, shouting out loud, "I can't believe it!" His brother just stared at him and whispered, "It's your turn on stage. We're late!"

16

They arrived late at Bir Zeit and found the band in a tight situation. The announcer had already introduced them and called them to the stage, but since Majid wasn't there, he'd given their turn to another group. And now that group was up on stage, singing and playing instead of Majid's band.

No one said a word. They didn't even look in his direction. They just sat there on the steps behind the stage in the campus auditorium. The audience had gathered around the stage and on the steps and on top of the walls and up in the trees, until there was no standing room left. Majid pushed his brother in between the band over to the farthest corner behind the stage and winked at him. But the wink did not help comfort his stunned brother. The scene was much bigger and fancier than he had imagined. The student audience was in the thousands, plus reporters and parents and dignitaries and scouts and security guards, and tanks too. That meant the occupiers did not underestimate the crowd and the music and the poems being recited. What would happen if things got out of control and the crowd went wild? What if their emotions were to spill over on hearing a poem or a song and they rose and flared up right there on the campus like a moth inside a lantern? A moth could fly away, and the glass of the lantern could break, and the oil could spill and the peace and safety could be shattered—the peace and safety of an occupation that had lasted many years, generations, continued and become routine, a way of life. But the moth was still hovering. It might get burned, or the lantern might explode and shatter.

Ahmad saw his father in the third row among the writers and journalists. He also saw Badr al-Washmi in the second row among the sponsors, the dignitaries, and the bigwigs.

How had he gotten there so quickly? The strange thing was that al-Washmi was right in front of his father, not more than a few heads and seats separating them. Al-Washmi's head was very conspicuous, very handsome, with dignified gray hair and northern features and blue-green eyes. He had athletic shoulders and an elongated neck that had been tanned by the sun to a golden, reddish brown, and he enjoyed a sizable stature. As for Ahmad's father, Fadel al-Qassam, his head was hardly noticeable, balding slightly; he had dusty dark features and was wearing an old jacket. The poor man had foregone his own needs in favor of the Italian boots and the leather jacket for his son the performer so his son wouldn't lose face in front of his peers. And now his son the performer was missing his turn, not appearing in the boots or barefoot for that matter, and no leather jacket, either. Where was he? And his dopey brother, where was he? What about the band and the music award?

He finally caught sight of his younger son on the steps leading to the stage, under the trees, so he waved to him, but Ahmad was watching the crowds of people from behind his sunglasses and his camera, taking pictures. Where had that crazy kid been? He waved his arms. Where did you guys go? Why are you so late? He waved until he became embarrassed in front of his colleagues for making such a fuss, and put his arms down and listened to the music.

The crowd clapped and cheered for the band as it finished, and someone yelled, "Palestine—free and Arab!" But his voice was weak and got lost amid the clapping and clamor of the people and the high-pitched sounds from the microphone and the buzz of the speakers and whistles of the crowd.

At last the band's turn came—the band with lead singer Majid al-Qassam. The announcer introduced them with great excitement, for he knew Majid's popularity among the students and the regulars and the music connoisseurs who heard him sing in hotels and at wedding receptions. "The *majd* band led by the glorious Majid al-Qassam!" The crowd cheered and clapped. Someone who was standing on the wall shouted, "Stand up! Stand up!" And others echoed, "Stand up! Stand up!" The stadium was filled with a loud roar, "Stand up! Stand up!" The band members entered the stage, one by one, and stood embarrassed by the welcome and shouts of the people and their compromised position after being late. But the crowd's excited reception and the sounds of people shouting made them forget their embarrassment and anger at Majid. If most of the band members had sensed it before, now they were certain that the applause and the acclaim was for the rising star Majid al-Qassam. They were part of his show, beneath his wings, a position that had benefits as well shortcomings. Indeed, all of Majid al-Qassam's short-comings—his negligence, moodiness, and self-aggrandize-ment—melted away the moment he stepped onto the stage. All that applause—was it not for Majid? All that cheering—was it not for Majid? All that excitement when they shouted his name, was it not a sign that Majid had become a star twinkling in the West Bank sky above the mountains of Galilee?

Majid did not appear immediately. He waited a few moments while the people yelled and clapped in unison. One minute they were clapping, the next they were shouting, "Majid al-Qassam! Play! Play! Tik, tik, tik, tik. Majid al-Qassam, let us hear your voice! Tik, tik, tik, tik. Majid al-Qassam, son of the revolution. Tik, tik, tik, tik. Majid al-Qassam, your nation is free. Tik, tik, boom, boom!"

His father was struck with awe. Was all that applause for his own son? His moody, flippant son with his foolish behavior and demands? Was he the one they were describing with such wondrous descriptions and applauding with such unified rhythm? Then it was true he was an artist. Then it was true he had talent. Then it was true he was the lead singer of an important band, the glory band, and those now on stage were the members of the glory band with its lead singer Majid al-Qassam! But his father had not heard about Majid or written about him, about him or them, because the band, it was said in Ayn al-Mirjan, was just a dance party band for teenagers. But these teenagers were not so teeny. They were young men and women. And here they were standing on the stage, smiling seriously and without affectation, shaking their heads acknowledging their audience, standing like soldiers in perfect formation and discipline, dressed completely in black except for small scarves they wore around their necks with the colors of the Palestinian flag and the kaffiyeh. So then why did the rascal insist on the leather jacket? Was he going to appear in the leather jacket and be different from the members of the band?

At last came Majid al-Qassam. He jumped onto the stage wearing black clothes and a scarf with the flag and the kaffiyeh, waving his hands in a victory sign. The crowd roared, "Play! Play! Son of the revolution, play! Play! Son of the liberators, play! Play! Revolution for victory and freedom!"

His father looked around in amazement. He saw the writers and the journalists following along with the crowd and chanting with the students, "Play! Play!" And clapping and looking all around the place—above the steps and the walls and the tree branches—with hopeful smiles on their faces and the excitement of youth in their hearts. It was as if the atmosphere had puffed them up, revived the hopes of the past and dreams of liberation and freedom, and brought back days they had lived before, the good old days, before the Naksa, when Gemal Abdel Nasser was like a rocket with the raging beauty of youth, like Omar Sharif. His son Majid was like that. He felt tears well up. He felt sorrow wringing his heart, because he knew what was beneath all the show and all the performance—he knew all about his son's madness and his faults and his clothes and his stupid shoes and hair gel. He felt the blade of an enormous, sharp knife plunge into his heart, the blade of contradiction: This would be their downfall; their dreams would fill them with false hopes like in the movies, like scenes on television; they were the onlookers who ate and drank but didn't speak or move; they were the ones who put their feet up and gulped down Coca-Cola and hamburgers.

"Stand up! Stand up!" the crowd shouted. Majid shook his head and smiled into the cameras and greeted the audience with his head bowed down and his hand patting his chest until he approached the microphone and said, "At your service. At your service." The crowd's excitement grew even stronger and their shouting louder: "Play! Play! Son of Qassam, play! Son of the brave, play! Son of the revolution! Son of nations." Boom, boom, boom, boom. They whistled and howled.

His father placed his head in the palms of his hands and closed his eyes. Now what? What was he hearing? True, his son's success and the audience's applause pleased him, as the father responsible for his upbringing. But as for the homeland, the people, the revolution, and faith? Yes, the boy was a true artist, born with music in his blood and rhythm inherited from his mother and his grandmother and people's weddings. But he was not the revolution, not the dream of the revolution, not the liberator of the country and the homeland. He was not the great freedom fighter Izzeddine al-Qassam. He wound up with that name by chance, inherited the title, inherited the meaning, but he was not that al-Qassam, and neither had he been. He was Fadel, the son of the camp, and Majid was son of the wishy-washy generation, a corrupt generation, with their constant clowning around and Coca-Cola and Italian boots. But people, people's minds, and true, mature work had nothing to do with such trivialities!

Out came the voice and the singing of the band and the roar of the people. "O my dear wretched countrymen!" The father's heart leapt at the words and the voices and the roar of the instruments and the singing. The hair on his arms stood on end, from its very roots. He cocked his head and listened very carefully to make out amid all the rumble his son's voice, which rang out like a call to prayer. The buzz of the crowd died down. Silence prevailed, except for the *mawwal* and the burning voice trilling with emotion and spilling over with sadness and strength. It came from the depths and rose to pierce the clouds, the mountains rocking and shaking the tallest trees. Heads swayed, chanting, "Allah, Allah!" Longing and desire ebbed in words that swelled with emotion and love. His voice came in warm waves, releasing the soul from its lodgings, freeing it to live the dream in all its details, young again, stronger, deeper, believing more than ever in freedom and humanity.

His father was moved. He raised his head and stopped thinking and analyzing and dotting his i's and crossing his t's. He was swept away. He melted into the melody with its twists and turns and became one with his son. Even he, Fadel al-Qassem, was incapable of saying anything but what the others were chanting. "Allah! Allah!" When the call to prayer ended and the rhythm went back to a steady beat and the tambourine shook and the drum reverberated and the clapping started back in rhythm with the music, he started clapping, too, and calling, "Play! Play!" He was a young man again, just like everyone else in the crowd, like the students and the reporters. He forgot about his son, forgot the frivolous son who dreamed of making a recording and a video and boycotted food for the sake of

Italian boots and a tub of hair gel. He flew on the wings of the melody. When Majid finished singing and the audience stood up, he, too, stood up. He stood up for renewed hope. And he whispered in a raspy voice through his tears, "An artist. By God, he's an artist."

17

The two of them were on their way to Ayn al-Mirjan, accompanied by Suad, Majid's friend from the band, who lived in Nablus. She invited them for a cup of coffee and a quick trip into the old marketplace and the main plaza. Then she took them up to her house in the old city to introduce them to her mother, who was a weaver. Her mother had a workshop with a number of young girls working for her and hand-powered machines and spools of thread like cotton candy: pink and blue and pistachio and yellow and all kinds of colors. Ahmad stood there enchanted, looking at all the wool and the hands going back and forth with unbelievable speed, and the bobbins of yarn spinning around like dancers. His brother was carrying on a long conversation with Suad's mother. While Suad went into the kitchen, Ahmad stood watching the girls from the corner of his eye and watching the threads unwind. He whispered to himself, "I should take a picture!" But he was too shy and let his eyes wander all around the workshop. He could see Mount Ebal and the edge of the forest from the window. He saw the cactus and the olive trees and milky white houses scaling the heights and standing out against the background, appearing speckled with gray and a little bit of green. A fragrant breeze wafted by, carrying the smell of Arabian jasmine, and he noticed on the ledge of the western window some old empty cheese cans with branches of jasmine and carnation plants sprouting from them, making a summery wall between the girls in the workshop and the neighbors.

He thought of the windows at the Washmi family mansion and the potted palm trees reflected on the tiles that shone like mirrors. The tiles here were etched with designs and had no shine to them at all. Voices came from behind the jasmine plants, a *qanun* solo on the radio, a child crying. An intense sense of belonging came to Ahmad amid these sounds and the girls' faces and the scent of jasmine. And Ebal stood right before him, so mighty he was awestruck. Here were the rocks and Mughr al-Thuwwar and the cactus and the sanctuary of Sitt Suleimiyyah and Sheikh al-Imad. Such was the history of this city and the history of Abu Suad and his family, too. Abu Suad had been in Ramleh prison for years, but despite that, his family survived without complaining and life went on.

Then, completing this perfect atmosphere, Suad served glasses of ice-cold juice flavored with orange blossom water. Ahmad relaxed for the first time since he and Majid had left Ayn al-Mirjan for Ramallah and Bir Zeit and the music festival. There everything had felt strange to him, but here people were without pretenses, without hidden agendas and secrets. The smell of jasmine mixed with the smell of food cooking, and the sound of the machines mixed with the tune from the *qanun* and the people's voices, and the mint and the wild cucumber and the smell of bread and a pickup truck blew its horn as it made its way through the marketplace, and the driver's voice shrieked, "Get out of the way!"

Suad took Ahmad up to the attic. Past an old bed and lots of empty spools, over in the corner, a cat lay on a lambskin with a litter box, water, and food beside her, and three cute little kittens playing and jumping over a ball of yarn. The mother cat watched over them with amazing poise. Ahmad asked Suad why the mother didn't play with her babies, and she replied very seriously, "Because she is a mother." She reached over, picked up a little white kitten the size of a baby chick, and held it to her chest and started petting its fur and talking gently to it.

She tried to give it to Ahmad, but he stepped back and turned his head away.

"You're afraid of a cute little, soft little kitten?" she rebuked. "Pet her, pet her—feel how soft she is."

So he reached over and touched her fur. The cat looked at him with turquoise eyes like glowing blue beads and a face as pure and white as jasmine. Her little face was like a beautiful human face, like a little baby, or a little angel, and her eyes were more beautiful than anything he had ever seen, full of understanding and intelligence and life. She enchanted him. He stroked her fur and she licked his hand with a coarse tongue like sandpaper. But he understood the gesture and understood she was content with him, so he picked her up. When he held her to his chest and started petting her fur, she started purring softly like the sound of a tiny narghile. But she was a living creature, as beautiful and tender as could be. He stared at Suad in amazement, so she nodded her head and encouraged him, smiling, "You should understand that animals love people." He nodded his head. He held the kitten and clung to it. From that moment forward, the kitten became the focus of most of Ahmad's pictures.

But what really surprised him was Suad's manner. Suad the serious, Suad the hardworking, became a child in that attic with the cat. "Cute kitty, kitty, Amber, my moon, so sweet, such a light-blooded soul." She used names and adjectives that belonged to cats and trees and plants. Suad studied biology, and to her all living things were connected: plants, cats, dogs, birds, and people, all together. And even though they didn't have a garden or a yard, their house, suspended above the domes and the arches, was filled with flowering houseplants and mint and jasmine vines that crept over the doorway creating a small arbor, much smaller, and much more beautiful than the gazebo.

"That is sweet basil," she told him, pointing. "And those are carnations. And that is *shama'a*—or, its common name, the seven years. Look at the flowers—they're like velvet."

He looked at the flowerpots and tin can planters and he felt as though he were indeed in the midst of a luxuriant garden. There was *mirjan* and a pepper plant and lilies and irises and vines and a honeysuckle shrub.

"These are living things?" he asked, smiling.

She pointed to the kitten on his chest. "And this is a living thing."

He thought about it and said, "A living thing, so it lives and dies?"

"All living things live and die, but death is not the end."

"What do you mean?"

"I mean, it is possible for us to die so others may live."

"But that means the end!"

She shook her head and smiled.

So he asked, still bewildered, "You mean we can still live after death?"

She pointed to the kitten on his chest, so he asked in amazement, "Like cats?"

"Like cats," she said confidently, smiling. "With nine lives."

She saw him sitting there confused and awkward, with embarrassment stumbling over his tongue, so she explained clearly. "All living things have souls, and when they die, the souls live in new bodies: a flower, a tree, a cat, a bird. Do you understand?"

He shook his head once, then many times in a row, and said, "No. I don't understand."

"I mean we shouldn't pick flowers and uproot trees, and we should treat cats like human beings, because they have the spirit of life dwelling in them, the spirit of the creator, and maybe even the spirit of a person inside them."

He looked at her and got the feeling she was pretending to be a philosopher for him, or mocking him, so he relaxed his eyelids and shut his mouth and decided to listen without asking any questions. She noticed that, so she said very seriously, without smiling, "Look and think about it."

She lifted the kitten from his chest and brought it up close to his face and said, "Look into her eyes. Think about it."

He looked into the kitten's face and saw how her face resembled a person's, a beautiful, living, breathing person, and he saw her little mouth like a ruby and her tiny nose like a peanut, and her white face like a full moon. He remembered Mira and her expressions and the freckles on her little nose. Bewildered, he asked, "And what about the Jews?"

She didn't hear his question, so she asked him to repeat.

He turned his face away and asked again, "What about the Jews?"

"What about the Jews?"

"I mean the Jews, how? I don't understand."

She said slowly, "Of course the Jews are people."

"And they have souls?"

She stood up in front of him and smiled. "You tell me."

"I mean, we shouldn't pick flowers and we shouldn't uproot trees and cats are like human beings, and what about Jews? Why should we uproot them?"

She asked sharply, "We uprooted *them*, Ahmad?"

He didn't answer. He took a few steps away from her, so she followed him, feeling his confusion and bewilderment. She asked him again, "You tell me. Who uprooted whom?"

He could not find any convincing and honest answer except to say simply, "They uprooted us." But Mira and the cat and Bobo and Suad and all the living things, all the souls, all the plants and human beings and creatures and sweet Mira was like the kitten, or was the kitten actually Mira? The kitten was purring softly on his chest like a motor, but she was not a machine, she was a person, like a person, with nine lives.

Suddenly he asked, "Is your father in prison?"

She nodded her head and said stiffly, "Yes, my father is in prison."

He lowered his head. The kitten lay on his chest, meowing, and the image of Mira appeared and disappeared, swaying before his eyes. "You're sad?"

He asked the question as if it weren't a question, as if it were fact, which is why she didn't feel the need to respond. She turned around and took a few steps toward the flowerpots and the tin can planters of jasmine and whispered, "Prison is our fate, like death. It has been written on us."

She turned toward him, smiled, "And after death…"

He whispered, "Does the spirit inhabit a new body?"

She pointed to the kitten on his chest and said, "Nine lives."

18

The cat became the most important creature in his life. He fed her milk and bread and yogurt. She would lap up the liquid and stay away from the bread. She was still a baby, the size of a chick, but over the course of a few weeks, she grew and started jumping and hiding behind the couch whenever anyone in the house startled her as she clawed at the fabric of the furniture. He tried to explain to Mira that cats were nicer than dogs, but she didn't understand. He used his hands and spoke, "Amber is a cat. A kitten." She didn't understand. "Meow, meow," he said. She laughed and said, "Meow, meow." He pointed to the dog and imitated its voice and said, "Lo aw aw like Bobo. Amber meow meow." She laughed and puffed some air and twisted her hand around and said "meow, meow" and ran around with Bobo running at her heels. He wished he could take Mira to Amber, but he knew that taking Mira to his house was impossible. What would his mother say? How would his father react? Not to mention that the distance was far and the terrain rugged between the settlement and Ayn al-Mirjan. He was able to bear the fatigue because he was a boy, older than she was and rougher than her, and Arabs were rougher than Jews and used to getting tired and crossing long distances. That was what his father had said to Majid. But Majid said with stifled sarcasm, "Rougher than them? If only we were rougher than them."

"I mean we've grown accustomed to doing without things, tiring ourselves, going hungry," his father said. "I mean, we're more patient."

"If only we were more patient," Majid answered. He yelled at the cat for going near his guitar and said to his brother, "Get that cat away from my guitar before I throw it out the window." Ahmad picked up the cat and went outside to the yard and set off with her toward the hill. He walked and walked, and the cat was quiet and still, looking all around and taking everything in. He got the feeling she was starting to understand, like a diligent child who observed everything. She looked at the world and she turned her head toward sounds and she gazed at him with the sweetest look in her eyes, as if to say, "I love you." He pulled her to his chest and to his neck and kissed the edges of her eyes and behind her ears and whispered, "Amber, my beauty, my darling."

But when he got to Mira's, the kitten was frightened by the dog and ran away and hid in the thorn bushes. He searched for her between the rocks, under the bushes, behind the yellow-flowered *tayyun* and the wild thyme, but his cat wasn't anywhere to be found, and neither was Bobo or Mira. Mira left him to look for the cat by himself. She looked at the cat and smiled and said, "Yofi," but when the dog barked at the cat, she didn't show any concern. The dog disappeared, the cat disappeared, and Mira took off. He was left all alone, anxiously searching.

He sat on the rock, bereft, waiting for his cat to appear, or for the sound of her in the thorn bushes. He missed her desperately, with a strange, special sadness. The cat had really started to take form in his mind as something more than an animal. A heart and soul moving at his feet and on his arms and on his chest when he picked her up and carried her around the house. This creature had a heart that was beating and ears that could hear and respond to being called. He would call "Amber," and she would look at him from any corner and any direction. Behind the tree, under the couch, on the bed, on the bench—as soon as he said, "Amber," she would turn and look and come running to him. At first he loved her because she ate out of his hand and depended on him. Then when she grew, he loved her even more when she started responding to his touch and made him feel as though she returned his love. Did she love him more than Mira? Did he love her more than he loved Mira? Or was the cat Mira, a substitute for her?

At first, he thought of her as Mira. He imagined her. He would put the cat on his chest in an embrace and whisper, "Mira," and the cat would say, "Meow." He would say, "I love you," and she would say, "Meow." Eventually the word took bodily form, as did the cat. The cat took on a personality within his own personality. She became a mirror of his thoughts. She would attack an insect, paw at it and pester it until it tired out, then she would strike it and eat it. At first he saw her as savage, disgusting and repugnant, but then he understood the story, the story of animals and nature, and the story of man and nature, and the story of defending life by taking life.

He said to his father, "If we give her enough to eat, she won't kill." His father smiled and said compassionately, "But nature, my boy, prevails over nurture."

"What do you mean?"

"An animal kills to live, was created to eat, and eats to live."

"And people?"

"Human beings kill in order to rule. What does that mean? That means power, it means politics, it means wretchedness, it means colonization."

"Like the Jews?"

His father looked at him curiously. "What do you think?"

He shook his head, picked up the cat, and carried her to the steps. He felt she was like a human being. She killed to rule. He punished her there above the stairs by locking her in the closet. Then he came back to make amends, because she was an animal that killed in order to live, and because he was stricken with an idea upon hearing about the attack on the settlement of Maaleh Adomim. The idea was that a person in this situation was like a cat. He killed to live. Like Suad had said about a person dying in order to live. Kill in order to live, die in order to live. In other words, life and death cannot be separated when we thought about freedom.

The cat took on human form. Sometimes she was a baby, sometimes a young girl, sometimes Mira. But Mira did not care about him. She cared about her dog. Amber, Amber loved him. She was his baby, his darling, and the closest being to his heart.

He was very shy and withdrawn, afraid of people. He stuttered and stammered and backed away cautiously from every frightening thing. The cat, on the other hand, attacked and took her time and toyed with the mouse before pouncing on it and striking the fatal blow. A little mouse the size of a cockroach, she'd eat and lick her lips in approval. Then she would sit on the grass and wipe her mouth with her small white paw with something like a smile on her face. He felt disgusted and revolted and then amazed. She approved of what she had done. There she was smiling and licking her lips. He smiled at her and said, "Amber, my beauty, I would give anything to see you smile like a human being." She turned and looked up into his eyes. She gave him a beautiful look, a turquoise blue look, like a precious gem, the color of sapphire and emeralds and clear, fresh water like the picture of the sea on the calendar. He had never seen the sea, never got there. But his father told him when he was little, "The sea is like sapphire and emeralds. One day I'll take you there. We must go back."

19

Suad came to visit them. She came with one of the young men from the band. They entered the bedroom and shut the door. Ahmad's brother raised his voice, "I am free to do as I please." Then his father came in. He had left the store and come home all of a sudden. He went directly to where the kids were. Then Ahmad heard a lot more shouting than before. His father was shouting and his brother was shouting and Suad was saying, "A scholarship to go to Rome!"

The door opened violently and his brother came out while his father shouted, "Behind my back? Badr al-Washmi? Son of a bitch!"

Majid turned and said, "I am free to do what I want." He picked up his guitar and his leather jacket and left the house. Suad came out and stood on the steps. "Come back, Majid!" But he got into a taxi and took off.

She saw Ahmad then, and smiled and stroked his cheek. "Don't worry," she said. "He'll be back tomorrow."

A tear dripped from his cheek, and he went outside to follow Majid. But Majid was nowhere to be found, so he came back inside and sat on the couch by himself, listening to the hum of the refrigerator and feeling very lonely and afraid. His brother was gone. His father was angry, and his mother was troubled, pacing back and forth and giving him a strange, questioning look, pressing the palms of her hands together and reciting the formula, "There is no power and no strength save in God." She walked toward the door then turned and came back, only to stare at him in fear.

Suad came into the room and stood there in front of him, looking at him. He was still crying silently. He had fallen into a void, into an eerie silence. Amber and his brother, the two dearest to him. She sat down beside him and put her arm on his shoulder. "He'll be back tomorrow," she said again. She looked around, her eyes examining various objects, and then asked him about the cat. He broke into sad, bitter weeping that he tried to conceal, but the sobs came out of him against his will. He stood up and left the house. He walked and walked, headed to the hill. The cat had taken on a new and much greater significance. She had become Majid, and Mira, and everyone dear to him. If Amber came back, he wouldn't feel so empty. He started muttering, "Amber, my beauty. You are most precious." A song came into his head, from his memory, a song his mother sang to him when he was little that made him cry. He cried with it and for it, and his mother laughed and said affectionately, "Look, your son cries to the song!" "O what strands of lovely thread, threads of silken hair, O what lovely threads of silk, how lovely Ahmad's hair… How lovely Amber's hair… How lovely Majid's hair…" He broke into more tears. "O Amber, you and Majid, you and Mira, you and me." He remembered her standing behind the glass, calling to him, sharing secrets with him, looking into his eyes with that look that seemed to say, "I love you." "Like turquoise," his father would say. "Like sapphire, like the sky and colors of the sea, one minute blue, the next green, and the next minute the color of oil or indigo. What amazing colors! God be praised! Praise to the Creator and the Innovator. Look how beautiful! Look how smart she is. So playful and active and childlike. She bounces like a ball. Damn your father, you're so beautiful!"

"No, don't curse her," Ahmad snarled. "Because I'm her father."

That made his father laugh. "Don't be a fool!"

"This cat is like a human being," he muttered, stubbornly. "She's intelligent. She understands me and talks to me and calls 'Daddy.' I feed her and I give her water to drink, and I carry her in my heart and my eyes and in her eyes I see the eyes of a human being." He wanted to say, "I see the eyes of Mira," but he was afraid of his father, so he just grumbled, "Amber, my beauty, you are my eyes." He took off toward the hill to see his cat, to see Mira, and to weep alone over the loss of his loved ones.

20

Issa saw him under the tree by the fence, so he went over to him and asked, "What's wrong? Why are you crying?"

Ahmad hid his face and continued sobbing quietly.

"Hey, Ahmad, shame on you! Tell me what's wrong."

He didn't answer. He continued to cry. Tears streamed down his face onto his palms. He licked them and tasted their saltiness and bitter flavor, and he remembered how the cat used to lick her mouth and then wipe it with her sweet little paw. Her soft, velvety paw, tender and puffy like a ball, like a sponge. He had said to his father, "Look at the cat's paw. It's padded. It's like a sponge."

"God be praised," his father said. "God created her. God created man in His image, and He created animals from flesh and blood, but without a soul."

"What do you mean, without a soul?" he had argued. "Amber has a soul just like a human being. Ask Suad."

"Who's this Suad?" his father had paused between bites to ask.

"You idiot!" Majid had hissed. "Don't you dare say any more."

"Why shouldn't he say more?" his father asked. "Speak. Come on!"

But Majid had left the room, left the house, in fact. Amber and Majid! And Mira, too! The tears flowed down Ahmad's face as if from a spout.

"Stop it, Ahmad. Shame on you, man!" Issa said.

He didn't answer. He turned his face to the east. Issa came closer to the fence and poked his fingers through the openings. Trying to comfort him, he said, "Who hit you? Your father?"

When Ahmad didn't answer, Issa tried, "If it wasn't your father, then tell me who it was so I can go break his head!"

When Ahmad still didn't answer, he said, jeering, "Was it that idiot Mira?"

Ahmad shook his head.

"That idiot Mira got a cat, a new cat like a bunny. White and cute with green eyes."

"A new cat?" Ahmad asked, forgetting his tears.

Issa grinned over his success. "A new cat."

"With green eyes?"

"Like turquoise."

"And her face is white?"

"Like jasmine."

"And she has a long tail like a palm tree?"

Issa stared. "How did you know?"

Ahmad stopped crying completely and felt anger burning his nose, so he wiped it and stood ready to challenge and start something. "Where's the cat?" he asked sharply.

Issa noticed the change in Ahmad's demeanor and laughed a little. "Hey, Ahmad. You've stopped stuttering and stammering!"

"Where's the cat?" he shouted, forgetting his tears.

"They locked her up in a cage like a suitcase and took her this morning to the doctor."

"Why the doctor?"

"To have her fixed."

"Fixed?"

"You know, they slice her open and cut out—" He made a cutting gesture with his finger, as if it were a knife, below his belly.

"Impossible!" Ahmad shouted.

He jumped onto the fence and started screaming, "Mira! Mira!"

"Hey. Lower your voice. Are you crazy?"

When Ahmad kept screaming, Issa left him there and went back to his work.

21

Issa returned and said that Jews loved cats. They had special medical procedures for them, too. Mira's neighbors' cat had its claws removed at the doctor's office, and they also cut off his balls and tossed them in the trash. The poor thing was like a lady now. Ahmad stared at him and went back to stuttering, "But Amber is a female cat, not a male!"

"It's all the same. Female or male, it's all the same." He looked at him and tried to lighten things with a joke, "They could castrate even you."

Ahmad trembled and shivered. He wasn't afraid of being castrated, because after all, he was a human being and far away from them and they weren't going to castrate him. But Amber! Oh Amber! He remembered her eyes and her fur, how so very, very soft it was to touch, and so warm, and so dear, and how her heart beat while she purred like a narghile. When he carried her like a baby on his chest, and she would lick his hand and nip at his fingers with her teeth, sweet little love bites. As if she wanted to say, "I love you." She wanted to say, "Thank you and God keep you for having fed me and given me water to drink and carried me around like a baby on your chest." She wanted to say, "You are my master and my darling and my father and my mother and my everything." And she looked at him with that look. "She's so beautiful," his father had said. "Like the moon, and her eyes are the sea. I see light in her eyes. Look how she understands. Look how intelligent she is."

"Like a human being?" he said, beaming.

"What? You fool, she's a cat. A cat without a soul. An animal."

"You mean, animals don't have souls and hearts?"

"No. They have hearts, but no souls."

"Tell me, what's the difference?" But his father didn't answer. He waved his hand in the air and said, fed up, "No soul. No soul. It means no soul!"

Exasperated, Ahmad yelled, "But she has a heart. Tell me what the difference is!"

Oh, Amber.

Issa said Mira bought Amber a wicker basket like a bed with a little mattress in it. And she bought her cans of tuna and little biscuits with pictures of smiling cats on them. The operation was necessary. Mira's mother said it would be better—cleaner and better. "'Do we need any more problems?' she said. 'The cat will get pregnant and start multiplying like Arabs. Do we need any more of that?' The bitch said 'Arabs' and smiled at me like it was some kind of joke."

"And what did you say?"

"I didn't say anything. What was I going to say?"

"But you heard it."

"Of course I heard it. I hear a lot of things, but I keep quiet."

"You don't say anything?"

"What am I going to say? Tell me what I should do."

"Okay, what about Amber?"

"Never mind Amber or any other crap or stupid talk! Let me get back to work and make some money!"

And Issa went back to his work. Ahmad sat on the rock and gazed into the distance. He started imagining Amber in the hospital and a sharp knife slicing into her, ripping her open, tearing her to shreds. The cat meows and stares in fear, cries and howls and turns in search of Ahmad's face and his chest, in search of his loving caress. How often he fed her, how often he gave her water, gave her milk when she was a baby, broke up the bread when she was little so she could eat it. Then she grew and began eating meat and chicken bones. True, he never bought her cans of tuna and little biscuits with pictures on them, and he didn't buy her a wicker basket with a bed in it, but he fed her his own food. She slept on his lap, on his bed. She was a person, a human being. She was Mira. But Mira had gone far away from him now. She was no longer his beautiful sweetheart. She had become a little settler in Kiryat Shayba, and he didn't like thinking of her anymore. He didn't hate her. Or he did hate her, but he didn't know how to categorize her.

Issa said that Mira kept Amber locked up in a big cage so she would get used to things, because cats run away and go back to where they grew up. That's what Mira's mother said, and that's what he had heard about cats from everyone.

"But, but…"

"But what? Amber is in a cage and her operation is on Thursday."

Ahmad went back home like a corpse. What could he do? What could he say, and to whom could he say it? Should he tell his father that Mira took the cat and caged it up in Kiryat Shayba? He would ask him who Mira was. And how did the cat get to Kiryat Shayba? Should he tell him that Mira used to come to him, used to crawl under the fence in order to play with him? And then his father would shout, "What, you little rascal. You've been playing with her? With the scum of the earth?" No, he couldn't tell. It was enough just worrying about the mess he was already in. If only Majid were around. If only he hadn't run away. If only he hadn't left him. If only he were here, he would understand everything, figure it all out, and go speak with them and get her back. He had worked there. He spoke Hebrew and English. If only Majid were around. But Majid had gone to Rome. And Issa, Issa was concerned with his work and couldn't care less about Amber or anyone else.

The next day he said to Issa, "Take me to Amber. I miss her." Issa refused, refused vigorously. But then he saw the camera and smiled at it. Ahmad hid it from Issa's view inside his shirt and said, "The watch. Take the watch. It's a very valuable Swiss watch. Digital and water resistant." Issa thought about it, and then he negotiated for the sunglasses, too. Ahmad removed the sunglasses and the watch, and with that they reached an agreement.

22

When Ahmad took off his sunglasses, the glare blinded him. The sky was scorching white. The timeworn pasture and the dry thorn bushes shimmered like wavy glass and the light dazzled and hurt his eyes. So he shut his eyes and imagined her. He saw her eyes looking into his, all the colors of the sea, and he thought of his father's description of the colors and his comments about cats being made of flesh and blood but with no souls. No way. How could they be without souls? Amber was like him, like a person. An intelligent cat that understood and spoke with him and called to him. In her eyes he saw the eyes of a human being.

Issa said he would not take him to the cage and the animal pen except at night when people were asleep. There was tight security at the gates and at the entrances, but the hole under the fence that the dog's belly and Mira's hands had carved out was big enough for him to fit through. He would go in through that hole in the middle of the night and walk along the back road, behind the olive grove and the greenhouses and the animal pens.

"But what about your father? What if your father sees you?"

"I'll take care of myself," Ahmad said.

"You won't make any noise?"

He shook his head.

"And you won't take her?"

He didn't answer the question, so Issa stared at him. He tightened his face and said, "Ahmad, the settlers are like demons. Each one has a rifle and a pistol and a machine gun. Don't you dare. Don't you dare!"

He shook his head and shut his eyes. Issa persisted and pressed him. "Swear it. Swear it!"

Ahmad thought a moment inside his head. I won't take her; I'll open the cage door and let her out, and when I let her out, she'll come back to me.

"Swear it. Swear it!"

"I swear to God. There. I understand!"

Issa looked at him out of the corner of his eye, and he looked at the watch, then the camera. Then he smiled at Ahmad and at his possessions.

23

Ahmad left the house silently. He transformed himself into a cat, with soft, spongy, puffy insoles. At first he walked on all fours, and then he sprang to his feet and took off running like a madman. Ghosts and spirits and stories of ghouls and jinns and spooks still haunted his thoughts. His mother had filled him with those stories and with an awful fear of the dark and night noises. But tonight there was a disquieting stillness. The night lights, the moonlight, his shadow lengthening in front of him, the rustle of the thorn bushes, the sound of wild dogs barking, and the croak of an engine, were all disquieting. The croaking sound became clearer and clearer the closer he came to the hill. He could see the settlement sparkling and gleaming with electricity and searchlights and barbed wire fences and pipelines and tall poles and antennas everywhere. Issa said that radar detected sounds, but his father said it detected images. Who was he to believe? His father, of course. And that was why he had to sneak around like a cat, with extreme caution, because the settlers were like demons. Each one had a rifle slung over his shoulder. But Issa fiddled with his new watch and smiled at it. "Don't you worry," he said confidently. "I know them. But swear you won't take her." Ahmad swore up and down, feeling quite confident that his oath was not a lie. It was the truth, because he was not going to take her. He was merely going to open the cage and let her out, and when she was set free, she would come to him.

"Hey, Ahmad," Issa whispered, "Why are you late?"

He lifted the edge of the fence where the dog and Mira had squeezed through. Ahmad crawled on his belly and the palms of his hands, trying to be like a cat. In fact, the cat had taken control of him. She controlled his mind and his senses.

The image of her was right before his eyes. The blue of her eyes and the way she felt to the touch and the murmur of love when she purred like a narghile and slept peacefully on his chest, on his hands, right under his neck. Longing so filled his heart that he nearly went crazy from the yearning. He forgot all the dangers, the spotlights, the fence of the enemy, the rifles, and Mira. Mira vanished from his mind. She was no longer his friend with soft cheeks like apricots. She had become one of them. His father used to say, "They took everything. Let God take them!" So should he call on God to take her? He imagined her as one of those wounded people on television. He thought of explosions and military operations and blood and police and cars and ambulances and trained dogs searching beneath the rubble and between the rocks and the thorn bushes and the trees. He felt his heart convulsing with fear and his knees trembling, and his head was filled with thick smoke that blinded his eyes and plugged up his ears and set the world spinning and rocking. Suddenly he saw the searchlights shining on him and casting his shadow, so he flung himself to the ground. He started bawling. Issa grabbed him by the shoulder and yanked on his shirt and pulled on him violently. "For God's sake!" he said sternly. When Ahmad wouldn't budge, Issa stood towering over him and said sharply, "Come on, come on. Do you want to go in there, or do you want to go back?" He peered at Ahmad's face in the dark and wagged his finger at him and threatened, "But you won't get the watch back." Ahmad buried his face in the dirt. Issa looked at him in disgust and then in pity. "Do you want to see her or not?"

"Okay. Just let me take a breath." He breathed inside the crook of his arm and the smell of the earth filled his nostrils and made him want to sneeze and throw up. He felt dizzy and his arms and legs were like milk and his eyes were hazy with fatigue and the vertigo of fear.

Issa whispered, "The cat is over there. In the barracks over there. That's it. We've made it."

Ahmad lifted his head, looked at Issa and said, feeling sick, "Where's the barracks?"

Issa pointed in front of him. "That's it. We're here. The cat is sitting and waiting."

"The cat is sitting and waiting?"

Issa smiled and started saying crazy things to shatter Ahmad's fear. "I told her we were coming and she said okay."

Ahmad smiled and whispered weakly, "She said okay?"

Issa laughed and joked, "Exactly as I'm telling you. I told her we were coming and I'm telling you she said to hurry up!"

"The cat said to hurry up?"

Issa didn't answer, but rather pulled Ahmad's shoulder hard. Ahmad got up onto his knees, then onto his hands, and walked a few steps, hiding beneath the olive trees and entering the dark shadows of a big barracks. He could smell the animals and the manure and the hay and the humidity. He lifted his head and saw from a distance a glass window and bright light coming from the nearby barracks. Issa pointed with his finger and whispered in excitement, "See? See? The cat is in there."

Ahmad approached the window and peeked inside. He could see lots of cages with dogs and cats and birds and turtles inside them. He asked in wonder about this place.

"It's a hospital and kennel for animals," Issa whispered. "The cat is in there. Can you see Amber?"

"No. I don't see her."

"All right, come on. Oh God. Let's go inside."

Actually Ahmad had seen her through the window, but he pretended he hadn't so Issa wouldn't say he'd held up his end of the bargain and say, "That's it. We're finished," and make good on his promise with just that. No, he hadn't seen her and he would not admit seeing her until he got up close to her and touched her and opened the door to set her free. And when he freed her she would come back to him. He remembered her eyes like the sea on the calendar. All the colors of the sea. The colors of emeralds and sapphires, deep blue and transparent green. He imagined her crying in fear and crawling on her belly the way Ahmad had and hiding from the scalpel and the operation. If he had been there she would have come to him, taken refuge in him, and said, "Save me from the scalpel!" After today she would not be able to have babies, or she could die during the operation, and he would never see her eyes again. She was going to die. She's going to die. Amber's going to die! Tears streamed down his cheeks, so he wiped them with his sleeve and whispered in agony, "Amber, my beauty. I'm coming. I'm coming!" He looked at Issa and said, firmly, "Let's go inside!"

Issa grabbed his arm and pressed on it to warn him. "I hear a noise!" he whispered. "Quiet. Don't move."

Ahmad stood still for a few moments, his heart pounding and his tears drying up, but he didn't move until Issa tugged on him and said once again with apprehension, "Let's go. This way. C'mon. Let's go inside." Ahmad followed behind him. When he opened the door, it made a frightening creaking sound like a long wail. A little dog started barking, then lots of dogs in cages inside and outside started barking. Issa tugged on him again and said sharply, "Go back. Go back." But Ahmad wouldn't stop. He pulled his hand away and rushed toward the cage to open it. But Issa held him tight and pulled him back, hissing, "The guards, you fool!" But Ahmad resisted and tried to wrestle himself free of Issa's grip. His eyes were fixed on her, but she was staring into the distance, a foggy, expressionless look in her eyes. Was she afraid like him? Did she sense fear? Was it that animal instinct for danger, like when there is an earthquake?

He called to her, "Amber!" She didn't hear him. She just kept staring into the distance. The dogs heard him, though, and started barking even more inside and outside the barracks. There were people's voices and Issa's grip on him. He started screaming, "The door! The door!" Issa smacked him on the head and he became even more distraught, struggling and shouting, "The door!" But her door wouldn't open. Instead the barracks door suddenly flung wide open and the security guards rushed in.

Amid the commotion and the soldiers' blows to his head and face and eyes, and Issa's screaming, and the dogs' barking, and the spotlights, and the cars, and the army vehicle, and the warning siren, and windows opening, and whistles blowing, and men and women out in front of their houses armed to the teeth with cannons and machine guns, and men standing in their pajamas with weapons in their hands shimmering in the light and the spotlights, he saw Mira. He caught sight of Mira standing in fear, wearing a little short dress with an embroidered hem. He started to cry in sorrow.

"Mira!" he whispered. And there was a loud whistle.

24

The long siege had begun. Streets were cut off from other streets and the cities were more like isolated cages than cities. Each city was a huge ghetto surrounded by soldiers, and tanks blocked the entrances with trenches and walls of dirt and checkpoints. Young men died at the checkpoints, and women gave birth at the checkpoints, and the sick died at the checkpoints, and there were sniper attacks and public demonstrations and laborers were imprisoned in their own homes and cut off from their livelihood. Cars were replaced by horses and donkey carts that crept along mountain paths. Riding on animals became the new fad, after we were raided by globalization and Israel.

But our correspondent Fadel al-Qassam, thanks to the newspapers and journals and media, looked after himself and clung to his Volkswagen (the mark of a journalist or television reporter) and displayed a kaffiyeh in the rear window to avoid being pelted with stones or bullets. That meant that the correspondent and his family did not have to feel quite the same isolation as most: they had a media car of a sort that only foreigners and important journalists and television cameramen owned. But thanks to his son's idiotic actions, he was prohibited from traveling between cities. He was a captive in the cage of the siege like everyone else. Despite his pride, he contacted Majid, who had read in the newspapers and heard on the radio and on television that his brother and his cousin Issa had undertaken a daring military operation and had been caught trying to infiltrate and plant explosives and mines in the settlement of Kiryat Shayba. The two of them were being held in an Israeli prison and were being interrogated and tortured. Majid's father called and told Majid that the person responsible for taking Ahmad's case would not be able to save his brother because he had neither qualifications nor connections and didn't know how to get around among the collaborators and the arbitrators and the military forces. He followed all that, in a disappointed and despairing tone, with, "I entrusted your brother to you. Do something!" And Majid immediately did something. He went to see al-Washmi and asked him to intervene on Ahmad's behalf. He found al-Washmi near the fountain, where he had visited him that morning with his brother and been offered grapes and wild cucumbers.

When al-Washmi saw Majid, he thought he had come to ask again about the scholarship to study in Italy, so he tried to put him at ease by telling him that the scholarship would come very soon, though he didn't know exactly when. All he had to do was sit tight a few weeks, and if things didn't work out within a few weeks, then maybe in a few months. That meant Majid should not be disappointed and he should spend his free time doing something useful. So what was he doing now that he had graduated and held a highly esteemed degree?

Majid went along with it and listened to him very patiently, waiting for an opportunity to break in and say something. But al-Washmi beat him to the point with a grave question that hit him like a missile. He asked nonchalantly, as he peeled some figs, "I heard your brother planted some mines in Kiryat Shayba."

"No. It's not true. It's a lie. It's nonsense."

Al-Washmi smiled sarcastically. "Hold on. Give and take. How can you be so sure?"

He swore on it. Every limb in his body trembled in anger. "I swear to God! Upon my mother's soul!"

Al-Washmi smiled and tried to calm him down. "Let the dead rest. What matters now is your brother. How? I don't know! But if we knew who and how…"

"What do you mean—who and how?"

"How means how, and who means who. Is it that hard to understand?"

He tried to open his mouth, but al-Washmi raised his hand and said, "Stop. Listen, Majid. Your brother is young. They messed with him. But if we knew who and how, we might be able to intervene."

"Ahmad has been wronged. I am certain of that."

Al-Washmi smiled and shook his head right and left and then down several times. That meant that the accusation had stuck to Ahmad, to them, had stuck to the whole family, Majid included. What was he supposed to do with this animal who was waiting to pounce on him and investigate him and was saying, "Who and how?" He imagined his brother being subjected to questioning and interrogation and beatings and torture, and he was sick in his heart. He could feel his tears ready to flow, so he swallowed his saliva and began muttering, "Oh Lord! Oh Lord!" Al-Washmi looked at him and said sadly, "Your poor father. What a disaster. And the house, they might…"

"Blow up our house?" Majid shouted in alarm.

"Everything is possible. But if we knew who and how, we might be able to intervene for him."

He gritted his teeth and asked, "How should I know?"

Al-Washmi noticed how pale Majid was. "You must know," he said calmly. "We must understand the meaning of the riddles."

"What riddles?"

"Cats and dogs and the black and white panther."

"You mean the little cat?" he asked in surprise.

Al-Washmi did not answer, but smiled a cruel smile.

Majid went on pleading, "My brother is innocent and the lawyer said it was no big deal."

"No big deal? The accusation involves mines and riddles and possibly premeditation and bin Laden."

"Mines and riddles and bin Laden?" he shouted, losing control. "Quit talking nonsense!"

Al-Washmi glared at him. Majid had gone too far, raising his voice. This lowly guitar-playing gardener—telling *him* to quit talking nonsense?

"Okay, okay," al-Washmi said. "Forget the whole thing. When I hear some news about the student exchange, I'll send it along to you."

Majid got up, feeling as if a glass of cold water had been poured over him. Al-Washmi looked him up and down, and repeated in a bored tone, "When I get some information, I'll send it to you."

Majid turned on his heels and took a few steps before speeding off until he bumped right into Laura al-Washmi. She surprised him with a long and drawn out "Hello" that sounded like a *mawwal*. He pushed her out of the way. "Move out of the way. No *hello* or *how-are-you*. What sons of bitches! What strange specimens!"

As he left the villa, Majid saw a young man watering the roses and flowers and spraying the grapes with insecticides. He gave him an angry, loaded look, which made the guy smile. Majid suddenly turned back and faced the door to the villa.

"You gypsy son of a bitch! Bin Laden, he said! Bin Laden!" Majid cursed and spat.

The young man stopped spraying the grapes, and this time he smiled plainly.

25

Majid woke up to the sounds of screaming, banging, slapping, and wailing. He left his room and stood in the walkway to the gazebo hoping he might understand what was going on. It was definitely not a simple robbery or some kind of family quarrel or anything of that sort. The wife was still in Canada, the grandmother was acting like a queen, and Laura could not possibly produce all that screaming and commotion herself. There were the servants and the guards and lots of loud voices and sounds. He crept out from beneath the grapevine toward the window and he heard the words, "They killed him. They killed him!" Then he heard cars and ambulance sirens clamoring into the night. He saw the police and security forces. There were at least ten of them hopping out of their jeeps with machine guns in their hands. "Surround the place. Surround the place," he heard them yell. It occurred to him in a flash that he would be the prime suspect, after that ugly meeting he had had with al-Washmi only hours earlier, and the way he had pushed Laura and swore at her and how he stood at the door and spat, and all that stuff about his brother and Issa and bin Laden. He heard his name mentioned several times. One of them said, "He left swearing and cursing and he mentioned bin Laden." Without thinking, Majid went back into his room, grabbed his clothes, and took off, still in slippers. He stumbled all the way to the cherry trees, where he removed his pajama top and put on his shirt. But he could hear footsteps coming his way, so he jumped over the fence with ease. Out of nowhere, unknown hands seized him and pulled him toward a car while a young man whispered, "Shh. Don't say a word." The car sped off quietly down a side street in the direction of the valley, then up mountain paths. Then the car parked inside a little garage behind a building. Inside the garage, and by the light of a flashlight, two guys got out and unscrewed the license plate and replaced it with an Israeli one. Then they took off again, and just like that, Majid became a fugitive in the hands of a band of revolutionaries, and just like that a new page was opened in the life of the young musician. He put down his guitar and picked up a machine gun.

26

The revolutionaries said to him, "You're one of us." He smiled in distress because the only thing he knew about the revolution were the words he sang at parties and concerts. He would feel the pulse from the crowd in the concert hall and it would spread to him and he would sing louder and the blood would rush to his heart and his fingers and the guitar would transform into rumbling thunder. His father said to him, "You moved people!" He muttered, "Sure, sure," but deep inside he knew his real motives. He wanted to make it to Marina and be like Amr Diab. But now here he was out in the wild, among the trees, under the olive groves, hiding like a goat in a cave carved out of the belly of the mountain. Today they were here, tomorrow over there, walking by night along the mountain paths carrying their belongings and their bombs and some dynamite. Sometimes they would blow up an army vehicle, or plant explosives, or steal into a settlement and blow up an electric plant or diesel tank. But deep inside, they knew the forces were stronger than they were. The Shlomos dominated world summits, from London and Washington, all the way to Moscow. Moscow was gone; the whole world was gone, only Cuba remained. But Cuba was under siege, like Palestine. Lenin was gone and Stalin, too, and they hadn't left any legacy but chaos and imbalance. The balance was lost and we lost the wager and reaped nothing but misfortune and widows and an army that never ran out of orphans and collaborators. We had one Washmi before, and now we have a multitude of Washmis. And organizations with turbans and medals and Mecca pilgrims and imams and trade by the millions. We are the millions. We are the orphans, like sheep without a shepherd. Damn shameful nation!

In the cave, by lantern light, he said to him, "Read." He smiled and said, "I am not a reader." He said once again,

"Read!" Majid looked at him and thought about his beard, and the hair on his hands, and his fingernails. Caveman, from the stone age, the age of stone, Mecca pilgrims praying to a god who didn't hear—what were they doing? They said, "Read and understand the universe and nature and human matters and the ups and downs of the stock market. Today it rises, tomorrow it drops—all you have to do is bet on the invisible world."

Bet on the invisible world? What kind of bet was that?

"Okay, then," they said. "Do you have another suggestion? We bet on knowledge and that didn't work; we bet on understanding and that didn't work; we bet on truth and conscience, and all we got was a forest and idol worshippers and stock markets. But we have something more powerful, more powerful than the atom at Hiroshima, more powerful than Bush."

And who was it, what was it that was "more powerful than Bush?"

"Faith," they said. "Read, read, and pray to God to bring us victory and break them. *La hawla wa la quwwata illa bil-llaah.*"

Majid shook his head. He didn't discuss it, didn't argue, just lowered his head and mumbled, "With God as your Victor, no one can defeat you." He went outside the cave to watch the Apache helicopters bombarding and leveling the villages and the cities and spreading destruction everywhere. He looked up and asked, "Five prostrations or more? What will satisfy you?" And when he didn't get an answer, he picked up his mat and spread it out there, outside his cave, and slept on it. He peered into the heights and said spitefully, "Even if you forgive, I will never forgive. If you fall asleep, I will never fall asleep. You ruled, but now I am the ruler." And he shut his eyes.

27

Ahmad jumped to his feet and said, "Majid, my brother!" His mother drew in a deep breath, and his father's face turned yellow as he stood up.

The man wept on the chest of the young man, but the young man did not cry. He stood looking around and examining each corner of the house. The television, the sofa, the dinner table, and the poster of Jerusalem in its prominent place. Then he searched the mother's face to see if she would greet him wholeheartedly or huff and puff in fear for her son as usual. "Welcome, welcome," she whispered in fear. Then she sat on the edge of the sofa and recoiled into herself.

So the father shouted at her, "Get him a bite to eat!"

She got up heavily and dragged out her movements, noting how the two brothers greeted each other. Neither showed the least bit of affection for the other.

The two brothers sat on the couch and the father sat on his chair in front of the television and the mother went into the kitchen. The father looked carefully at the two boys and noticed right away the secretive, suspicious harmony between them as they sat together. Neither one showed the least bit of interest in the other. They didn't hug; they didn't shake hands; they didn't offer a word of endearment. Ahmad didn't shy away and he didn't blink. He was staring off in some direction with his ears pricked up, not showing any expression. The boy had changed; indeed he was more a young man. He had become serious and spoke with brevity and unsettling calmness. And Majid was different, too. His hair was short and dull, his shirt was dirty, and his face had been darkened by the sun.

With sorrow and worry in his voice, the father said, "It's a strange world. Who would believe?"

Majid lowered his head and with seriousness and weightiness he said, "Dad, the situation is getting worse and worse."

"Worse than this?"

"Worse, much worse." Majid looked around nervously. "There is a military convoy and there are tanks and thousands of reservists. Prepare yourselves."

His father smiled bitterly. "Prepare ourselves? Prepare what? We have no army and no weapons and no backbone. What preparation are you talking about?"

The young man stretched out his hand and said, at a loss, "Rice, sugar, flour, oil—you know. Provisions."

"Worse than this?" the man whispered again. He thought about the conditions of people's lives. Thousands of workers lined up every morning in front of the government offices looking for work and food. The siege had drained their resources and their ways of earning a living. The labor market in Israel and everywhere in the West Bank was closed, with no opening in sight. There were tanks surrounding the cities and there was no longer the smallest opening for a cat or a dog to sneak through. And with daily clashes at the checkpoints in every village and every city, they were greeted every morning and every evening with fresh casualties and funerals and demonstrations replete with fireworks, angry young people, and slogans. Even more horrible was realizing that there was no end in sight to that long tunnel. Now Sharon and his government and the far right were threatening to invade the cantons and evacuate the inhabitants. Evacuate them to where? He had been forced to leave Haifa when he was small, and he lived his childhood in the refugee camp. His father had died in that camp, atop the crate of spearmint gum he was selling on the sidewalk after having been forced out of his carpet shop. And here he was now, witnessing with his own eyes his two sons becoming vagabonds. There was nothing he could do to fix it. That meant that three entire generations of his family had lived with this struggle. Generation after generation would be expelled. It was an unequal war without hope. It was a whirlpool that sucked its victims into a swamp. Death was cheap. How were these young men supposed to face all that power? Power fortified with airplanes, tanks, rockets, and the most modern weapons and deadly contraptions America could produce. What could his sons and their generation possibly do?

Suddenly and without thinking the father said, "Turn yourself in."

Majid turned around and Ahmad stared, but neither uttered a single word. They both knew their father was beginning to fold under the pressure. No one was buying books anymore—a loaf of bread was more important. And *Al-Quds* wasn't selling anymore, because television news coverage was broader and faster. And the security forces raided the house every couple days. If the Jews stormed the West Bank cities, there was a very good chance they would demolish their house. How was their father supposed to bear more than that? The two boys exchanged glances, which caused the father to become angry. Pointing at Majid he said sharply, "I am not blind. This boy… Shame on you!"

The younger boy interrupted with alarming brevity, without stuttering, "I am not a boy. I grew up in prison."

The father noticed for the first time that the boy wasn't stuttering anymore. With astonishment he thought maybe prison had changed him, or something else, some other thing. But despite these thoughts he said, "Oh yes, you are still a boy. Just yesterday you were wearing shorts and coloring and playing with that cat. How did you change? Why did you change?" And pointed at Majid. "It's all your fault."

Majid put his hand on his father's knee and whispered affectionately, "What's wrong, Dad? You've changed!"

"I am a father, Majid. I am a human being."

Unexpectedly, the younger brother spoke again. "Dad, what should we do? Tell me, what should we do?"

The father was surprised by the question and withdrew, mulling over his indecision and fear for his house and his children. He remembered what he used to write about and the things he used to call for and prod Majid to do. Hadn't he said to Majid, "Take him and teach him?" Hadn't he made fun of the boy for being like a girl and having no muscles? Hadn't he been afraid for him because he was so gentle and shy and stuttered all the time?

After a brief pause, Majid said, "This is our fate."

And he smiled his pale smile and added sorrowfully, "They're playing a death dirge, and we're required to dance to it."

The man imagined his two sons carried upon shoulders, wrapped in flags and flowers like the others, like the martyrs and victims of all ages. Why death? Wasn't there some way besides death and destitution and running from the army and the police?

He spoke calmly, trying to appear logical and convincing, "I am of the opinion that you should turn yourself in and prove to the authorities that you are innocent."

The brothers exchanged skeptical glances, so the father said sharply, "If you are innocent, turn yourself in."

"And if they ask me who murdered him?" Majid asked smiling.

His father didn't answer. Majid raised his voice, "Should I say who murdered him?"

When his father didn't answer, Majid went on. "If I turn myself in, there will be an investigation, and possibly torture. I might weaken. Do you want to take responsibility for that?"

The man didn't answer, so Majid asked again, "Do you want that responsibility?"

The man whispered weakly and sadly, "And you would lose your life and your youth and your future?"

Majid lowered his voice and asked gently, "What do I do, Dad? Tell me what I should do."

The man did not answer. He felt himself melting away inside his skin with shame and fear and confusion. He could no longer think straight. He had lost control of his nerves and his brain was paralyzed. He was losing his wits. Did he want his son to rat on people and other people's children?

He took hold of his son's hand and pleaded with supplication and a broken heart, "Look at me."

Majid looked at him curiously, wondering what he meant.

"Look me in the eye," his father repeated. "And tell me the truth, on your mother's soul."

The young man looked at his father with compassion, because he knew that the pressure had begun to take its toll on him.

"Look me in the eye. On your mother's soul, did you kill him?"

Majid shook his head. "Al-Washmi, no."

"Someone else then?" his father yelled.

He didn't reply, so his father repeated, "I'm your father. Honor me and tell me the truth."

Majid didn't answer. He withdrew his hands, stood up, and headed for the door, his brother following behind him. He stopped at the door, turned to his father, and said with emotion, "Father, give me your blessing. It is what I must do."

The father was stricken with the calamity of the situation. Their destiny had already been decided; there was no longer any doubt about it. His son had already become a martyr. This same kid who used to sing and spike up his hair and behave so childishly! And his younger son was waiting his turn to do the same. Just like that. *They're playing a death dirge and we must dance to it.* Was this going to be his children's future? Was this going to be the future of all the children?

Majid, seeing his father frozen in his place, staring, as if he had lost his senses, called out, "Father. Please give me your blessing."

The father responded. "May God be pleased with you, son of Shahira," he mumbled in a daze.

He heard his wife shouting after him. "And what about my son?"

"And your son, too," he whispered, still in a daze.

He flung himself onto the couch, and then he remembered that his son had not eaten. He tried to get up to go after him, but he heard movement and voices outside, so he sat back down, muttering, "And everyone's sons."

28

The town got divided up into cantons, and families were cut off from their sons and the government. The government was in one valley, and the young people were in another. The government labored for the present, not the future. Yet the future was what concerned families and their children. What would happen to the young people? The present was a fog, and the future was in the hands of an afreet, they said—all violence and loss and ruin. Even that boy, even Ahmad, the delicate, shy, sensitive one, didn't stutter anymore. He no longer sat around reading and drawing and watching Michael Jackson. Now he jumped up from his seat and left the house and didn't return until late at night. What did he do? And where did he disappear to? What was he thinking? And what about school and his studies? The teacher said, "Of course, yes, he has definitely fallen behind. What did you expect from your son? That experience made him grow up fast. It stole his childhood. But tell me, is there any news?" The father pretended not to understand, because it was essential to be cautious. The town was full of collaborators and al-Washmis. So he said, obscurely, "There's no news except about Sharon and his winning the election. He'll do to us what he did in Sabra and Shatila. God help us."

"I mean about Majid," the teacher whispered.

"God help us," the father said stiffly, staring at him. "Good-bye." And he walked away without taking a polite leave or apologizing. What could he do? Fear was frightening. Even those you knew before, you didn't know anymore. So-and-so's son had become an agent, and the grocer's son had become an agent. And Abu Yusef's son, too, and the doughnut and date-cookie seller, and the lupine bean seller carried his tray around into the neighborhoods trying to obtain information. We're all, the father thought, a bunch of sellouts. We're trash. And the attacks did not stop. A bar was blown up, some explosives blew up, and kids who had lived through years of filth and occupation and the shackles of imprison-ment had now become bombs. They were without hope, and so they sacrificed themselves, made themselves into bombs that walked around on two feet, penetrated and hit deep inside, challenged the security forces and the prevention forces and the checkpoints and a strangling siege that had lasted one year, then two years, then many years.

Was there any hope? Was there any escape?

From a telephone on the street near her house, Majid called Suad. "Get ready. There is a military convoy and tanks and thousands of reservists."

"I know," she said.

When he showed up at her door, she led him up to the attic.

He knew that she knew, but he wanted to feel as though he was a person in the ordinary world, an ordinary person who loved singing and music. He wanted some companion-ship, some warmth. The life he was living had caused him to wither and harden. His heart had rusted. His senses were deadened. His previous hopes of living for music had died. Here he was now, drowning in pools of blood and breathing in the smoke of volcanoes. Why was he no longer afraid of death? Like everyone else in his generation, born and raised and living under the occupation. The occupation meant contradictions: revolution versus debasement, collaboration versus sacrifice, vileness and depravity and espionage versus the ultimate sacrifice, blowing oneself up. Majid was hanging in the balance—or rather, in the imbalance. The matters of nations were supposed to be measured with wisdom and in best interests, but here all calculations were performed without compasses. In simple terms, that explained why he had sung Mahmoud Darwish songs and chanted, "Leave me alone, people. Let me go where I want to go." He was the child of a generation that spun up and down and knew nothing but defeat and self-contempt. The reaction to that was to pump oneself up with a poem and a burning dream. A nozzle that pumps one full of gas—eventually the dream blows up.

Suad returned carrying a dinner tray. She sat out on the ledge of the roof while he ate. "There are lights coming from the army and the tanks over on top of the mountain," she whispered. "They've surrounded Nablus. Not even a cat could escape. How did you sneak out?"

"That's a trade secret," he said, smiling and chewing. He was quiet a moment and then added, "Even if they build a wall from the ground all the way up to the sky, we'll still get to them and blow them up."

They both fell silent while he ate and people slept. Nablus was drowning in silence and apprehension. The hunger of the poor, the loss of young sons, airplanes bombing targets all over the city, and the powerlessness of the residents to lift the siege or return fire made them see that stones no longer served their purpose. Can you combat an F-16 with a slingshot? That became a popular thing to say among the locals, and they joked and mocked the spontaneous encounters between demonstrators and tanks, and airplanes, and rockets, and a new type of tank-like vehicle they nicknamed Aziza, which they said could not be destroyed or blown up even by a nuclear bomb. But one guy wrapped a load of dynamite around his waist, snuck under it, and blew up himself and Aziza. People became convinced that dynamite and live bodies were the way.

"The attack on Natanya," she said. "So many people died!"

He nodded his head and tightened his lips and didn't comment. Bewildered and hesitant, she said, "It's terrible. Civilians … housewives … human beings."

"And what about us?" he said. "What are we?"

She became quiet, because the subject had been hashed out to the point of exhaustion. People went on and on about it, some calling it permissible and legal, others saying it was sacrilege and forbidden, while others gloated at the misfortunes of the enemy. The gloaters were more numerous, in fact they were the majority, because the majority of people were in a state of suffering. Oppressive and unyielding suffering does not awaken in a person the language of charity. That was their life and reality.

He tried to change the subject. He wanted to have a pleasant conversation, a lighthearted conversation, a happy moment to make him feel that he was human. Hiding himself during the day and sneaking around during the night had made him feel as though he were a bat. He was being pursued by the Jews on the one hand, and by the Palestinian Authority on the other. And even though the Tanzim had claimed responsibility for the killing of collaborators, among them Badr al-Washmi, his cooperation in other operations made the idea of his appearing in broad daylight impossible. And thus it had been written for him to live the life of a bat.

"Do you have any news?" Majid asked.

She turned to look at him and see if he was referring to news of the heart—in other words, news about Laura. But he was gloomy and hadn't shaved in days, so Suad didn't dare mention her name. The last time she mentioned Laura, he had snapped at her, "News about people. Forget Laura! News about people!" So she rattled off the various bits of news of family, news of the street, news of the neighbors, news of everyone except Laura. Why leave Laura out of the category of "people"? How could he forget her? Could a man forget his feelings just like that? Suad hadn't forgotten her own old sweet story, and the shadow of that man loomed in her memory. That man, that feeling, that flood of longing. Where was he now? They told her he was in Ramallah. Right here in Ramallah. But he might as well still be far away. Her dreams were always unrealized. She felt jealous of Majid and his ability to forget and to change and make changes in his life. What was it with men? Did they forget so easily because they had more opportunities? Their lives were not so fraught with obstacles; they suffered only one siege. Then she looked at his gloomy, worried eyes and his scruffy beard and felt sorry for him.

She said in a whisper, as if not to bother him, "People's news is the same as always, but Laura…"

"What about her?"

"She's reporting the television news now."

He didn't comment, so she continued, "Laura's talented."

He looked at her and said wryly, "Laura's talented?"

Suad studied his profile in the darkness, lit only by the streetlight. "Laura *is* talented. She speaks many languages and she has connections and she's used to Western customs."

He gazed into the distance, not wanting to stir up that subject, because it was a point of weakness, a stain on his memory he wished he could wipe away. He had been childish and arrogant in his youth, as he called it now, weak when it came to material things and fame and riches.

"Laura called," Suad said. "She said the army was everywhere."

Majid didn't comment, so she pressed, "She asked about you."

He looked alarmed. "She asked about me?"

She didn't answer, but kept talking, as though to herself, as though grappling with her own conscience and the conscience of the night, "The poor girl. We didn't treat her right. She was looking for a clean purpose in life. Maybe hearing some news from us would help her."

"Or screw her up. And us, too."

He turned his face in the other direction, toward the lights and the minarets and the people's houses crammed into the neighborhood, under siege. Those people were the ones to feel sorry for, not Laura. Laura on the news? Who could trust her?

"People's news? Our news?" he said angrily. "Laura al-Washmi? There's a war going on!"

"If there's a war, does that mean we have to become harsh?"

"Of course we have to," he said sharply. "Harshness is a means of defense. This enemy is like a machine, a bulldozer that doesn't leave a single green branch in its wake. People are like ants before it. In order to confront it we have to harden and be solid. We have to be like stones, like a rock that doesn't budge."

She looked at him and then at the mountain and the light coming from people's houses, and then at the opening between the two mountains. The crescent moon on the western side was dying out and illuminating the sky in an ice-cold light. She whispered sorrowfully, "This enemy is like a machine, and now we're going to become like machines. Is there any hope?"

29

They hid themselves inside the cave, and then they spread out. Majid disappeared beneath the olive trees and the shadows of the fig trees. But the Apache helicopter continued circling overhead. Every so often it would spray bullets, other times it would drop bombs, all the while he hopped from valley to valley and between the trees and between the rubble until he reached a very dangerous cliff overlooking a deep gorge. But the danger of being bombarded from above was even worse, so he jumped and rolled among the thorns, descended into the slope and disappeared.

When he woke up, the sun was glaring like a spotlight in his eyes. He shut his eyes, but his head was pounding and he could hear the sound of flies buzzing around him, attracted by the blood on his head. He moved his head and the world went black.

He heard someone whispering his name. He opened his eyes. The sun was setting, and the red horizon was like a curtain soaked in blood. There were people—kids—like ghosts. He heard their voices. One of them said, "He got hit in the head by shrapnel. His head is broken open!" And he fell unconscious.

30

Suad stood over him, then Ahmad. She whispered, "This is glucose, and these are fluids. Try. Maybe. Only God knows."

Ahmad looked around and remembered the day they went up into the attic and he saw the kittens playing with the yarn. Through the window he could see the dome and the minaret over the marketplace. From where he was, suspended in the attic above the world and away from people's eyes, nothing could reach him but the call to prayer and the sounds of machines and the meowing of the kittens.

A little cat came over to him out of curiosity, so he whispered to her, "Here kitty," but she didn't respond. She hid under his brother's bed.

He inspected his half-dead brother and the tubes carrying glucose to him and keeping him alive and breathing. Every once in a while he would groan a little, and then he would go back to his motionless silence.

He couldn't believe that Majid wasn't moving, wasn't feeling anything, wasn't talking. That was why he kept looking at him and at the cats and at the glucose dripping and flowing into his body.

Suad handed him the biology book and said, "This book has lots of pictures. Take a look at it." He took the book and held it near his brother and started reading out loud, so Majid could enjoy it, too. Ahmad started reading. He raised his voice. He heard his own voice. Louder. Louder. But Majid didn't move. Ahmad called to him, "Majid, can you hear me?" But Majid didn't move. He abandoned the book and listened to the sounds of the world around him, the sound of machines and cars and the sound of footsteps approaching.

He stopped reading and looked toward the door. A woman dressed in black appeared. She was old and toothless and was carrying a bag. She dropped the bag onto the floor and sat down, panting. He didn't recognize her. She looked at him, still panting, and asked him how Majid had been hit. Ahmad shrugged his shoulders and stared at her. She became angry and asked, "Don't you know who I am?"

He didn't answer, so she drew closer to Majid and bent down to examine him more closely. "Tell him, Majid. Tell him I'm your grandma."

She bent closer to kiss him, but he didn't move.

"Where did your father go?" she asked Ahmad, irate.

"He's in Ayn al-Mirjan," he answered. "The roads are a mess and there're checkpoints… His blood pressure is up and his heart is weak."

She removed her head covering in one quick move, pulled her dentures from her breast pocket and popped them into her mouth. "What a mess!" she said angrily. "Mountains and valleys and every other step there're tanks and airplanes and people running all over like it's a war. It's worse than a war. They told me my grandson was gone and had said his good-byes. I thought it meant he was dead and it broke my heart. But thank God, he's okay."

Ahmad whispered, "He was hit with shrapnel in his head. He has a cerebral concussion."

"What does that mean?"

"It means his head."

"He can't hear and he can't see? Stop talking nonsense! Get up, grandson. Get up, Majid, my dear, my darling. Get up."

She started shaking him. The bag of glucose started to sway over his head and nearly fell.

"What's that?" she said angrily.

"Glucose."

"What's that mean? What's it for?"

"Fluids to nourish his body."

"And why doesn't he eat?"

"Because he's not conscious. He's not aware."

She stared at Majid and slapped his cheeks several times.

"Majid, my grandson. Get up, sweetheart. You rascal, acting dead! What a faker! Come on. Move."

Majid made a small moaning sound. "See! See!" she called out with joy. "Didn't I tell you? He's a faker; he's always liked doing that sort of thing! Come on, you faker. Move!"

But he didn't move. She reached into her bag and pulled out a box of snuff. She sniffed a few sniffs, started sneezing, said "God bless" and thanked God. Then she picked up a few pinches of snuff and put them under Majid's nose. He sneezed several times and the bag shook again and nearly fell on his head.

"The bag! The bag!" Ahmad shouted.

She waved her hand. "Never mind the bag and all the junk and nonsense. Give me my bag and give me a cup."

She pulled out a white cloth from her bag. It was wrapped around a strange powder. She dipped the cloth into the cup of water and started squeezing it between his lips. But he didn't move. She was frightened and whispered, "Someone must have put a spell on him!"

Ahmad didn't answer. He kept staring at her half-dead face and thinking, astonished, Camera. Camera. He wished he could photograph her face—its creases, the wrinkle of the chin, and those eyes stuck on like buttons.

31

"He opened his eyes!" Ahmad shouted and jumped to his feet to get a closer look at Majid's face. But he went back to his seat, muttering in disappointment, "Maybe I'm dreaming."

She greeted the angels as she started her prayer. She turned to look curiously at Ahmad.

"He opened his eyes for one second and then shut them again," he said.

"Two or three days and you'll see, he'll wake up for good. Come on; let's massage his back and his legs. Come on, grandson. It's grandma."

She started massaging him and singing in a hoarse voice the popular Egyptian song, "I wish I were a bird so I could fly all around you... wherever you go my eyes are upon you..." And Majid blinked and Ahmad shouted, "He blinked his eyes!"

"Stop talking nonsense. Massage him. Massage him."

Still, she stole a glance at Majid's face and saw his eyelids twitching like a tiny muscle twitching beneath a fly on a horse's rump.

They heard some footsteps, so Ahmad went outside the room and stood on the top step trying to see who was coming. He rushed back and said, "Issa, Issa."

Still massaging, the grandmother said, "He's finally decided to show up? Let him come in."

Majid blinked his eyes and moved his eyelids up and down. He wanted to tell her that Issa could not be trusted, and that the visitors to the workshop could not be trusted, and that no one anywhere could be trusted. The situation was very dangerous. But his grandmother didn't pay attention. All she cared about was massaging him and bringing life back to his body.

Issa came in carrying a canister of butane gas. After he had been imprisoned and kicked out of the settlement of Kiryat Shayba, he had started working as a gas delivery boy. He traveled around in a pickup with an old, toothless driver. The old man drove and Issa delivered the fuel. He would carry the canister on his shoulder and the wrench in his hand and climb flights of stairs into buildings and deliver to whorehouses. He would stumble and pant and cough and blow his nose, the whole time with his armpits stinking like a toilet.

The grandmother said, "Go to the bathroom and wash off that stench."

"Why wash?" he muttered, with an idiotic smile on his face, looking at the body laid out before him on the bed.

"Go take a bath!" she shouted in disgust.

He shook his head and took a few steps toward the bathroom, muttering. He hated taking a bath, couldn't stand it. If not for the call of nature his feet would never touch a bathroom floor and his body would never touch a drop of water. When he woke up in the morning, he went into a crud-covered bathroom and the rats jumped out from the walls and stared at him while he squatted over the hole in the ground, and they weren't frightened and didn't run away no matter what he launched into the toilet. He had been born poor. His parents died when he was a baby and he was brought up by an old relative who worked as a maid in people's houses. She retired as soon as hair sprouted under his arms and he started working for the shopkeeper and the greengrocer. The bales of American clothing they would get were half good and half rags. He would sort through the clothes and stack them into various piles. One pile was the "okay" clothes that could be sold to poor people because at least they had tags on them with sizes. Another pile had slightly better quality clothes that he would fold and hang out in the street under a sign covered with cobwebs and birdshit that read: Latest European Fashions. And there was another pile that was not good and was sold to garages and oil change stations or to the upholstery shop at the far end of the market place where it would be chopped up finely like parsley and used to stuff mattresses and comforters for poor people. When they built the settlement of Kiryat Shayba, Issa was the first person to go work there.

"Listen to grandma, Issa," she said. "You and Ahmad pick Majid up and carry him and we'll leave Nablus in the middle of the night before the assault."

Majid blinked his eyes. He wanted to tell her that Nablus was surrounded by the army from every direction, and there was no way out even for a cat or a dog. And also, Issa was not to be trusted. He was stupid and practically illiterate and didn't understand. Issa was a cheap lowlife who was easy to bribe. How were they going to carry him, and where were they going to hide him, and what if they slipped?

"I'll carry him on my shoulder like a butane gas canister," Issa joked.

"No. You and I together," Ahmad insisted. "I'll take his shoulders and you take his legs."

They went on negotiating over the easiest and best way. Majid was tall and his shoulders were broad and his arms and legs were way too long. If they carried him lengthwise, his legs would dangle, and if they carried him sideways, his arms would dangle, so what should they do? The grandmother suggested that they sit him on a chair, tie him to it, and carry the chair from both sides and take him down the stairs one step at a time. And after the stairs? Issa said he would steal the pickup truck with the butane gas canisters and stretch Majid out among them and cover him with bales. Ahmad said that the Jews would discover him there, because he was no needle in a haystack. But Issa said he would drive the truck on the road that leads to Altour mountain and from there to the village in Area C where there were no inspections or surveillance. The grandmother smiled with approval and encouraged him, "Bravo. And do you know Areas A and C?"

"From delivering butane," he said proudly. "I know everything from delivering butane. They said we weren't allowed to deliver butane except in Areas A and B."

"And what about Area C?" Ahmad asked with doubt.

Issa gestured with contempt. "Is it that hard to figure out?"

"And you know the way to Ayn al-Mirjan?"

"Is it that hard to figure out?"

"So you know it?"

"Hey, man, have some faith. Have faith and leave the rest in God's hands. Come on, let's try."

They tested it out on the grandmother first. She sat on the chair and relaxed her body. They tied her hands and her legs and tested which method was best and safest—horizontally or vertically or diagonally. And while they were carrying her and arguing back and forth, she saw Majid. He was staring straight ahead, and there was sadness and pain in his eyes. He appeared to feel and understand. She shouted to them, "Wait a minute! Untie me. Untie me." But they were right at the climax of their excitement and were intent on completing their attempts to carry her down a few steps. She kept shouting and they shouted, too. "Raise it up. Lower it. Up. Down. Pull. Turn. Down. Down," until they reached the first landing and put her down so they could rest a little and catch their breath. So she screamed again, choking from all the agitation, "Untie me. Untie me. He opened his eyes. Untie me. Untie me!" Issa stared at her, not comprehending, and Ahmad worked at untying her for a second, and then turned and ran up the stairs two or three at a time. He looked over toward the bed and found his brother exactly as he had been before, his eyes shut, motionless.

32

As they left, Nablus was drowning in silence, except for the casbah. Young men like ghosts in the night were transporting boxes of provisions and ammunition. Their possessions were meager: primitive light weaponry, bread and dry grains, gauze and cotton and antiseptics.

They passed by a mosque that was brightly lit and abuzz inside. There were teenagers in sweatshirts and jean jackets or clothes from the bales. There were young boys and girls and old men.

"Now listen to your grandma, Issa," she said, up front in the truck, between Issa and Suad. "If you don't know your way, maybe Suad knows and can help you."

He shook his head, looking into the mirror. "I know the way, I know the way."

He was slow, and she wanted him to get moving before dawn broke, because light was the enemy of movement.

"Why are you going so slowly?" she asked nervously. "Come on. Get moving."

He didn't answer, just kept staring in the mirror and seeing the shadows of the young men carrying boxes to the mosque and rooftops and storage depots. Ahmad was standing in the back of the pickup among the gas canisters and getting in Issa's line of vision. Issa opened the window and craned his neck outside. "Get down, why don't you," he shouted. "Get down."

The two women yelled, "Look out! Look out!" as the pickup nearly went off the road. So Issa put his head back inside and smiled his idiotic smile. The streetlights reflected onto his face, and Suad saw a face that she recognized and didn't recognize at the same time. She didn't know him personally, but his face was the familiar face of a young Arab man, half villager, half city-dweller, poor, without ambition, smudged with motor oil, unable to read anything except the signs written in large, bold script hanging above stores or for street names.

Suad turned and asked nervously, "Is this the way?"

He shook his head without answering her. He was thinking that this annoying girl with her pants and short hair and tennis shoes and sweater was not so great, not so special. She was just another of those stupid idiots. He knew her and knew her type. There were many just like her at the university and the colleges and the parks wearing pants and tight clothes and carrying their books so everyone would know they were educated and well-bred and respectable. And they were nothing but tramps. They were only good for that kind of thing. And despite that, they held their noses in the air. Girls puffed up like stinkweed thistles—if you poke them just the tiniest bit, they explode and spray their stinky juice everywhere. What a sight! God is great!

"Are we going the right way?" Suad asked him again.

"Yes, this is the way," he said sharply. "Don't you recognize it?"

"Shut up and keep quiet," the grandmother said. "She's just asking a question."

"She's asking a question and making a big deal out of it," he said. "From the moment we left Nablus she's been asking, 'Is this the way? Is this the way?' If she's so scared, why'd she come?"

The grandmother squeezed the girl's hand so she wouldn't respond to what he said. The situation was already nerve-racking enough. They already had plenty to worry about. They had the poor wounded patient in the back with the load of butane canisters, and his younger brother freezing in the March cold and dampness, and Nablus was in a state of fear and anticipation, and the army had surrounded its two mountains and all its entrances and exits, and this road out would either lead them straight to hell or straight into a tank.

In fact, they hadn't gone more than halfway up the ascent to Altour when they came face to face with a huge tank that rose up before them like a blimp, blocking the way to the summit—the roadway and the view. What could possibly be worse? What a catastrophe! The two women screamed and covered their eyes from the glare of the spotlights.

A soldier yelled, "Stop. Stop. Get out, driver. Get out and stay put."

The grandmother whispered, "If they ask you, tell them I'm your mother and Suad is your sister and Ahmad is your brother. Don't mess up!"

"Get out. Get out. Put your hands up."

Two soldiers approached. One was young and the other was older. They had on all their war gear and their metal helmets, like they were from outer space. There was another one at the top of the tank guiding a cannon nose the size of a huge smokestack. And there was a fourth soldier looking out of a small porthole in the belly of the tower. The sound of the tank was like the sound of a huge airplane with multiple motors and jets. The rumble of the air surrounding it was like a helicopter.

"Lower your window. You stay there, and you get out."

Issa got out with his hands up and stood exposed to the lights. He spoke a few inaudible words and tried to pull out his identity card, so one of the two soldiers charged at him and struck him with his billy club on the back of the legs. His knees buckled and he fell to the ground. He raised his arms instinctively to protect his head as the soldier struck him with the butt of his weapon until he collapsed onto the edge of the sidewalk. The grandmother wagged her hand behind the car window and shouted, "Shame on you!" And she started pushing on Suad's shoulder to let her get out. "Let me get out and talk to him." But Suad wouldn't let her and said, "No. Let me get out." She opened the door in a quick motion and the younger soldier jumped in front of her with his weapon in his hand and shouted at her, "Stop. Stop."

She stopped immediately and put her hands up. The door was half open and the grandmother was uttering a series of invocations and recitations and saying to Suad, "God is with us. Don't be afraid." So Suad nodded her head, brought her hands down and held them close against her chest. She took a breath and looked directly at his face. She saw the face of an adolescent Ahmad's age or a few years older. The spotlights were transforming the darkness into daylight, making his soft face look like a girl's face. She looked at him and he looked at her. He continued to hold his weapon drawn and didn't move. She wanted to say something to him, to talk to him, but with that weapon and those clothes and the metal helmet and the tank, he looked strange. What was the point of talking? But he wasn't scary. Despite the weapons, he wasn't scary; despite the nightmare and despite hell. She looked at him and he looked at her. She sensed his confusion and his inexperience. He had yet to harden and develop thick alligator skin. She, on the other hand… Suddenly all the scenes of her life, ever since she was a small child, came into her memory. Stopping at checkpoints and standing in lines. Raids on university campuses and the arrest of young men. The arrest of her father over a quarter century ago, when she was still a baby. She had lived her whole life without a father. Then the Tanzim, and the pamphlets, and the posters and the student council and Majid's songs. Dear Majid. The most important thing is that they don't find you.

One of the other soldiers circled around the back of the pickup. He pointed his gun at Ahmad and gestured. "Get down." She saw him get down with complete calm while the soldier nervously inspected him.

"Put your hands up. Up! Up!"

He nudged Ahmad with the nose of his weapon and

made him stand near Suad, then he moved both of them away from the door.

He looked at the grandmother and she looked at him and said with fear, "*Adon*. Please, my son and my daughter."

He didn't reply. He came closer, opened the door all the way, and looked inside examining everything—the floor of the cab down near the leg area, behind the hajji, and below the steering wheel and the pedals. Then he turned toward the back and she started to tremble. Her dentures made a chattering sound she could hear, which made the ringing in her ears louder and her fear even greater.

"*Adon*," she called out. "I'm old. An old wrinkled woman."

"*Sheket*—Be quiet!" he shouted and continued looking in the back among the canisters. Suad approached and said, "May I?" The big one turned and looked and shouted in understandable Arabic, "Silence. Not a word." He glared at the younger soldier, rebuking him and commanding him to be harsher. But the young one looked at her and she looked at him and she said sweetly, "May I?" So he looked at the older one, but he didn't make a move. Then the older one came over and looked at her, and she saw in his face a bad omen. He was big. A heavy corpse. A tawny face. A black moustache. Creases and wrinkles in his face. Were his looks Eastern, Arab, or European? East European, perhaps? She didn't know yet. She would never know.

He said sharply, in bad Arabic, "Show me your ID card. Your permit."

She turned away from him and tried to go back to the car to get the ID and the permit, but he yelled at her, "Stop right there."

She pointed to the pickup and said calmly, "ID card and permit."

He pointed to one of the other soldiers who came and stood at the door to the pickup with his gun aimed toward the inside. The older soldier pointed inside indicating that she could get what she wanted. She went near the younger one, looking right at him, but he did not look up and kept avoiding her eyes. She reached in and got her purse from inside. The older one yelled, "Stop. Stop. Throw it on the ground."

So she picked up the bag from the bottom and dumped out what was inside: a wallet, house keys, a toothbrush, chewing gum, a pen, and some papers. He moved toward the pile of things and poked them with the end of his machine gun. When he was sure there wasn't anything explosive hidden among the things, he shouted in bad Arabic again, "ID. Show me the ID card. And the permit."

She handed him the ID card. "Permit," he barked, mispronouncing the word in an irritating way. "Show me the permit." She clenched her lips and her fists and whispered, "I don't have a permit."

"No permit? Go back. Go back. Nablus not allowed."

The grandmother leaned her head out the window and said in a shaky voice, "Please, God keep you, I'm sick."

He smiled sideways with rage and disgust and turned to Issa. He looked him over and then hit him with the billy club. "Get up. Let's go," he screamed. "Get up. Go back. Go back."

Issa tried to get up. He dragged himself and rose up a little and then tumbled back down. "Let's go. Let's go," the soldier yelled. He kicked him again on his backside and Issa stood up straight and rushed toward the car. Suad got in and Ahmad stayed where he was, waiting for orders. The soldier pointed at him with the end of his gun, "Get in. Get in."

And as he climbed into the back, the soldier gave him a hard farewell kick.

33

All of a sudden, machine guns started firing. The two soldiers dropped to the ground, and the tank began firing and turning in every direction. East, west, in the direction of the trees and the rocky mountains and the heights and the road down to Nablus. The older one shouted, "The butane! The butane!" but his shouts disappeared amid the bitter fighting and the hand grenades and machine guns and a cannon firing missiles that left deep craters in the belly of the mountain and the surface of the earth. Ahmad threw himself down among the canisters near his brother, underneath the bales.

"Don't be afraid. Don't be afraid. Be strong."

The sound of the whisper entered Ahmad's ear, then his middle ear, and inside him it overpowered the sounds of the bombs and the bullets and the screaming and cursing of the young men on top of the mountain. Ahmad raised his head, gripped the bale tightly and tore through the rags with his chin, searching for his brother's face and his brother's voice. Was it real? Was that his voice? Or was he terrified and the thought of death was making him imagine all sorts of things? He called to his brother, forgetting his fear. "Majid, Majid, are you conscious?"

He put his face up against his brother's and started kissing him and hiding his face with his brother's face and then hiding his brother's face with his face. His own was cold and burned like ice, while his brother's face was warm beneath the rags. Ahmad's teeth chattered like a seismograph. He was weeping loudly. "Are you conscious?"

"Hours and hours," his brother said, and then the current of life died out and he stopped. His waves of consciousness came all of a sudden and then broke up and disconnected like a current through rusty or loose wires. Touch the wires together, the light goes on, then the wires loosen and the light goes off. And at that glorious moment, the moment in which one meets his maker, Majid whispered in agony, "Hours and hours." But his brother heard his words and understood the meaning and realized that his brother, despite his inability to speak, despite the blow to his head and all the misery and the cannon fire and the screams of the soldiers, had been conscious... for hours and hours. Therefore the paralysis wasn't real, and the cerebral concussion wasn't real, and the alleged coma had been the wrong diagnosis. "He is clearly in a coma," the doctor had said, though his grandmother said, "That's nonsense. God's guidance told me he's asleep and he's conscious." Suad had added optimistically, "I hope so, Hajji. I hope he's conscious. I hope so! I really hope so!"

Ahmad shook him again. "Are you conscious?" But Majid didn't move, so Ahmad began to sob. Ahmad forgot all the sounds around him, the gunfire and the shouts of the soldiers and the hand grenades and the cannons. He felt a hand clutch at him and then drag him far away from his brother. He tried to hang on and stay where he was. The butane canisters tipped and rolled onto his brother's head, so he caught them with the edge of his shoulder and looked back. He saw the soldier with the helmet, the metal helmet, gripping him hard and pulling him back violently away from the bales. Ahmad wanted to fight him and thought about hitting the soldier over the head with one of the canisters, but out of fear that his brother would be discovered, he gave in and let himself be pulled out of the the pickup. The soldier pushed him off the end of the truck and he fell to the ground near the soldier's feet. He lifted Ahmad up with one hand like a sack of flour and took him to the younger soldier, who was lying on the ground. He hit him with the end of his billy club and yelled at him to move. The younger one looked up. He was crying. He had tears in his eyes and all over his face and chin. Ahmad saw him there on the ground, balled up like a wounded dog, his soft face like a girl's face. There was a flash, one flash like a camera, a quick glimpse, a picture enlarged under rays of light, not colors, just lights, and lightning and thunder and shrapnel and the khamsin wind. The older soldier threw him on top of the younger one and the two were joined together. Ahmad could feel the young soldier's body tremble. What a tragedy, or rather, what a comedy! Moments ago he had been on top of his brother, and now here he was on top of this guy. Ahmad badly wanted to strangle him, to take out all his anger on him, but the guy was trembling and shaking like a girl. Ahmad's heart was torn and his tears flowed ice-cold. He buried his face in the other's back and pressed hard on him, and so the soldier calmed down and surrendered, waiting for either death or mercy, one or the other. The two found themselves in an awkward position, one embracing the other feverishly and trembling, both bawling uncontrollably, like girls.

The older soldier picked up Ahmad and Issa. He pushed them out in front of him as human shields for the soldiers. The sound of machine guns died down and the cannon continued to pound the rocks and the belly of the mountain and the olive trees where the sounds were coming from and the machine guns and the road down to Nablus. A few moments later Ahmad and Issa were tied onto the front of the tank in the shape of a cross, and the tank moved along with them tied like that to the front, down the dreadful path through the olive trees, following shapes in the dark that jumped about in the night like ghosts. They all disappeared— the soldiers and the tank and Issa and Ahmad—while Suad stayed put in the grandmother's lap. "Mommy, mommy," she was crying, with every hit and every bomb. "Mommy!" she screamed and buried her head in her bosom while the mother recited prayers and begged God and the angels to intercede for them and told Suad, "Say Amen."

34

After using them as human shields, the soldiers left Ahmad and Issa at the foot of the mountain. From there they crept into the old city and headed to Suad's mother's workshop. They were surprised to find Laura al-Washmi there, accompanied by a foreigner and a television cameraman. Everyone was horrified to see the bruises and contusions covering Ahmad and Issa.

Suad's mother rushed to them, slapping her hands against her cheeks to see them in that state and consequently expecting the worst for the remaining passengers, especially her daughter Suad. Ahmad was quick to set her mind at ease. "We left them under the olive trees. They were fine." And he summarized the scene as briefly as possible, but Issa kept interrupting him and telling them about the terror and the bombs and the machine-gun fire and the huge tank that he described by stretching his arms wide open and saying, "It was ten times the size of this room!"

Laura took Ahmad by the shoulder and led him away from the others.

"How is Majid?" she whispered.

His eyes dropped down as he thought, Laura al-Washmi—do we really need more problems?

She put her hand over her mouth and whispered, "Is he conscious? Paralyzed?"

He glanced at her quickly, enough to see the agitation in her eyes. But she was the daughter of al-Washmi. Al-Washmi the slain. Al-Washmi the collaborator. Al-Washmi who had caused him and his brother so much loss. Ahmad had lost the kitten and Mira. Mira and Laura, Laura al-Washmi, Laura and foreigners and television.

She noticed that he was paying attention to the camera and not to her. "Listen, believe me, Ahmad, you can trust me."

She took his hand in both her hands and repeated in a shaky voice, "You can trust me!"

He looked at her and he saw transparent tears and a reddened face, free of make-up or anything fancy. In fact her entire appearance was not fancy—a dust-colored wool jacket and blue jeans and an old wool scarf. Her hair, which was pulled back tightly and held in a knot with a metal hair clip so that her forehead appeared unframed and dry and flaky, drew his attention. How was it possible that she was working as a TV news broadcaster?

He pointed to the two men and asked dryly, "Are they from PBC?"

She didn't look in their direction, just kept holding his hand and staring into his face, as if she was trying to win him over and make him trust her and tell her how Majid was doing. But he dropped his gaze and kept quiet. She walked away from him and turned to the window and wiped her eyes. She went back to the group and handed Suad's mother a little card and said quietly, "This is my card with my address and telephone numbers. Say hello to Suad for me. And if you need anything, anything at all, I'm at your service."

She gestured toward the foreigners as if to say, through them or with them or with their help or something like that. Suad's mother nodded and said, "Thank you," and that was that.

As soon as she knew they were gone, Suad's mother ran to the two boys and started asking them about the pickup truck and Suad and Majid and about what happened to them.

She told them that the situation was bad. Ramallah and al-Bireh were blockaded. An attack was imminent and the young men in the neighborhood were taking cover and holing up in the courtyards and in mosques. What were they going to do now that they had returned to Nablus? And what about the pickup truck? What about Majid and Suad? Of course it was impossible to go back for the truck, because the town was surrounded by trenches and tanks, and there were checkpoints and barricades. Where would they sleep?

And just like that, they found themselves joining in with the other young men behind the barricades in an enclosed courtyard in old Nablus under the archways and the arcades.

For the first time, he saw the police and the security forces on good terms with the townspeople and Hamas and the members of all the various groups, factions, and organizations of every background and every ideology. As far as he was concerned, and many others like him and like his father, the Palestinian Authority was a government, a quasi-government, that brought them nothing but disgust. After the revolution in Beirut, after the great struggle, and the grand ideas of enlightenment and freedom and Cuba and Moscow and the poetry of liberation and freedom, along they'd come with a system of government just like all the other Arab governments: chaos, corruption, taxes, systems of repression, and an old-boy network. Where was the work they'd promised? Where was the economic growth? Where were the ministers and representatives of the people? How often did he hear his father say loudly and clearly what his pen was unable to capture. The result was an ugly picture, a fuzzy picture without focus, or in Arabic, "with no aim and no target." What exactly was liberation? Land being swallowed up? Water being depleted? Fences and checkpoints and settlements, and security forces forbidding us to speak the truth or complain and responding to everything by saying, "This is Oslo, the road to peace!" Here was peace and Oslo and the Palestinian Authority and the security forces all down in the streets in a bitter quarrel, under a microscope.

"You go with them," they said to him and dressed him in a white jacket and taught him how to bandage broken bones, how to wind the dressing tight, and how to give an injection. Issa was sent to the cooking and food distribution team, but two days later Ahmad saw him with the mine-setting team near the mosque. He was carrying a coil of wire and a cellphone and a transistor. "Who would have thought I'd end up an engineer!" he said, laughing. So one of the guys yelled to him, "Hey, come on, Issa, hand me the wire." Issa winked and said boisterously, "See how important your buddy has become? You'll see me tomorrow when they enter." What he meant was when the Jews entered… if they dared. Indeed who would dare raid the town and the squads and the security forces and the police now that they had all come together, united for the first time since Oslo and the establishment of the government? Who would dare? The security forces, Hamas, Fatah, and the Jihad, and the Popular Front, and all the rest were carrying flags and raising banners and shaking their weapons above the frightened heads of people exiting the mosque and people who were congregating in the municipality building and at the gate to the main square. They spoke words larger than themselves and promised victory and freedom through sermons and the numerous flags they were carrying and the many factions involved and by firing their weapons into the sky toward the antennas and the minarets. Who would dare?

They planted mines at the entrances. They divided the forces into groups, assigned roles, set up makeshift hospitals in the mosques, pushed together barricades, placed guards on the rooftops, erected telescopes in the minarets, and sang anthems of victory through the night.

Ahmad felt that he belonged to this people, to this hastening pulse and these freedom songs. The words raised his spirits high above Mount Ebal, where he would become like a bird with two wings and see the world like a movie screen with noble battles and martyrdom. He forgot his mother, forgot his father, remembered what he had encountered when they arrested him over the cat and when they tied him onto the tank and turned him into some shield to protect them, a tattered human rag. At that time, in the beginning, he cried and got scared like a child and wished he could hide himself under the stairs or in a garbage bin behind a building, as he used to a long time ago. Then after a while, after hearing so much hatred and resentment from both sides, he too became resentful. He was filled with such anger it shook his very being and made him feel as if his nerves were taut strings which, if plucked, would explode into a raging melody, into a song of death. He remembered his half-dead brother. And he remembered the bombs and the machine guns and the way he felt when they kicked him and slapped him, when he was unarmed and defenseless. But now he was not defenseless, and despite not being armed, there were young men from every ideology and every faction, there were security forces at the entrances, and mines and cooks and minarets and telescopes and night watchers. All of that made him feel protected, not defenseless. That was victory. He was engaged in jihad, he was engaged in faith and noble death and martyrdom.

He stepped aside into the mihrab in the makeshift hospital inside the mosque, read the *Fatiha* three times, wiped his face three times, and prayed to God to give them victory, for they were on the side of righteousness.

35

Laura found them just as described, under the olive trees. She didn't see Majid, because he was hidden in a cave. It wasn't until she cried and shook her hand in Suad's face and said with bitterness and heartfelt pain, "You can trust me. I am clean!" that Suad let her inside the cave and let her see his face. His face reminded her of her past, though it was only months ago. She had been spoiled, the daughter of al-Washmi, the daughter of dignitaries and banquets and high-society parties and the gazebo. Her father had been like a curtain behind which the world was hidden, and what she saw, she saw as through a fog, with no edges or clear outlines. When he was destroyed, the curtain was destroyed, the clamor died down, banquets and parties stopped, and she woke up. No one asked her where she was anymore, so she hardened and became rigid. Her mother fled, her grandmother put on black mourning clothes, and the servants went on vacations, long vacations, and then disappeared for good one by one. Likewise all the friends and relatives fled. They were afraid of being accused or held suspect. Al-Washmi ceased to be their key to success and quick access to high positions or lucrative deals. Instead he and his past and his reputation and his mother and his daughter and all his possessions were now counted among things absent and things lost. He no longer wielded power, so people stopped mentioning him. His mother and daughter were left with nothing but deep sorrow and fear, which might come in the form of a beggar or police officer or gardener. They put up an iron gate and iron bars on the windows. They fired the guards and the gardener. Their garden went to ruin and their mansion turned into a ghost house. The two of them had a very difficult time trying to adjust. The grandmother went back to doing oil paintings and reading Rimbaud and Baudelaire. She started calling people, with a great deal of caution, foreigners and journalists, and inviting them in for tea and Nescafe. And that was how the media entered their home and her granddaughter became a journalist.

36

"What a nice painting," the hajji complimented. "My goodness, it's a carbon copy."

Madame al-Washmi didn't answer. All she said was, "Hush, hush," trying to silence her, but the hajji wouldn't be quiet. Indeed, the lady of the house's dry and cold manner threatened to drive them away from that palace with its restful atmosphere—which her grandson so desperately needed—where Laura was bending over backward to satisfy Suad and where there was plenty of food and drink and one could sleep in a bed with sheets and feather pillows. And what was more, the road to Nablus and Ayn al-Mirjan was completely closed, so how could she go back? Where would she stay? And how could she leave her grandson in this condition? And also, the pretty girl was crazy about him and treated her and Suad so kindly. But that lady was a big snob. The hajji was used to her type, the snobby, high-society ladies with roots in foreign countries who spoke English and French and couldn't pronounce their r's correctly. She knew her. That is, she knew the type. The type who took pride in having acquired the most expensive things. The type who mocked Arabs and Easterners and wore hats and colorful things even during mourning. If she was in mourning, then why were her fingernails so nice and long and freshly manicured, and why was her hair dyed and her face all made up? What kind of mourning was that? That was grief for the dead and respect for the lost one?

"This afternoon I have visitors coming," the grand lady Madame al-Washmi said.

She wanted to add, "So hide yourself, disappear, keep out of view, because the sight of you is suffocating," but she couldn't. The kid belonged to an organization and had followers and God knows what else, and such things were not said openly, but rather behind the back. So she whispered angrily to her granddaughter, "Did we really need this mess?"

"What mess?"

Laura pretended she didn't understand what the problem was. But she did understand. She understood very well. She understood that Majid's presence in their house was dangerous. Despite his innocence in terms of her father, he still—she had been told—did some horrible things, such as setting off explosives at the checkpoint, and smuggling weapons and ammunitions, and planting mines. His name was on the list of wanted criminals, at the very top. But she paid no attention to the government and the criminals. She was above the government and the Authority, above the occupation and the checkpoints and the siege. She was Canadian-American and worked as a correspondent for the television station. In other words, she was protected all around by a level of security even Arafat did not enjoy, nor even Sharon. The former was afraid of America and Israel, and the latter was afraid of peace and the Muslims, but she was protected on both sides, because her father had provided undefined services to those involved, and he was still owed favors from both sides. And despite his death, thanks to the television stations and their far reach, he still represented what they kept hidden from people's eyes. She was above the leadership, above the government, above the convicts, above the organizations and the nationalities, because she was Canadian-American and her grandmother was a third-generation Turk and she had roots possibly stretching to Serbia. And over and above all of that, she worked for PBC.

"I don't understand," her grandmother said with surprise. "Have they run out of young men? This guy's a terrorist!"

Laura smiled, because her grandmother insisted on mixing Arabic with English and because the word "terrorist" to her was merely an expression they used to describe any action they didn't like. Who didn't like? Sharon didn't like? And who was Sharon? Who was Barak? Who was Shamir? Who were those guys? Weren't they just like him? Worse. And he was more handsome than them, definitely more handsome, taller, with a nicer voice, and he played the guitar. How many had he killed? Five? Ten? Those other guys killed thousands. In any case, he didn't kill anyone, he trafficked weapons and ammunition and blew up an army vehicle. He was not a murderer, but a risk taker, like Hemingway and Sir Walter Scott. And the issue was relative. As far as their people were concerned, he was a resistance fighter. And to the others, he was a terrorist, a saboteur. But she had crossed through all the categories and had tasted the bitterness of being al-Washmi's daughter and came to know that the language of the news, any news, was the language of particular TV stations and political opinions. The news was relative.

"Even if he is innocent and unjustly accused," her grandmother said, "he is unconscious and unaware!"

"No," Laura said stubbornly. "He is very aware."

She left her grandmother's room and went directly to Majid in the attic.

37

Madame al-Washmi turned off the television and shouted loudly, "You call this martyrdom? This is a crime!"

She turned and looked at the old hajji with anger and disgust, which made Majid's grandmother feel like a worthless refugee, an unwelcome guest, unknown and ignorant and poor. A buried feeling reawakened: she belonged to the lowest, most wretched class of downtrodden people. Yet at the same time a malicious joy came to her, because she knew that Madame al-Washmi was also the wretched descendent of gypsies. She turned to the two girls and said, "What's it to us. Let's change the subject. Put on Future TV, Suad. Let's watch *Superstar*. I love that show. If it had been around when I was young, I would have kept it on all the time."

Madame al-Washmi turned her face away and whispered in disgust, "*Superstar*!"

The grandmother added in a hoarse, sing-song voice, as she gazed up at the chandelier, "Oh, how I miss the good old days. The crystal in Haifa and Yaffa sparkled like diamonds. The evening parties and gatherings in the orange groves. We reveled till morning in those groves. I was young and cute as a baby doll, and my voice rang out better than Umm Kulthoum's. When I sang "*Ya Layl*"— the stars in the sky would tremble along with the tarbushes of the pashas and beys as they sang along and became dizzy with joy. Once a man sat down before me on the ground and said, "Dear Lady, Asmahan and Umm Kulthoum pale in comparison to you." And when Abd al-Wahab heard me, he begged me, implored me to act with him in the movies like Layla Murad and Umm Kulthoum."

The two girls laughed and the Madame muttered to herself. Then Laura shouted, "Abd al-Wahab? *The* Abd al-Wahab?"

"The one, the only, the great."

Madame al-Washmi rolled her eyes and picked up the remote control, flipping through stations and mumbling to herself. Her granddaughter looked at her sharply and said with forced cheeriness, to prevent the evening from ending as sourly as the night before, "Wow! Abd al-Wahab? The Abd al-Wahab? He used to come here? Here to our own town?"

"What used to be your town," Suad commented bitterly.

"It is my town and your town," the hajji said with excitement. "In spite of them and in spite of you, and whoever doesn't like it can go drink the sea. We are steadfast as the mountain, unshaken by any wind."

"Long live Abu Ammar!" Suad said.

The hajji nodded and said lovingly, "Long live Abu Ammar. Yes, long live Abu Ammar."

"Why do you say it like that?" Suad asked her.

The hajji smiled but didn't elaborate. So Laura asked her, "You've seen him? When?"

She nodded and lied, "I've seen him and he's seen me."

"When did you see him?"

The hajji waved her hand and said obscurely, "I've seen him and that's it. What's it to you?"

"And he's seen you, too?"

"Of course he's seen me and he said to me, 'What a beautiful voice, dear lady.'"

"And why did he say that?"

"Because I sang."

"You sang for Abu Ammar?"

"Of course I sang for Abu Ammar. If I haven't sung for Abu Ammar, then I haven't sung for anybody."

Madame al-Washmi let out a sarcastic snarl. "Hah!"

Her granddaughter ignored her. "How did you sing? When? Tell us. Come on. You sang for Abu Ammar?"

"Of course I did, and when he heard me he said, 'Oh my, what a voice!'"

"What a voice," Madame al-Washmi scoffed in disgust.

The two girls exchanged glances of laughter and tried to suppress their giggles while the Madame sneered with disdain and contempt. But the hajji withdrew into memories of the good old days. She got so carried away telling stories that even she couldn't tell if they'd really happened or if she'd just wished they had. But it didn't matter. Now was a time of misfortune and calamity; it was enough for a person to remember or imagine anything that helped ease the pain of the current reality. She went on, "I wish we had stayed on our land and hadn't been humiliated and forced to experience such hardships."

The two girls shook their heads, but they didn't say anything. What was the point of discussing it? What was the point of grieving over what was lost? But Laura was drawn into the hajji's stories. Out of fear that the hajji would become disheartened and her grandmother would cause another problem, Laura continued egging her on.

"So, what was it like to sing for Abd al-Wahab?"

The hajji's eyes wandered off and she sighed. "Oh my," she said, returning to her memories and dreams.

"It was in a beautiful orange grove, all lit up like diamonds. There were marble fountains and the fragrance of orange blossoms filling the air and the sky was like velvet, velvet studded with diamonds. And when I sang '*Ya Layl*' the stars stood up and the tarbushes flew off and the worry beads twirled about and the ebony staffs were raised. And they cried 'O God' from so much dizziness. When Abd al-Wahab heard me he said, 'Bravo! You've torn Umm Kulthoum to pieces! You must come and act with us in love scenes like Layla Murad and Umm Kulthoum.' But I refused."

Suad didn't comment, only smiled, as did Madame al-Washmi. Laura, however, took the bait. "You refused? Why did you refuse? Would anyone refuse to act and sing with Abd al-Wahab?"

The hajji shook her head in sorrow and regret. "Yes, I refused."

"You refused?"

"Yes, I swear I refused."

Madame al-Washmi suddenly blurted out a question. It surprised everyone, herself included, though her tone, full of sarcasm, didn't. "And why did you refuse?" she asked.

The old hajji didn't really notice the tone of the question or who was asking it. "I was crazy," she said, distressed. "I wish I had said yes."

Madame al-Washmi continued probing. "And why didn't you say yes?"

"Because I was crazy and stupid."

"Why stupid?"

"Because I had fallen in love."

No one said anything. The two girls lowered their eyelids out of politeness, or maybe out of sympathy. This was an 80-year-old hajji, or maybe she was in her 90s, and she still clung to her past. It was a past filled with dreams and fantasies and joy. What was was and would never come again. She had been young and beautiful and she had great renown and she had lived her happy days in Yaffa in its glory. And now there was no more Yaffa, no more renown, no more glory, and no future. That was sad, truly sad. Quiet reigned over them for a few moments, but the hajji couldn't stop.

"I was very young. I was pretty and fresh. When he called me his life—*Inta Umri*, he said—I believed him. He was the son of the bey. He was beautiful like the moon with blue eyes and blond hair. He was incredible. I went crazy and got pregnant."

"You got pregnant?" Laura squealed.

The old hajji hastened to add with some confusion, "But we got engaged, and we wrote the marriage contract and he married me."

Madame al-Washmi asked her as if it were an interrogation, "The bey's son? Which bey?"

The hajji shook her hand and said, "The bey and that's all."

The Madame persisted, "Which bey?"

The hajji didn't reply, just kept silent. So the Madame kept after her, interrogating her with stifled anger. What bey or son of a bey would seal a marriage contract with this, this, this woman! She examined her with disgust, feeling she had been stabbed in the back. Was it not enough that she had opened her home to these people and invited them to eat what she ate, and sleep where she slept, and sit in a room no one but dignitaries and important people and those who held rank and power ever had any place being in and now along came this woman, this decrepit piece of junk, to lie to her and brag to her—with such nerve—that she had been the wife of the bey or the bey's son! So she pursued the question, "Which bey? I know every one of them, and I've never heard of any of them or their sons marrying a... a... someone like you."

The old hajji snapped out of her dream state and asked angrily, "Someone like me? Why—what's wrong with me?"

The Madame didn't reply. She turned her head, grabbed the remote control, and started flipping through the channels. The hajji went back to whispering, and without raising her voice, she asked again, "What's wrong with me?" She knew that anything she might express while angry could bring further affliction upon herself and upon her afflicted grandson. Certainly it was already enough that she and her grandson and this poor girl had lost their way and no longer had any place to take refuge but at the house of al-Washmi! What should she say to her? No, she would say nothing, not a word. But Suad got up angrily and said, "Get up. Let's go."

38

The next evening the atmosphere was different. Suad filled the hajji's ears with stories about the Washmis' gypsy origins, and told her that the Madame would never kick them out no matter what they did, because she was afraid of the Tanzim and of Majid's buddies. "What's the big deal about us and the Tanzim?" the hajji grumbled.

"It's a very big deal," Suad said. "And if she says anything, just say 'Tanzim' and she'll shut up right away. Do you understand?"

"I understand, I understand," she said and weighed the matter in her mind all night long. She decided it was true. "He's with the Tanzim, and I'm with the Tanzim." And she settled on this opinion.

To test the atmosphere, Suad said, "Have you ever been in love, Hajji?"

She looked at her without answering, because she didn't understand what Suad was after. Last night Suad had told her not to hold back anything from the Madame, to get her back good by mentioning the word Tanzim if the Madame dared open her mouth. The hajji thought Suad wanted her to talk about things related to poltics and the Tanzim, so why was she bringing up love? She stared at Suad, trying to understand what she was after. Suad winked at her and said slowly, so she would understand, "Hajji, I mean before the bey, who did you love?"

"I fell in love lots of times," she stammered, confused.

"How many men were there, Auntie?"

"I swear I don't know," she said, confused and embarrassed. "I never counted."

Suad kept after her, winking, "Maybe ten? Twenty? Maybe more?"

The hajji put her hands up in a sort of surrender and said, "More. Maybe more."

"More than ten? More than twenty?" Laura squealed, amused.

"More! Did she say more?" Laura's grandmother said disapprovingly.

"Really, Auntie?" Laura shouted with surprise and joy. "Who did you love?"

The hajji went along with it, following Suad's winks. "I loved too many to count."

"And were they gentlemen? I mean, important men?"

Suad said, "Of course they were important men. They were ambassadors and ministers and every one of them shook the universe with a nod of his tarbush."

"I was wondering what shook up Israel!" Madame al-Washmi remarked wickedly.

Suad recoiled. The remark struck a chord deep inside her, because of how much she despised them—the men with the tarbushes and the turbans and the robes. She was always saying, "They are the crux of all our problems. They brought us the bad luck." And now the Madame was reminding her that those men were the ones who backed down, because the ones in high posts and in the arsenals were up to their ears in the likes of women like the hajji in the glory days. If the men with the tarbushes in their high posts were without their *señoras*, would we have ended up with no place to go? Would we have taken refuge in the house of bad luck?

"Tell me, Auntie," Laura said with merriment and lightheartedness. "Tell the truth. Which one was the handsomest?"

Tenderly, because men at that age and in the memory are like children, she said, "They were all handsome."

"No, Auntie. That's impossible. One of them had to be handsomer."

With complete seriousness, she said, "The one I was in love with at the time was the handsomest."

Laura squealed with surprise and awe, "The one you're in love with at the time is the handsomest? And then what happens?"

"Afterward, they die."

"They all died?" Suad asked in disbelief.

The hajji shook her head and said wearily, "No, they didn't die. I was talking about the love."

"Love dies?"

Madame al-Washmi broke in, passionately, without any preface, "That's not love."

The hajji answered serenely, "Of course it was love."

"That's not love," the Madame shouted angrily. "That's lust, infatuation, childish—silly. That's not love!"

The hajji shook her head. "Of course it was love."

"That's not love," the Madame shouted again, as if she had taken a blow to her honor and her character, "That's lust."

And she picked up the remote control and began flipping through the stations, muttering, "That's not love." Then she noticed everyone's eyes on her, so she tossed the remote aside, opened her cigarette case, lit a cigarette, and started puffing on it. She became conscious of herself. What was she doing? Why was she shouting? She was defending all wives, defending herself, the lady of the house. She was defending every decent woman with a sense of virtue against everything vile. This animal of a woman lived in shame and sin. She seduced and stole men away, enticing them to leave their wives and go to her, just as he had done. She remembered all the lonely nights. She remembered the feeling of degradation. She remembered what he said to her and what she said to him before she slipped away. She went here and there, but secretly, without any scandals, without any bells. In other words, out of a desire to protect the family and the family name and her name and even the children's name. This woman, though, had none of it—no home, no name, no children—because she was a fallen woman with no morals.

She said calmly, trying to appear composed and reasonable in front of the two girls, "A well-balanced, respectable woman lives and dies with one love in her heart, one great love."

Suad nodded without commenting. Love was not a game to be played, it wasn't an infatuation that wilted so easily. Great love was like the cause, like politics, like Palestine, and it lasted forever, until they themselves were wiped out and it was wiped out along with them. Love was not a game, but a principle. An oath and a commitment. And then she remembered him. He appeared to her, as if peeking in from some far off place. She whispered in sorrow, "No. Impossible!" And started searching inside herself for things by which to measure what was true. She saw him fade away—he was far off in the distance, and her heart was no longer beating, but pounding. He was neither in love nor against it. He was in her memory. He was part of her principles. He had been a great love. Had been and was and always would be. Like the cause. Like Palestine.

Laura said in disbelief, "Really, Grandma, you only fell in love one time?"

"Yes, really."

Laura laughed and said, "So why are you upset? Are you upset?"

"No, I'm not upset."

She blew out the cigarette smoke and withdrew into her own thoughts. What was the meaning of love? What was its shape? How long did it last? Did love remain—as she said—until the end of time? Rage engulfed her. That lowlife had come out of nowhere and shaken her beliefs, or at least what she believed in front of other people. Deep down, she knew that what she kept repeating to her granddaughter was not the truth. Maybe it wasn't exactly a lie or a deception. Maybe, most likely, it had been a sacrifice for the sake of another love—for her children and the family name and honor. That was love. That was what she meant.

"Great love lives forever, Hajji," Suad said. "It dies when we die."

The hajji shook her head and said, "No, my girl, that's not love—that's your idea of love."

Laura laughed and stared at the Madame, but Suad didn't budge. Indeed she started defending her position. Suad said, "I know exactly what I'm talking about."

The hajji shook her head several times and didn't elaborate. Suad said, "Love, Hajji, is not a game. Love is a commitment."

The hajji considered that and said, "You mean Tanzim."

Laura clapped and laughed and made trilling sounds and stared at Suad as if she were daring her. Madame al-Washmi said, looking in Suad's direction, "Then you and I are in agreement!"

Suad whispered with dismay, "No. That's not possible!" What was going on? She and the Madame were aligned? She and the Madame together, against the old hajji? She and the Madame with the hair dye and the fingernail polish and peacock feathers and French and English words and the mispronounced r's? She and Madame al-Washmi, mother of *the* Washmi, were together in this palace, this lair, this trap, against a woman who who had eaten and drunk with her and accompanied her on her journey across valleys and wilderness? A woman who had tasted with her the bitterness of fear when they saw the tank and comforted her when she was afraid, and read to her the sura of Yassin and the verse of al-Kursi, and sang to her and to her own grandson in her scratchy, affectionate voice, and told her about the past and the son of the bey and Yaffa and Haifa and Abd al-Wahab? No, she would not lie. Abd al-Wahab was true, and the son of the bey was true, and the nights filled with diamonds and ebony staffs and orange groves, it was all true. It was real. "You've torn Umm Kulthoum to pieces"—maybe that was a dream. That's allowed. Is it forbidden to lose ourselves in our dreams? As for Madame al-Washmi, she was all dye and make-up. She was the epitome of fakeness, a person with no identity and no depth. Suad began to feel her principles slipping away, and with them the cause and everything she believed in. She felt such intense anger, she didn't know what to do. "Get up, Hajji," she said. "I want to go to bed."

39

Madame al-Washmi insisted that everyone go home. People were fluttering in the streets like birds, traffic was bumper to bumper, the streets clogged like sewer drains. The sun receded behind the rain and the cold clouds, and all the broadcasting stations blared what Sharon was saying: The person responsible for what was happening was Abu Ammar. The television screens from the East and the West and all the way to New York showed the aftermath of the attack and the military operation, and the dead and wounded on stretchers. "This is Arafat's fault," they said. "Blame it on Abu Ammar."

Madame al-Washmi said that the assault would not spare them. The Jews' invasion of Ramallah would mean searches and raids. In other words, disaster. House demolitions were likely. Any house or building harboring young men or security forces would see true massacres and fire and smoke and catastrophe.

"I will not stay. I will not stay. It's either him or me."

Laura became upset. "Now? At this time? When he is in such a sorry and weakened state?"

"You're the sorry and weakened one," her grandmother lashed out. "Your heart is soft and your mind is soft and you don't know that any love in this world eventually wilts and dies in time."

"But what about a respectable woman's love?" Laura asked, dumbfounded. Her grandmother didn't answer. She rushed to the window to make sure the assault hadn't started. She saw the lines of cars taking off quickly, like missiles, and she saw the neighbors and scattered crowds of people, all carrying a bag in each hand: bags of flour, breadsticks, bread, dry milk, fruit, and Pampers. The security forces in their jeeps rushed here and there, and ambulance sirens pierced the air, rattling the fogged, wet windowpanes and shaking the frozen raindrops from the rose bushes. She repeated, "It's him or me."

After a great deal of conversation, it was agreed that the only suitable place for Majid to go was the president's headquarters. There were soldiers there and security and nurses and fire extinguishers. All this was at Abu Ammar's headquarters.

He opened his eyes and shut his eyes and muttered in despair, "Not Abu Ammar!" But no one heard him. Everyone was in a state of confusion. The radio and the television and the cars and the security forces and the loudspeakers were blaring and saying, "Imminent attack!" Young men carried rifles and machine guns around the traffic circle and the lighthouse and in the streets and in buildings and at the president's headquarters.

He opened his eyes and shut his eyes and saw an image, of al-Aqsa Mosque and Abu Ammar. He knew immediately that the place itself represented defiance and refusal, and the thing that was being rejected and refused had become reality, had become Abu Ammar.

To him, Abu Ammar was merely an image, a picture he saw everywhere that gave him a strange feeling he could not fathom. He was for defiance and refusal, because reality was a big trap. But defiance was also a trap. Between this trap and that one, the rejected and the rejecter spun in a tornado, never to meet. Or if they met at all, it would be in another storm. The one would discover in the other what he himself lacked, and struggle would be reduced to the blurry image of a man, motionless, frozen, a still-life with no frame.

Majid found himself in a room full of boxes and closets and a bed surrounded by maps and an enlarged picture of Abu Ammar. And under the picture he saw his grandmother doing her ablution, praying and begging God to give us victory and bring us back to our consciousness and bring

Majid back to his consciousness before the beginning of the attack. She said, "Dear God, for the sake of the heavens and your angels, set him free, and fill his days with happiness and light." So he asked, surprised, "Grandma, am I conscious? Is it possible?"

She looked at him, smiling, and said, "Of course it is possible. The angels told me that you were conscious; asleep, yet conscious. Sit down, my darling, so I can tell you the story of this place."

"I know, I know," he said, astonished.

PART TWO

1

The shelling started. But before that, they cut off all the lines
and the telephones and the antennas, and the cellphones, too,
and the water network and the electricity and the television.
Nothing of the world reached us anymore except the echo
of dogs barking into a silence that promised death.

It began with the dawn, on a rainy and windy day. A
thick fog that covered the world with white icy vapor, in
which people looked like floating ghosts. Hundreds of tanks
rumbled in the night through the fog. At the crack of dawn
they came from several different angles toward the president.
Guards stood on tops of buildings, waiting for the onset and
prepared to fight back. But against whom? White fog and the
rumble of thunder mixed with the sounds of machines and
tanks and warplanes and the quiet that promised death.

Their leader looked at him and said, "Don't move. You
stay here with the second line, at the president's door." He
and his comrades were to respond to an attack on the
president's door, they were to protect the president; if the
situation required, he should give his life to defend this man
who was a stranger to him, a man he didn't know and didn't
understand and didn't believe in. Why die for a man he only
knew as a face in a picture? The picture of a system that had
done nothing to avert danger, but rather had brought it upon
him. If it hadn't been for that system, if it hadn't been for the
Authority, if it hadn't been for an agreement that wasn't
getting anywhere on a land that spun round and round on no
axis, would he have disappeared from the world and lost
consciousness? Would he have suffered that concussion out in
the wilderness amid the flies and the wolves of the night,
while Apaches strafed and hit those destined to fall?

The officer said, "Fire," and started firing from behind
the sliding door at a distant target that was difficult to discern.

The sound came closer. Closer. Closer. He could see him, for the first time. His colleague stood up to salute him, but the president motioned with his hand and so his colleague went back to his original position. There was a flash, and then silence. With the blink of an eye, the situation changed. The man was shorter than he had imagined, and his eyes were gentler, and so were his gestures. The look of worry in his eyes resembled what was grinding in the depths of his own soul. Fear and anger, sadness and anger, despair because the world had orphaned us. We had no family and no friends. The world disappeared; the leaders fell silent. America voted; the Arabs were stifled; Sharon won. No, not yet. Sharon wouldn't get to him. He would not destroy him. He is at the center of a huge color picture featuring all of us. We were all in the blurry picture. Hand in hand. We were sticking together. Like a solid wall. Fire, Uncle. Fire. Rafiq collapsed. Majid picked up his weapon and the attack intensified. Another fell, and three were hit at the entrance. The wall collapsed from the eastern side, then from the west, and we were left with no barricade to protect us from the mouths of their cannons and their tanks. Bulldozers crushed hundreds of cars, squashed them like cockroaches, along with the cement and the rocks and the presidential compound. They penetrated the information bureau, and came on like imminent death, a few more meters. The president descended to the second floor. He passed right by Majid and touched his shoulder lightly, slightly, a touch that was enough to revive within him some warmth and sympathy. The goal was clearer than before. He looked toward the president to exchange another glance, but a door came crashing down and he was thrown behind it amid a pile of rubble and smoke from the fire.

During those moments, the inner gate of the compound was witnessing a very heavy battle between the president's guards and security forces and the occupying forces, which were fortified with tanks and armored vehicles. The metal-clad barricades that the president's guards had erected in front of the main gate didn't hold, and that was where, during the first few minutes of battle, an officer was killed and more than eighteen soldiers from the president's guards wounded.

With continuous shelling, the occupation forces were able to make cracks and holes and penetrate the intelligence bureau building. With that, the eastern wing of the president's quarters was completely occupied. All that separated the occupiers from the president's rooms was a single wall. The situation became more dangerous as the Israelis attempted to advance further toward the government headquarters, where commandos who were charged with defending the life of the president were stationed. The battle escalated. Clashes were now face to face, room to room. Occupation soldiers were approaching the government headquarters through the main gate and through the openings in the walls. Everyone inside the headquarters recited the *Fatiha* and the *shahada*. Bullets rained down from every direction. And actually, after an hour and a half of fighting inside the rooms of the government headquarters, the commandos were able to halt the attack.

When they finished, Majid went up to the second floor, where the president was, and slipped quietly between the guards. And then he saw him up close, from mere meters away. He scrutinized him, thinking, Is this man really Abu Ammar? His grandmother had said many times that he was a giant of a man, with a voice like thunder and piercing eyes as sharp as knives. And now he saw that he was a regular person, not a giant, and his voice did not thunder and froth. But his eyes—truly his eyes *were* piercing. Majid lowered his own eyes before them. Despite his lack of sleep and continuous exertion and strain and his age, his eyes were still sharper than awls. They pierced and cut like knives. He inspected everyone there, one by one, as if he was searching among them for the secret of life. Who among them had died, who was alive, who had weakened or surrendered. This was the age of misfortune, and these moments were decisive. Either you collapsed and surrendered, or you made it through. There was no middle course. This enemy showed no mercy, did not compromise. This enemy wanted all of you, your name, your body, your heart, your soul, your dreams, and the heritage of your ancestors. You would not retain anything but your shame and a few crumbs tossed to you to lick from beneath their feet like a wretched dog. Are you a dog? Are you wretched? Would you accept being caged like an animal?

He was still inspecting them, searching among them for the secret of life, the secret of fear and courage, and he said in a voice closer to a whisper, like a farewell prayer, "Welcome to death for the sake of life."

"Welcome to death," one of them shouted.

So Arafat raised his voice to correct him, "For the sake of life!"

He looked carefully at them. He stared at them and saw tears in the eyes of a young man he hadn't seen before. But no problem, this was how it was. This place was their refuge, or their final trap. He came closer to him and examined him at arm's length. Majid stiffened and lowered his eyes and prepared himself for any question. And the question came. It landed on his head like an ax. "Are you a fighter?"

He swallowed his saliva and the disgrace of his tears and the humiliation of a life wasted on bad luck and occupation and unconsciousness. He answered, trying to sound strong, "I am a fighter."

He came closer. More. Closer. He whispered in his ear, "And what about these tears?"

The question sliced into his flesh. He wanted to defend

his weakness and his sensitivity and say, "I'm an artist," but he was afraid and felt shy in front of the commander and his fellow fighters, so he said with apprehension, "Because I'm human."

Arafat shook his head and walked away. One of them shouted, "With our souls, with our blood, we sacrifice for Abu Ammar!"

They shouted in refrain, so the whole building shook with the thunder of their voices. He raised his hand and corrected them, calming them in a tone that was closer to prayer, "With our souls, with our blood, we sacrifice for Palestine!"

They repeated after him, "With our souls, with our blood, we sacrifice for Palestine!"

The building shook again, or what was left of the building. Majid looked toward the commander, then toward them, one by one, and he felt warmth in his heart, because their eyes, all their eyes, were filled with tears, though he was the one who was an artist.

2

I am writing so I don't lose my memory or slip back into a coma.

All the lines are cut off. The cellphones, the antennas, everything that could possibly connect us to the outside world and the rest of life. We are in prison. We fell into the trap. The siege has intensified.

The president shouted into the radio transmitter, "He's crazy. He's a criminal. Do something!"

Sharon heard the radio, so he ordered his troops to step up the bombing. Bombs and missiles came from every direction. Hellfire. The president looked at the civilians who were there—journalists and workers—and said to them, "Move the cabinet in front of the window and get down on the floor. Hurry up, get down." They got down and lay flat on the floor, reciting suras from the Qur'an.

Quiet prevailed for a few moments, allowing them to hear one of the guards in the corridor saying goodbye to his uncle on the walkie talkie. "I ask for your forgiveness, Uncle," he was saying. "Please forgive me." And another guard wrote on the wall in large, bold letters, "Welcome sweet fragrances of heaven." We were all convinced that heaven and the angel of death were lurking at the threshold. So we asked God to have mercy on us, and we remembered those who would remember us. Who would remember me? Ahmad and my father, my old grandmother, Laura, Suad? Would they forgive my foolishness? Would they remember my merits? Do I have any merits? Forgive me, Dad. Forgive me. And you, Laura, have I hurt you?

The other man repeated, "Forgive me, Uncle. Forgive me." And I felt death draping itself over me like clothing and over us all. Some of us fell into a strange sleep. One of us slept squatting, and another had been in a deep, lethargic slumber for several days and didn't even wake at the sounds of the bombs and missiles and whizzing of bullets and the curses of the men.

Sharon heard the radio transmission, so he decided to go down to the square to carry out the order with his own expertise. And as he was strengthening his plan and organizing his team, his war minister was announcing to the world and all its leaders that Arafat and those with him were safe. They were safe and sound. So Arafat shouted into the radio, "Liar. Liar. Sharon is a liar!"

Sharon heard that insult and decided to put an end to everything. And as he sped to the east, he was told that things had become difficult and that Arafat was jumping for joy. Why? What was going on? He was told that aid had arrived from peace activists of every color and nationality: British, Germans, Americans, Italians, and even Jews. Jews? That was what really surprised us. Because all along we thought the world had forgotten us, that I had no family and no friends, that I was an orphan at the banquet of the wicked. But they came. They really came.

And I am writing this in my journal so I won't lose my memory and fall into a coma again: They came carrying signs and chanting protests. The soldiers shot bullets above their heads to try to stop them, but they were not deterred. They moved forward toward the square until they reached the entrance gate and the barricades. The guards prepared to receive them by opening a space in the fortifications, and they passed through and came into the headquarters amid applause and jubilation. Our president welcomed them with kisses.

The Frenchwoman in charge of the delegation, Claudia Le Postec, said to us, "When I heard what was going on in Ramallah, I feared there would be another massacre, so I decided to come at any cost." She also told us that the members of the delegation believed that the Palestinians' brave stand strengthened the fight against globalization and against American and Israeli hegemony. The Palestinians and those on their side would win in the end; Sharon was the loser. Then the Jewish-Canadian, Nataya Golan, interrupted and said, "I want my children to live in love and peace. In the shadow of the occupation, no one will live in peace."

Throughout their visit, the forty members of the delegation refused to be treated as special guests. They did daily chores along with us, whether it was cooking or cleaning. One of the volunteers insisted on cooking the rest of the meals. They had brought us candy and distributed it a little at a time, and during the night hours, they distributed themselves among our rooms to act as shields against the expected attacks.

They worked like bees. Sixty-year-old Professor Gerard wrote day and night, preparing articles and editorials about what was happening. The sweet young girl Julia tore her own shirt to bandage one guy's wound. Muhammad bin Baraka from Morocco, despite learning of his own father's death, remained in the president's headquarters. And despite all the sadness, we celebrated Nicholson's 55th birthday. As a surprise, Nicholson went around with a tray of *halawa* and tomatoes instead of cake. He blew out a candle amid cheers and well wishes for a happy birthday. Then we gave him a gift. The flag of Palestine and the 2000 Bethlehem Medal of Honor and lots and lots of kisses. After that we took pictures of that strange and unusual party.

I am writing in my journal so that I won't lose my memory and fall into a coma again. But will I live to see it published?

3

They distributed chunks of bread, hunks of cheese, and sips of water from droppers, but not enough to satisfy our thirst and hunger. A bitter battle had begun inside our intestines. Going to the bathroom was torture. If you entered, you suffered red death, and if you didn't, you suffered cramps and anxiety. Rats and pigs lived better than we did. Patience was the key. That's what the guy next to me said, but the next one over said the key was faith. The third one claimed that thinking about food and family weakened whatever strength was left and jarred the mind. I said "Amen" to that, but my heart increased its longing for my old grandmother and my hunger made her food my constant obsession. Stuffed squash, stuffed grape leaves, *msakhkhan*, and fresh *tabun* bread. Oh, grandma!

When the bombing stopped, the worrying began. What were they intending to do? When would they hit? From which direction? How would we resist, and with what weapons? We had no provisions and no ammunition. At last we decided to take a chance. One of the storerooms was still intact, the one with bottles of water. It hadn't been blown up yet. They described it in detail, and I remembered the place. We had been sitting there, my grandmother and I, on the bed, a few hours or a few days earlier, I didn't remember. I had opened my eyes and seen a picture, and below the picture was my grandmother. I said, "Grandma, I'm awake." "That's right," she said. "You're asleep and awake." Then she vanished and my mind slipped into unconsciousness. Then I remembered. The attack began.

And now a number of commandos were going to risk death for the sake of water. "Take me with you." They refused point blank. They had discovered I was not normal. One minute I was conscious and could remember, the next I left the real world for the world of dreams.

In order not to lose my memory, I am writing—what is happening, what they say to me, what I say to them, and whatever crosses my mind.

Of course I remember what I was before getting hit, before al-Washmi and Laura and Suad and music. Here life has no music. But sometimes one of us hums or chants prayers and I feel my tears welling up and spilling, despite myself, and I yearn for my grandmother and Ahmad.

The commandos crept from the conference hall on the third floor through a window on the first floor that led to the warehouse that had been taken by the enemy forces. They put into practice the art of deception and sneaked into the place. Despite expecting to fall into an ambush, they insisted on getting the containers of water. And truly they advanced with agility and nimbleness, holding their breath, and after less than ten minutes they came back with the water and started passing it in through the windows. We felt victorious and relieved after such a long wait. Everyone insisted that the first gulps of water should go to those brave young men.

I would die for the sake of fresh air, and they would die for the sake of water. And they say this is life!

I began to feel tormented by my thoughts, and I wished I could slip back into unconsciousness. And again I nearly died in search of fresh air. I went out to breathe, because this place is like an animal pen. They blocked all the windows with furniture and sandbags and reinforcements and rubble. The bathrooms! I was suffocating. Dying. I went out to breathe. I climbed the stairs. An officer saw and welcomed me. "Coffee?" "Yes, of course." In this situation, this condition, with this hunger and thirst and this blockade, a cup of coffee! A royal feast I never dreamed of having. A scrumptious banquet. I was very grateful. I sat down beside him drinking the coffee. Suddenly, in the blink of an eye, the cup flew out of my hand and I went flying along with the chair. An LAU rocket shook the universe and pasted me like a ball of dough against the wall. I lost the royal feast. I lost the coffee and the cup. A fleeting incident. One in a million. A drop of water in the sea of this siege. And they say this is life!

4

Ahmad clung to Umm Suad. She was a substitute for his own mother. She was the type he liked—firm, but also affectionate and generous. She fed him whenever he came to visit. *Sambousek* and thyme bread and all kinds of sweets. When she found out it was his birthday, she made him a beautiful cake and decorated it with orange leaves and strawberries. He liked the cake so much he took a picture of it. He also took pictures of the cats playing with balls of yarn. He still loved the cats, despite the misfortune of having been sent to jail over one of them. But when he told Umm Suad the story of going to jail, he said, "If it weren't for the cat, I would never have woken up and gotten involved in all this." He pointed to his Red Crescent gear and his badge. She pointed to the camera, wondering what it was for. "A hobby," he said shyly and showed her several pictures. Pictures of cats, of Mira in Kiryat Shayba, and Issa and Majid up on the hill with the swings of children from Kiryat Shayba in the background showing through the barbed wire and the fence of fear. She asked him why he called it the fence of fear. "It's a fence to protect them," he said.

"Does it protect them?" she asked, smiling.

"Protect them?" he asked. "I went under the fence and so did Mira and Bobo and Amber."

"And after jail, could you get in?"

He thought seriously, and whispered uncertainly, "Maybe. Maybe. God knows." He looked at her, wanting to know why she was asking, because he knew about her past and her present and her jailed husband and her daughter Suad, but he became shy and swallowed the question. This woman was like his own mother to him, even though she was not his mother. Rather, she was the opposite of his mother. She was strong and firm and generous and had a tongue like a knife and a laugh that echoed and shook the whole neighborhood. Her voice was as loud as a cannon when she called to the grocer and the baker and the mint and anise seller, "How are things?" One would say, "Fine," and the other would say, "They're going to raid us soon," and another would say, "Send down the basket." So she would wrap the basket in rope and toss it from the roof or from the window, saying, "I have guests. Send me up some bread and meat and wild gundelia and a bottle of olive oil." Then she'd look over at the girls in her workshop and yell, "Get going! What are you stopping for? I have guests. I have to go cook!" And she'd turn to Ahmad and say to him, "And you, Ahmad my sweetie, today you have to eat with us." His face would turn red and green and he would cast his eyes away upon seeing the girls looking at him. He would try to get away by saying, "I have to work," but she would yell from the top of the stairs as he descended them. "Come on, now, sweetie, I'll be upset with you if you don't. Today you have to have lunch with us." And he would return at noon to eat lunch, despite his shyness and her shouting in front of the girls. In spite of himself, he would return to eat, because he still loved his stomach, and because she made him feel at home.

5

The bombing began. "People of Nablus, get ready," came over the loudspeakers. "The Jews are attacking." Umm Suad laughed and said to the girls, "Hurry and get to work. What are you stopping for?" She wanted to finish the order and collect payment before the attack began. After all, she was responsible for opening the house and the workshop and for paying the girls. Ever since her husband had been locked up, she had been a very strong woman. Before that she had been like other women. She kept close to home, cooking and huffing and puffing and getting pregnant and having babies like a cat. Each year she had one in her lap and one on the way and one clinging to her knees until every corner of the house was filled to the brim and there was no more room for a new hatchling. Then along came the Jews to spare her. They took the prize rooster and left the hen and all her chicks behind. She screamed and yelled and pulled out her hair, and then she got up on her feet and went to work. She sold her heavy gold bracelet and bought a weaving loom, then another, and another, until the house was filled with the machines. The children grew up and Saeed left to study in Syria, Aziz went to Morocco, Marwan to America, Mahmoud was killed in a battle in the Jordan Valley, Jameel left, Imad left, and no one remained except Suad. How come they say girls aren't worth anything? How could she not love Suad? Of course they called her Umm Suad. Suad, it seemed to her, was the whole world, a blossoming flower. The father of all those children left them nothing but worry and fear and distress and an entire household of bills and expenses. And there was the lawyer and the costs of the visits, and money for his cigarettes and his food and drink when she visited him. She began preparing the basket days before a visit. *Kibbeh* and *sambousek* and sesame breadsticks and date-filled breadsticks and cheese and *halawa* and semolina cakes. At first, she didn't pay attention to his expenses because of the children and the children's needs, like food and drink and school and this shirt and those pants and that dress and books and pencils and notebooks and water and electricity and cooking fuel. It was horrible! All this and all that for the sake of whom? Thanks to whom? To a husband who had never spared her? When he was around he'd been like a mule, a numbskull. He'd bellow and shake the whole house with his voice. "Hey, woman," he'd say to her. "Hey, stupid. Hey, idiot." And she'd say, "Okay, okay, just calm down. Be patient." And she would run here and run there, wipe up after this one and breastfeed that one and help her old mother-in-law hobble to the bathroom. Then he was put in jail, her mother-in-law died, the children left, and she remained. She was stronger. If he were to come back today and say, "Hey, stupid," she would bring the world crashing down on his head. But truly, in jail he improved. In jail he became better natured, calmer, nicer, kinder, and told jokes and flirted with her. They taught him that in jail. He became a human being. Twenty years. Twenty-five. That was no small amount of time. When he went into jail he was in his late twenties. Now he was more than 50, and she, too, was 44. Laughing, he said to her, "You're 44? An *Umm arba'a w-arba'een?*" She burst out laughing so loud it rang through the whole jail. Even the Jews were frightened of her. Pointing proudly with her fingers adorned with gold and money she said, "*Umm arba'a w-arba'een?* Go ahead. Marry a second wife!" He laughed and winked at her and said, "Me take another wife? Where would I get one?" Then he kissed his index finger and blew her a kiss from behind the bars and said, "I swear if they were to bring me the houris of paradise and tell me to go ahead and choose, I wouldn't choose anyone but you, you crazy fool." She burst out laughing a second time and the Jews kicked her out. It was amazing. Because of the Jews he had become a gentleman!

She said, "Ahmad, dear, come help carry these." So he carried sacks of rice and bottles of oil and cans of lard for her. "Call Issa," she said. So he called Issa, and he called Khalil and Ruhi and Hamza. They lined up the sacks of goods on the floor of the inn, in the kitchen between the archway and the vegetable garden. She gathered all the women in the neighborhood and delegated jobs—four to make rice, four to make dough, four to cook and peel the fava beans and the potatoes and to cut off the ends of the green beans and the okra. It was a great kitchen that could feed hundreds of fighters and all the inhabitants of the neighborhood of Hosh al-Atout. The neighborhood of the poor, of the revolution, the neighborhood of darkness and open space and light that shines on all the downtrodden. Do you want to eat? Come to us. Do you want to drink? Come to us. You want a water pipe with honey tobacco? And cinnamon and cumin and tamarind? We provide benefits like the mosque, like a shelter, like a restaurant that feeds you for free. Come on in.

Some people said, "The Jews have reached the traffic circle." The young men said, "Let's see who's going to enter!" They had set booby traps and planted mines at the entrances. At every alleyway and every garden, and at every entrance to the casbah, in front of the mosque, the gate to the town square, the market area, and Fisher's Monastery.

The Old City, the casbah, Byzantine Napolis, Canaanite Shakim, Yabus, Himyar—the most ancient city in the world. Jericho was older, but ancient Jericho had sunk into the sea and was lost in the water, as were Sodom and Gomorrah. Nablus, on the other hand, remained like the bride of night, the bride of day, the bride of the past and the present. A museum of ruins with its minarets, its mosques, its domed marketplace and baths and the smell of cinnamon and soap and jellied pumpkin and *halawa*. This Nablus remained an unchanging bride throughout history. She grew up, achieved greatness, lived her youth, lived old age, became a matriarch, and despite all the years, she remained beautiful and fragrant with history. Her air was amber and her soil sugar and her insides almonds and pine nuts. She was a great love.

6

Ahmad rushed to Umm Suad and said, "The Jews have attacked." She didn't believe him, because the Jews had promised several times that they would attack and occupy, or at least they would reoccupy the various areas under the Sulta. The areas under the Sulta were more like chunks of *salata*— that's what people on the street would say, with frenzied laughter: the *salata* security forces, the *salata* government, the *salata* chaos. The areas under the Sulta were geographic shreds, a torn shirt with its pieces strewn in different valleys. The collar was here and the sleeve over there and pieces of the front and the back and all the buttons were missing. On the map it looked like drops of oil in muddy water. It was disheartening to see something with no shape and no border and no demarcation line. As for the leadership, the areas under the Sulta consisted of family groups and tribes and organizations like cucumbers and tomatoes and radishes and lettuce and parsley all packed into a cardboard box with no bottom, no top, and no sides. They brought it in from the salty soil, shredded it like the bales of clothes, stuffed it like the mattresses and sold it to the farmers and the poor and the widows. The people were like salad, too. This person was a farmer from Tubas, that person was a Bedouin from Khan Yunis, and that one was an educated man from Ramallah. Some words in Arabic, some in English and girls playing in shorts and wives wrapped up in traditional gowns and scarves. A strange mix. And it was an even more amazing mix when you added the settlers from Canada and Paris and Rome and London and Bulgaria and Romania and the black people from Ethiopia. It was something no one would ever think up on his own, this strange vat over which some ghoulish cook was holding a hexagonal ladle and stirring us like soup for him to eat.

The important thing was that Umm Suad didn't believe it. She looked at the girls and yelled at them, "Get going. What are you stopping for?" The bullets and the sound of rockets were normal, an everyday occurrence like listening to the radio or the noon call to prayer or a few minutes of TV news before getting back to work. But Ahmad shouted at them, "It's the Jews, I'm telling you!" And he stared at them like a madman in the middle of the room until each one in her turn snatched her scarf and ran out the door.

Finally, Umm Suad was convinced and started going down the stairs with a ball of yarn still in her hand. She had started working on a sweater for a young man who had been cut off from his family in Gaza. He was a handsome young man, neat, and young, Suad's age or even younger. He told her he was a newlywed and his mother's only son among seven daughters and that he had been cut off from his family since the beginning of the siege. He worked for the Authority, in the security forces, and was wearing baggy khakis like traditional *serwal* pants. He told her he was cold and coming down with something and that the air in Nablus penetrated through to his bones. He couldn't bear the cold because he grew up on the coast, in Gaza. "I'll warm you up," she said. "I'll knit you a sweater with my own hands, Gaza boy." And that's exactly what she was trying to finish in order to fulfill her promise to the Gaza boy, the newlywed only son among seven daughters, before the attack began.

One of the girls came back. She was holding an infant and had another child in tow who was pulling on the hem of her gown. "The Jews," she cried in fright, "The Jews! They came in from the east. They demolished our house!"

Umm Suad dropped the ball of yarn she was holding and ran to the window. She looked east and saw a convoy of tanks surrounding the traffic circle. She looked west, but couldn't see past the tightly packed houses and the minarets and the antennas and the satellite dishes on the rooftops. She couldn't see anything but the mosque and the rising smoke of a fire. Then she heard something rumbling like a waterfall, swishing and splashing and spewing. It was an ancient soap factory, older than time, engulfed in thick smoke, burning and exploding with its oil and caustic soda. Then a rocket fell onto their own roof and the building shook. Things went flying and flipped upside down. The wool and yarn and spools went everywhere, and the glass in the windows and the door and even the television broke into shards. She ran to the stairway and yelled, "They've attacked! They've attacked!" but not before Ahmad said, "I'd better go. No doubt the hospital is full." He ran down the stairs and into the Gaza boy. He asked him what he knew—how far had the Jews gotten? The Gaza boy stared at him. "You're asking me? Ask yourself!"

The boy from Gaza was just like other fighters and security officers. He didn't know what was going on. The leaders had told them that the Jews, with their huge armies and their tanks and their armored vehicles and their warplanes, would not be able to penetrate the little alleyways of the marketplace, because the alleyways were full of twists and turns and lanes and there were domes and low roofs that were tighter and darker than what they could deal with. The Jews, despite all their high-tech weapons and warplanes, were worthless on the ground when it came to house-to-house battles with small arms. We, on the other hand, had grown up in the place and knew every corner of every alley and every entrance and exit and every secret hiding place and every little neighborhood. They would surely get lost, because our alleyways and back roads were truly a labyrinth. No one but its own inhabitants could find their way through. When the battle takes to the surface of the earth, outside the walls of the tanks and the armored vehicles and the wings of the Apache helicopters and the warplanes, they should get ready to face death. We will be like demons to them, jumping out at them from behind the houses in the dark, and from above and below, we'll come at them like jinns and show them death and make them see stars at noontime.

But the battle never came. The Jews stayed inside their tanks and their armored vehicles, and they dropped bombs from their warplanes and shot rockets into the alleyways from armored cars, a single one several stories high. There were only cannons and antennas and cameras that took pictures from above and pierced through the darkness and the light. And then there were the Issas and the Moussas who sold them out and foiled their ambush attempts and defused the booby traps they had set. The guys shouted, "Traitors! Traitors!" and ran to take cover from fire. A freedom fighter blew himself up next to a tank and there were some other extraordinary and valiant attempts, but the tanks and soldiers and lasers and armored vehicles rumbled through the air and in the alleys trampling, burning, and blowing up everything in their path. The flames raged out of control, the buildings were pulverized and the Jews shouted over the loudspeakers, "Surrender yourselves. Surrender. Surrender. People of Nablus, you whores, we're coming to screw you." And our men shouted, "Retreat, into the heart of the marketplace. Hurry! Retreat!" So this one retreated, and that one backed up, and another was killed in his place, and a fourth hid behind the walls until they smashed them down onto his head. People were shouting, women and children screaming, and the wounded wailing. The city was a terrifying chaos, and its people were in a state of shock. It was like an earthquake or a space invasion in a horror movie. Or like the final judgment day we've always heard about. Like the day of resurrection we've heard about.

7

They were still cooking and serving plates of rice and bean stew. The women cooked and the security officers served food to the poor and the unfortunate. People fled in large numbers from the outskirts to the center of the city. A few pockets of resistance continued to fight valiantly. Memories of the famous battle at al-Karami in Jordan still beckoned to them to vanquish the enemy. But the chaos and paucity of weapons and information made the pockets of resistance more like children lost in the forest, separated from their leader, not knowing how to get back or go forward. Each one stayed where he was, shooting and dying right where he was standing, no one knowing what happened to the others. As for the inhabitants, they fled right away. They picked up their children and their blankets and took off into the alleys and the darkness like mice. This kind of attack had never been seen before, nor could they even describe it. Even the catastrophe of 1948 had not been as terrifying. In 1967 it was worse than 1948, because the Arabs were defeated without a fight. In 1973 it was distant, in the desert, and we heard about it on the radio and read about it in the newspapers and journals. But this—this bloody massacre and this space-age warfare with its armies and tanks and rockets and planes and armored vehicles and bulldozers that could crush entire buildings in the blink of an eye and steamroll the fanciest Mercedes flat as a sheet of filo dough—people had only seen this on television and in American movies about the conquest of space, like *Star Wars*, with heroes like Rambo and James Bond and the bionic man, heroes who killed the enemy, laughing all the while, joking, falling in love and feigning desire and screwing all the girls. What was happening could not be described in the real world. So running away was the best idea. Run. Run. The inhabitants ran to the center of the city, and the courtyard filled with the unfortunate and the wounded and the wails of children. The wounded were crammed against the walls and into corners, because all the beds inside the mosque were filled with hundreds of gunshot victims and amputees and mutilated and burned corpses. There were horrific odors from the gases and fumes and from burst bowels and people urinating on themselves and children vomiting. And there were the remains of a dog burned to a crisp, and a gunshot victim crying, "God help us," and dozens of others crying, "God help us." But God was with the victors inside their tanks and had forgotten about the mosque.

In this terror, Ahmad stood with his mouth gaping and tears frozen in his eyes, not knowing what to do or how to begin.

"Give them anesthesia. Give them blood," the doctor yelled. A nurse shouted back, "There's no anesthesia and there's no blood. We've run out of anesthesia. The blood's spoiled because of the electricity." The doctor turned and stared like a lunatic at Ahmad standing there, as though he were lost, in the middle of all the wounded who were reaching out to him and grabbing his legs and pulling on his feet while he stood like a statue. "You! Move!" the doctor shouted. But Ahmad stayed where he was. Again the doctor shouted, "Hey! Kid! Yeah you, you idiot, come on! Get moving!" A hand grabbed at his pants and scratched his leg and elbowed him. He collapsed. As soon as he fell, he started to come to and get back on his feet to escape, but the nurse caught him and shook him by the shoulders and slapped his face. He woke up and said, "What's going on?" The doctor shouted, "Hey, you. Come here." The nurse pushed him from behind, and when he got there and saw the gaping abdomens, the flesh and the blood and the blackened bodies, he passed out.

When he woke up, he started to cry, but the doctor said, "Come on, hero. This is your day. People are dying." He got up, slowly at first, then quickly. At first he closed his eyes as he held a young man who had been hit by shrapnel and whose leg was amputated. They were forced to amputate his other leg without anesthesia. Ahmad held onto him with all his might, ferociously, and shut his eyes. Then, with time, he opened his eyes and began tending to the wounded. He stitched wounds, cleansed burns, bound and set broken bones, administered shots. He became numb. He walked around hearing people scream in pain without showing the slightest bit of emotion. His main goal became to give something to these people, give them something from his heart or his blood. If it were possible, he would give them his soul, or more, because these people were like orphans with no refuge, no food, no God to watch over them. What did they do to deserve this? What did they do? Had they stolen? Plundered? Killed? Burned? Wasn't their sickness and poverty and unemployment and nakedness against the cold enough? And then here comes America and Israel with all this? Why, Lord? Where are your eyes?

The sheikh heard Ahmad shouting, "Where are you, God?" and so he placed his hand over Ahmad's head and began reading the sura of Yassin. "Repeat. Repeat. Repeat after me. Say, O Almighty one. Say, O Subduer. Say, we have given unto You so lift from us this tribulation and this evil and this sinfulness. Pardon and forgive us and make us Your servants in Heaven, O King of All. Repeat after me." Ahmad said it again and again, until he calmed and his tongue grew tired. He fell asleep in the middle of all the slaughter, saying "Forgive us, O King of All."

8

They were still cooking and eating. This was the fourth day of the incursion, and the Hosh al-Atout kitchen was still handing out what it could. The Gaza boy came and said to her, "Umm Suad, do you have something warm I can wear? An old scarf or something?" She turned to him, feeling terrible about his being cold, because the attack had started before she had a chance to make good on her promise. The sweater still had no sleeves. She said, "Watch the rice. I'll go take a look." He stood over the pot of rice, removing the lid every minute or so to make sure all the water didn't dry up. She was gone for a few minutes and then came back with one of Suad's old sweaters. It was girlish and light-colored. He looked at it and smiled shyly. She said, "Put it on, young man. Who's going to notice?" He stood in the corner, took off his jacket, and put on the sweater, tucking it into his khakis. Politely he said, "Anyway, the jacket is too big." She smiled at him and joked, "I'm sure they stretched it out so it would be big enough. They knew!" He smiled at her, because he understood what Umm Suad meant with her sharp tongue. And what Umm Suad meant was that the Sulta, which he was part of, knew all along that we would be bombed and screwed. These days there was no big difference between the suit and the person wearing it—they stretched out the suits and stretched us out, too, so we would be big and roomy and get screwed. So he smiled at her, and she smiled back at him. He clung to her as Ahmad did. He, too, was delicate and shy and in need of warmth, just like Ahmad.

Ahmad entered like a ghost. They'd given him a short break of a few hours so he could sleep. "The situation there in the hospital…" He raised his hands and shook his head. She understood what he meant, took him by the hand, and pulled him into the pantry, where there was an old bed and a blanket and pillow. He threw himself onto the bed with his shoes on and tried to sleep. He couldn't. He covered his face with the edge of the blanket and started mumbling what the sheikh had said. "O King of all, forgive us. O King of all."

She came back with a plate of rice, meat, and beans. She sat down beside him and said, "Eat. You have to eat so you don't collapse. You need to stay strong to be able to go on helping." He nodded and said, "I'm sleepy." She patted him on the back and said, "Get up, my son. You must eat. You must be strong so you can live up to this responsibility." He shook his head and said, "I'm tired." She patted him on the shoulder again. "You should eat, because you're young. You have your whole life ahead of you. Eat so you can grow and become an adult."

"Grow? Become an adult?" he shouted without thinking. "For what? For who? I'd rather die than grow older and go on seeing what is happening and what will happen."

She hit him on his back and started lecturing him. "What are you saying, you fool? Have faith in God. He put us through this trial in order to test our faith. This is just a trial. This is His wisdom. They think they can come at us like tough guys with their tanks and airplanes and missiles, but with our faith, we are stronger."

"What faith, Umm Suad?" he shouted. "What faith?"

He started sobbing while she patted him on the back and recited all the suras and prayers from the Qur'an that her mind was capable of remembering. The brain, in a situation like this, loses its capacity to retain and remember things, but the believer remembers. "Say there is no God but He—the living, the self-sustaining Eternal. No slumber can seize Him, nor sleep. His are all things in the heavens and on earth. Say the name of God. Mention the name of God several times, ten times, twenty times or more." She heard the Gaza boy repeating along with Ahmad after her, "O King of all, forgive us. O King of all."

She put her finger over her lips, gesturing quiet. She picked up the plate of rice and beans and said, "Come. Let him sleep." She went out and sat on the bench by the door. She spread out a bamboo mat and a cushion and said, "Sleep. It's night, and you should sleep, too." The Gaza boy shook his head and sighed and said, "Who can sleep? I haven't slept in two days."

He took out a picture of his pretty seventeen-year-old bride, and told Umm Suad that he had been married three days before they took him to the West Bank to join the security forces. He had not seen his young bride for three years. Three days and three years. He was a newlywed for three days, and then he was with the security forces in the West Bank for three years. "Which is better?" he asked, sighing. "To be a newlywed or a soldier?" She didn't answer him. She took the picture and looked closely at the face of his seventeen-year-old bride.

"I miss my mother, Umm Suad," he said like a child. She shook her head and remembered Suad and Saeed and Aziz and Marwan and the rest. And she remembered her own husband behind bars. "Why, God, do You cut us off from our loved ones while they're alive? Why do You separate us, and make us widows and orphans, and only half alive in this life? O all-powerful God. Have pity on us and forgive us. There is no doubt that people have blasphemed and lived sinfully and that's the reason for this kind of punishment. But God, O God, O God."

He said with his childlike tenderness, "I can't sleep. Let me clean the kitchen and do the dishes."

She stared at him, understanding what he meant, and said, "Okay. Go ahead and clean up." He had told her that he had promised his mother he wouldn't fight—and here he was and it was time to fight. Should he fight, or shouldn't he? Should he break his promise and fight, or should he heed his mother and keep his promise? She thought about it for a few minutes. If she said, "Fight," that meant she was directing him toward wrong, as he would be breaking his promise, and a promise to a mother was a holy thing. And if she were to say, "Don't fight," that meant she was encouraging desertion and treason, and he was a soldier! But he was not really a soldier, and not even a policeman, or a military man of any sort. What exactly was he? She didn't know, and he didn't know, and no one understood or knew, including those who came up with the solution and with this khaki uniform. Then she thought carefully about the khaki uniform, and realized that because it had no purpose and no logic, it made him neither a soldier nor a policeman nor a military man, nor anything having to do with the commonly held notions about fighting. So why would he then break his promise and kill or be killed or even fight? And what was the point of fighting, anyway? If every mother asked her son to make the same promise, would we still kill and fight? And that Jew inside that tank, didn't he have a mother? And would he kill and fight if his mother had asked him to make such a promise? Anyway, the important thing was, why should this newlywed Gaza boy fight? No. It was not treason nor cowardice not to fight, because he hadn't been employed for the purpose of fighting in the first place. With that in mind, she became convinced of the right answer. "A promise is a debt, Gaza boy," she said resolutely. "Don't you dare fight. You must heed your mother's words." He shook his head, but he still seemed lost and indecisive and nervous as he smoked.

"Let me clean up the kitchen," he said to her. "And wash the dishes. I can't sleep."

"Okay. Fine. Go ahead and clean up."

He picked up the bamboo mat from the floor, rolled up his pant legs, and began mopping up the grease and dirt and drops of blood from the kitchen floor.

When he was finished, she sat with him on the bench. "Now let's have some coffee," she said. "Okay," he said and got up to boil the water for coffee as if he were one of her children. She had come to feel as if he really was hers, her own son, a boy from their neighborhood, from Nablus. This newlywed boy from Gaza. Her children were gone far away now, and he too had been estranged from his mother for three years. If only he would return to his mother, and Saeed and his brothers would return to her. But luck and making a living and opportunity and the future... There her sons had a future. Here, what would they find—what this boy from Gaza had found?

She looked at him, at the Gaza boy, and saw how handsome and tall he was. She saw how young and gentle he was, like a girl, because he was the only boy among eight children. His mother spoiled him, so he turned out delicate and unable to bear the sight of blood. He had come to Umm Suad, panting, two days earlier, running like mad when he saw a man who was bleeding. "The blood. The blood," he started shouting. "They cut off his legs and cut his stomach open."

"Say God is one," she told him. "You're a man. What's wrong with you? Pray to the Prophet and be strong."

He started crying and muttering, "I'm not used to this. I've never seen such a thing in my life!"

Of course he had never seen such a thing, a man cut open like a slaughtered animal, parts chopped off and strewn all over the place. His head squished like a fig. Of course he had never seen it, but now he would. Why should this only son from Gaza see such a thing? "Sit. Sit." She took him by the hand. He was sobbing like a girl. Now here he was making coffee.

His comrades came. Three comrades came and said, "It's your turn, newlywed from Gaza." He tried to get out of it.

They exchanged angry looks, but there was no time to argue. They had to talk to him at his level. One of them said, "The situation is good, and it's safe at the checkpoint. All you have to do is stand at the checkpoint and call us if you see anything." He went along with that and said, "Okay." As he was heading out the door, Umm Suad called to him. "Stay and drink the coffee!" But he left, clearly upset, and refused to drink the coffee.

A few minutes later she heard a missile pound the courtyard. One of the comrades went out and came back screaming, "It's the poor guy from Gaza!" She ran out, barefoot, her head uncovered, searching among the rubble and the glass and the mud until she found him there, in pieces, his stomach cut open and parts strewn all over the place. She began striking herself in lamentation and screaming hysterically, "A newlywed! With his whole life ahead of him! God help me! What a sight! Your poor mother, what grief! You poor thing!"

She pounded her fists and wept and trembled like a lunatic. Ahmad grabbed hold of her and dragged her inside. "Come on! Let's go home!"

She turned to stare at him and saw him staring back at her. "He made me the coffee, but he didn't drink it," she said, hysterical, "and I knitted him the sweater, but he didn't wear it. A newlywed with his whole life ahead of him. His poor mother, what grief!"

He shook his head and said stiffly, "Come on. Let's go home. This is his fate."

9

"People of Nablus! All you whores! We're coming to fuck you!" That's what they shouted from loudspeakers that had been placed on minarets everywhere for the purpose of calling to God, but God was far away, and Nablus was burning.

"Ask for God's forgiveness, Ahmad," she said. "God has visited this affliction upon us to test our patience." He waved his hand as he walked away and said, "Get off my back!"

He had heard quite a lot about that patience and that faith and that strange and amazing test God was administering to his steadfast and patient servants who were able to withstand more than any other people on earth, because they were made of a miraculous kind of clay mixed with the water of demons. That was why they were called the mighty ones. But now that Ahmad had seen what he had seen and heard what he had heard, he couldn't bear that explanation anymore. Because really, what kind of explanation was it, claiming that God tested people with all this. What kind of heavy-duty test was this? Was there no end to it? How long was it, exactly? And how wide and how deep? Fifty years or more, generation after generation, three generations, four, five, ten, wasn't it enough? Wasn't it enough?

The sheikh at the mosque said to him, "Ask God for forgiveness, Ahmad. This is fate. My fate, and your fate, and the fate of Abu Rami and the Gaza boy."

Abu Rami had been a high-ranking officer in the security forces. "The poor Authority. They really got a bad deal!" Abu Rami had said, laughing, as he ate rice and okra one day at Umm Suad's. "The Authority is our authority, Ahmad. Are we bad?"

Ahmad looked into Abu Rami's eyes. They were like the eyes of the Catholic priest at Deir al-Latine, the Catholic nursery school where Ahmad's mother had sent him as a child. The old priest there was like an angel, with his white hair and black gown and a cross around his neck the size of a frying pan. He used to pat Ahmad fondly and let him play with the ends of his rosary beads. The priest made up a jingle for Ahmad: "Ahmad, Ahmad, sweet little Ahmad, how his mother loves him so, and his father even more. Which is better, please tell me, a necklace or a rosary?" Ahmad would look at him, not understanding, and keep fiddling with the priest's rosary that dangled from his robe, and the priest would muss Ahmad's hair and then pat it down. His eyes were like milk or a dove or a summer sky or a gentle breeze. Abu Rami's eyes were like that priest's eyes.

"The poor Authority!" Abu Rami was saying as he ate. "They really got a bad deal!"

"And what about us, Abu Rami? Who shortchanged us?" Umm Suad asked, still in anguish over the Gaza boy.

"Israel," he said.

"They drove us crazy with Israel," she said. "Being mistreated by your own people is much worse, much crueler."

Gently, he said, "Umm Suad. For goodness sake. Who is the Authority? Is it not you and I? We are Palestine. But Palestine is still a baby, or still in a state of labor, and when it's finally born and matures, so will its brain. Am I right or am I wrong?"

She shook her head and stirred the ladle against the bottom of the pot. "You're right," she said.

"Good for you. Are we friends now?"

She looked at him. The tears in her eyes spilled forth and she said, "My heart is broken over the Gaza boy. My eyes can have no rest while our children are dying and being slaughtered like sheep."

He nodded his head and puffed on his cigarette. Staring into Ahmad's eyes, he said to her, "Patience. Patience, dear queen. Dear wonderful lady of ladies. Dear mother to the entire quarter. Madame Mayor. Most beautiful mother." She smiled, feeling solace, because Abu Rami, in front of the young men and the feisty youngsters—the lion cubs and the women of the quarter and all her female neighbors—called her "the queen, dear mother to the entire quarter, Madame Mayor." The guys laughed, as did the neighbors, and they would tease, "Are you Madame Mayor or Mister Mayor?" With pride she would reply, "I am Madame Mayor, mother to the quarter. What do you say?" In unison they shouted, "We'll say Amen when we eat." And now, here she was, feeding them and giving them water to drink and weeping over them when they died, while the sheikh says to her, "This is fate. This is our destiny." Then she in her turn says to Ahmad, "Don't blaspheme against God. This fate, this destiny, it's all a test from my God and yours." And Ahmad grumbles, "Get off my back," despite the fact that Abu Rami and the others call her glorious Madame Mayor, wonderful lady of ladies, mother of the quarter.

But Abu Rami was gone, too, had said his good-byes, and she wept over him even though he was old, over sixty. She saw him die the day of the surrender. The day of the surrender, that same evening, hours before he died, he had sat in her kitchen eating dinner and drinking coffee. He had said to her, "Umm Suad, death is inevitable, a destiny from which there is no escape. So if there's no getting around death, why die like a coward? To die for our country is the best death, because martyrdom is the best visa for entering directly into paradise without the help of a middle man." He laughed and so did she. "Correct," she said. "God bless that tongue of yours!" She thought of her husband behind bars. He loved to make jokes like that and loved to laugh even at death. Death as a visa. Death as a medal, as testimony, a way into paradise without an agent. How sweet talking about death is when it comes without torture, she thought while stirring the pot and remembering the newlywed from Gaza. "My heart goes out to you, Gaza boy. And my heart goes out to you, too, mother of the newlywed from Gaza. The only boy among eight children. May God help you. If I'm feeling such agony, what about you, poor woman? And what about that young bride of three days, three days only, and now she's going to wear black? You poor dear and your lost youth. You're still so young, a baby, younger than Suad, much younger. And where are you, Suad? Where on Earth are you?"

"She must be in Ramallah, Umm Suad," Abu Rami had said, trying to calm her. "And Ramallah is in good shape. Better than here. They're just trying to hit the president. But Ramallah is fine, a thousand times better than here."

"Thank God Suad wasn't in Nablus and didn't see what happened. Thank God. But, really—one little phone call, one little word, a message, a letter. But no, we got no word, no phone call, no message, no letter, everything's cut off, including the electricity, the air, and the water. Everything's cut off. And even the storage tanks on the rooftops have been emptied. They sprayed them with bullets and all the water spurted out of them like fountains. Or they pissed in them, shit in them. Why, to leave a souvenir?"

"Don't worry about it. I'll go and check," Abu Rami said.

"How are you going to do that? How can you possibly check?"

Smiling, he said, "Don't you worry. Tomorrow I'll go and check." He walked off, laughing, into the courtyard where the young men were. He nudged some and teased others, handed out cigarettes and licorice. He was very affectionate and loved children and young people, and above all he loved his stomach, just like Ahmad.

Ahmad said, "I wish my father were here with us."

"Leave your father there to tend to his own worries,"

Umm Suad said. "Is it not enough that his children are each stuck in a different valley? You here in Nablus and your brother is out there in the wilderness or in Ramallah, who knows. And maybe Suad is with him. Only God knows if they're alive or dead."

"They're alive," Abu Rami said. "I guarantee it."

She looked at him and smiled. "You guarantee it?"

Confidently, he replied, "Of course I guarantee it. I'm your leader, and the leader always tells the truth and always makes guarantees."

She clapped and said, "Long live the leader! Long live the leader! Some joke!"

He winked at her and said, laughing, "Let it go. Dump it in the saddlebag!"

"The saddlebag is full to the brim," she shouted. "There's no room left." Then she remembered the Gaza boy's jacket and his baggy pants. Sadly, she said, "The saddlebag may be full, but it's been stretched out like us after all this bombardment and getting screwed. They knew. Am I right or am I wrong? They knew all along."

At dawn when she lost him she didn't tear her hair and slap her face the way she had over the Gaza boy. Rather, she wept silently and remembered what he had told her and what she had told him and how he had given away his cigarettes and licorice and how he used to sit on the wicker chair by the door eating humbly. She remembered what a patient man he was, his big heart. She could hear the ring of his laughter and funny jokes and remember his love for the young people. He'd been their father. Better than a father. Then he left them behind like orphans. But at least he had lived more than sixty years. He didn't have his whole life in front of him like the Gaza boy and Ahmad and Suad and those thousands of young men and young women on that never-ending list of people. Our poor, dear country. O glorious lady, lady of ladies,

Madame Mayor. O mother to all young men and women and mother to the Gaza boy. His mother spoiled and doted on him. And Umm Suad raised a bunch of baby birds and when they grew up she set them free to try their luck in the world, and now here she was, doing it again. Cooking and feeding and dressing them in her sweaters to protect them from the cold. And Nablus was bitterly cold that spring, the kind of cold that you feel in your bones. Despite all the fires and bombardment and shooting, Nablus was still cold as ice.

That morning as usual, or maybe not as usual, as if he was saying good-bye, Abu Rami handed out cigarettes and shekels. He gave out licorice and chewing gum and mints. He gave to this guy and that guy and to everyone regardless of what front or unit he belonged to. One was from Fatah, another was from Hamas, and there were some communists and PFLPs and the rest of the mess. He didn't discriminate. He was a father to them. He was the leader, and the leader is a father. Better than a father. That was how he would always explain it while sitting at the doorstep on the wicker chair, eating okra stew, bread, cheese, thyme mixed with oil, or whatever was there—there was no special treatment for the leader.

"I wish all the leaders were like you!" she said, looking at him with kindness and admiration. "I wish all the Authority people were like you."

"They are like me, and more," he said tenderly. "It's just that they're still young, because Palestine is still young, and when Palestine grows up and matures we will also become mature. Right?"

"God bless you and that sweet tongue of yours! If only all our leaders were like you."

He shook his head. "God is generous, Umm Suad. God can do anything."

Yes. But God took the leader, the humble leader, the people's leader, the one with the big heart and big mind and left us with the small-minded ones. What can we do? Why does God take the good ones?

"Because God likes the good ones," he said, laughing, just before he died. "If God takes me ahead of everyone else, it's because God likes the good ones."

He had smiled at her, and now she was crying over him. She was crying and thinking, Have mercy on him, please God. Have mercy on his soul. He was the best father, the best brother, the best leader in the whole world, and his death makes us all orphans. Why, God, why? Because you like the good ones? Well, I'm upset with you, God, our Lord, King of all. Why do you take the good ones and leave us with the lowlifes?

She opened the window a crack from under the blanket, an old black one the color of night. The storage room was dark as night, but outside it was daylight. She saw Abu Husni against the wall with his hands up. And she saw Abu Shaban glued to the wall, and he, too, had his hands up. She realized right away what was happening. "The Jews. They're definitely the Jews," she said. She opened the door to the front yard and saw the soldiers. They were in khaki outfits, too, and they had moustaches like Arabs. Khaki outfits everywhere. She soon realized that not all khakis were equal—their khakis were newer and better. They had helmets with antennas attached to them, and they had new weapons and grenades and lots of shiny things. One of the officers smiled at her and said, "Greetings, Madame Mayor. Go and tell those inside that we're finished. It's all over. We've gashed the drums and stopped all the songs. Tell them that they should turn in their weapons if they don't want to see another river of blood."

The son of a bitch speaks Arabic! Good Arabic. Better than us. She closed the door and ran back inside to the young man who was Abu Rami's replacement. "Young man," she said to him, "Good man. The Jews are out in the front yard and are saying we should surrender our weapons." He gasped and froze in his place. It seemed that all the bombardment and lack of communication and being cornered in the quarter and all the noise and the missiles had made it impossible to know what was happening. The Jews came in, swept through the marketplace, killed the young men, and defused the mines. When they were finished, they broke through the walls with their bulldozers and tanks and entered from one room into another and from one house into another and from one neighborhood to another, until they reached Hosh al-Atout, where the detention camp was, and the end of the line.

There was chaos among the men. Some said, Let's surrender. Some said, Let's die. Let's fight and die and never surrender.

The loudspeakers roared, calling to evacuate the casbah, the entire old city. It was to be blown up from one end to the last stone of the other, from al-Khuder Mosque and Fisher's Monastery all the way to al-Husbah, it was all to be blown up, within minutes. Leave the city!

Everyone started running toward the west, toward Yasmina and the monastery. Run. Run. Barefoot, naked, with slippers, with sandals, with children and without children, old people and the handicapped and wounded. Run over the rubble and the stones and the broken glass and the smoldering garbage and the dead bodies and people with wounds of all kinds—this one's hand, that one's leg, this one blinded by the intense bursting flames, this other rendered mute amid the screams of the wounded and the blare of the loudspeakers croaking and saying, "This area will be bombed! Give yourselves up!"

10

O my dear country! And you, dear mother of young men, lady of ladies, glorious Madame Mayor. Are you alone in your worry? You are not alone. Thousands of people, millions, downtrodden and miserable, are right here beside you. Look around you.

Umm Suad looked around her and saw piles of human beings stacked everywhere in the auditorium of the same public school her daughter Suad had attended. She used to come here for school parties and Mother's Day and graduation, and Suad would sing Fairouz songs and the national anthem and other patriotic songs here. Now Suad was out in the wilderness somewhere, or in Ramallah—God only knew! Umm Suad's sons were all in different countries and their father was still in jail and here she was amid piles of human beings listening to the weeping of other people's children and the lamentation of mothers and orphans and the wailing of the wounded who had not received medical attention from the Red Crescent or UNRWA because it was prohibited. The curfew had gone on and on, extending over days and weeks and months. There was no movement except for what came across the television screen. People demonstrated by the millions on TV screens and then faded away. That was the way it was—demonstrations, demon-strations—and then nothing. Demonstrations, demon- strations, and inaction. And that's the way it stayed. We were glued to the television, waiting for some relief. Was there any relief in the news? Even the news forgot us, because new news was so much nicer. Our news had gotten old. News about Iraq, news about Yemen and Saudi Arabia, news about Yugoslavia and Rwanda, we took a back seat to all that. We had become stale. We were old merchandise.

Then at last someone came to the rescue. He came stumbling over the people, plowing through them and stepping over the arms and legs of human beings lying on blankets and foam mattresses and straw mats. He came to say, "Umm Suad, your daughter is okay, Majid has regained consciousness, and I am going to fight in Jenin refugee camp."

She looked at him and saw his long, unkempt hair that looked like a rooster's feathers, and she saw some scattered chin hairs that had grown long and twisted into sorry little circles. And his eyes—well, a hyena's eyes were nicer than his. How could anyone look like that? What had they done to him? He was still wearing his white jacket and his badge, but the blood, what was all that blood? Were there still casualties and wounded during the curfew? Many long days had passed with them locked up in this chicken coop. Were they still killing people? Hadn't they had enough?

He sat down beside her on the ground and said, "I'm sick of it. Don't talk to me about God or Muhammad. I'm not awake and my heart is heavy and I can't think about anything but killing. I must kill."

She looked at him and the tears rolled her cheeks. This young man—no, this child—had become like a hyena, a wounded animal that writhes with hunger and dreams of killing. What would become of him when he grew up? He had seen what he had seen, and he had heard what he had heard, and here he was now, writhing and dreaming of killing. They killed his heart. They killed his mind. He had lost his feelings and logic. Did he have any weapons? Did he have leadership or organization, what did he have to fight with? It was all over. There was nothing left of Oslo. They killed Oslo. They attacked the leadership, they attacked the people, and they attacked Oslo. So how was he supposed to fight? He didn't answer her. He just sat on the ground beside her, silent.

It was clear he didn't know what to do. They had bulldozed Jenin, he told her, and his brother contacted him on the wireless from the presidential headquarters, and the president, too, was locked up, and maybe Ahmad's mother and father as well, God only knew.

"We've lost everything, Umm Suad. We've lost everything. The country is in shambles. People have been kicked out of their homes and farmers have had all their trees uprooted. They demolished houses and blew up mosques and wounded hundreds and jailed thousands. There is nothing left to live for, Umm Suad—what can I tell you? I'm out there riding in an ambulance and I'm unable to help a single human being. Streets were plowed over and erased without a trace, turned into dirt, turned into playgrounds for tanks. The traffic circle that was full of flowers—completely destroyed. They ripped out the fountain, cut down the palm tree, rode over it with their tanks, smashed the dadunya plants and burned them. There's not a single sidewalk, not a single traffic circle, no lights and no electricity. They even sprayed the traffic lights with bullets. And the poor police station and the post office and the *baladiyyeh*. What can I tell you, Umm Suad?"

"Talk. Keep talking. Tell it to me and get it out of your system."

"The ambulances—even the ambulances didn't escape them. Twenty vehicles or more—all of them white, with the Red Crescent or the Red Cross on them. They flattened them, drove over them with their tanks like they were cockroaches. I was in one of them and was saved only by a miracle. Umm Suad, what can I tell you?"

"Talk," she said. "Keep talking. Let it all out."

"And they ruined Jenin, too," he said. "They burned it completely. They plowed right through it, kicked everyone out of their houses. Some people had their houses demolished right over their heads, and then the Israelis rode over them with their tanks. Other people went out of their houses into the rain and the cold winds. Even nature did not have mercy on them. Have you ever seen such a harsh and cruel April? Rain and storms and high winds and cold. People not knowing where to turn or where to hide from the cruelty of the skies and the earth. Have you ever seen such a thing? I don't know what we've done to deserve it. Sometimes I say death would be a blessing. Other times I say we must have blasphemed, the way we always deceive ourselves and deceive the people around us, and that's why God has struck us down. Maybe because we didn't speak up about those who betrayed us and sold us out. Maybe that's why God didn't look our way. Issa sold us out, Umm Suad. Issa and scores like him. Hundreds, perhaps. Everyone said Issa and the others with him told where the mines were and gave us away. When the Jews entered, they walked right in, right over the severed wires, because Issa and all the others like him had exposed the wires and exposed us. But eventually we found out who did that. That's what they're saying. And they killed him, with an axe, right in front of me. I'll never forget the look in his eyes. He looked at me, crying and calling out to me. "Ahmad. Ahmad." I couldn't bear to watch. I couldn't open my eyes, and I couldn't shut them, and I couldn't feel sorry for him either. I really don't know if Issa was guilty or not guilty. Was he a spy or not—I really don't know. I don't understand. Could Issa really have betrayed his own brothers? Could he have sold out his family? Sold out his relatives, his people, his friends? I was with him through it all, and he never said anything to make me think he was a traitor. How could he be a traitor, Auntie? How could he betray us?"

She lowered her head, then lifted it and looked around at the people stacked up like goods in a big warehouse waiting to be sold. Just like sheep in a slaughterhouse, waiting to be slaughtered. Just like dates tumbling to the ground, onto fallow land, with no one around to pick them up. Like beasts of burden, like worms, like trees, like stones, like soil, all for sale.

He asked again, "Is it possible?"

She shook her head. "Of course it's possible."

He jumped up and said, "I'm going to Jenin, to fight and kill."

She called after him, but he didn't hear her over the noise of all the people. She bowed her head and whispered, "My heart goes out to you and your lost youth."

Then she remembered that he was still young, a baby who didn't know his top from his bottom. And she remembered his mother and her suffering, like the suffering of the Gaza boy's mother. She threw up her arms and whispered sadly, "It's all one and the same."

11

I return to my journal, so I won't lose my memory again and slip back into a coma.

It has been eight days since the siege began, and the buzzing in my head still comes and goes, reminding me of the concussion and the crashing down of the wall. And it seems that the wall caused my own collapse, for I no longer understand what's happening around me or which way to turn or how to respond. After all the heavy, incessant shelling I've lost my ability to concentrate. No building was spared from the explosions, the bulldozing, the bombing, and the demolitions, and we all ended up crammed into a tiny section of a building that had been bombed but at least had one slice of wall still standing. The peace activists left us and we remained alone there, ridden by fear and worry and distress that they would put new leadership into place, like Karzai in Afghanistan, and we would all die and be forgotten by the world.

Sharon had stated several times that he did not like Arafat and that he has been after him ever since Beirut and Tunis. Now he finally had his chance to get rid of him. As for Oslo and all those peace promises and the conferences and handshakes for everyone in Washington to see, and the baskets of flowers and the microphones and the loudspeakers and the cameras and the hundreds of millions of television viewers watching Rabin (half asleep) and Arafat (showing off his headdress) and Clinton (astonished by his own ability to bring these opposing parties together)—such matters did not please Sharon one bit. That was why he brought in his bulldozers and tractors: to demolish Arafat and whoever was with him once and for all. Naturally we were very scared. Arafat rushed to the highest floor, where I was blasted into the air along with my cup of coffee, and announced his position and our position with three words: "*Shahidan. Shahidan. Shahidan.*" And that meant the *Fatiha* had been read, peace be upon our souls.

Was that a maneuver by Arafat? How could I know, when I was just one of his guards, one of his second- or third-line guards—the commandos were his main guards, along with the security forces and Squad 17 and ten other kinds of guards who stood watch at his door and wouldn't let the likes of me talk to him for even a second in order to find out what he meant and what he was thinking. That's why I started listening to rumors and gossip and stories, in order to understand what the man was saying. To understand what had happened to us and what was going to happen. When I caught sight of his headdress as he came up the stairs, up to where I had flown into the air with my cup of coffee, I followed him and crouched behind a half-standing wall to eavesdrop. I heard him say to the reporter in his first cell interview, "*Shahidan, shahidan, shahidan.*" I knew in that moment that our hour had drawn near. It was over for us, and history would forget. That is honestly what I thought the man meant. "*Shahidan. Shahidan. Shahidan.*" That each of the three "*shahidan's*" should be multiplied by a hundred. Three hundred all together (which was how many there were of us) would bear witness unto death. I threw up my hands, thankful I wasn't holding the coffee cup this time.

But then I was told that the president was maneuvering. What did that mean? It meant that his message was three-dimensional, going along three waves toward three directions. The first wave meant we would fight to the death and Sharon would not be able to enter our half-demolished building without committing a veritable massacre. Such a massacre would make a martyr and a hero of Arafat and set him as a great example to his people. That, of course, would not please Sharon or Bush or Blair.

The second wave was directed at us, the ones fishing in troubled waters. It said there was no place for making behind-the-back agreements. Behind the president's back, that is.

And the third wave was for America. It said, "Get lost, this is the end of the road," to Bush and Blair. The martyr ruled, and this martyr was still here on the face of the earth and people were on his side.

And that's exactly what took place. People went out into the streets, from the first street in Ramallah all the way to Aswan and Saudi Arabia and the Sinai and the Sudan and Sumatra. There was not a single soul in the whole world who wasn't shouting, "Long live Arafat!" myself included.

Have you ever seen a martyr make political maneuvers? I have. On the third floor of a half-demolished building, where I was thrown into the air with my cup of coffee and where I crouched behind half a wall to hide from the Squad 17 security forces. There I discovered that Karzai was not coming here, that I was going to live, and that Sharon was going to get the message.

12

I started following every story about Arafat; he really amazed me. What did he eat? What did he drink? How did he pray? And why was he still alive? He held onto a nightmare of a dream that Palestine—no matter how small it became, or how big, or how white-haired, or how aged—would exist. He maneuvered and spun round, headed left then right, up and down, until death—and still Palestine had to exist. He played this game and that, backgammon and chess, blind man's buff, and still Palestine had to exist. Even in death, still Palestine had to exist. But what about us? The ones under siege in prison, under blockade, crammed behind a wall with no food, no water, no bathrooms, in a half-demolished building whose other half was surrounded by a graveyard of crushed cars and soldiers and snipers on rooftops and behind windows. What about us? "Sing," they told us. What do you mean? "Sing," they said. Why? What does it mean? Is this the time for singing? "Sing to show how powerful you are and let the Jews hear us and Zinni, too. Let him know we'll keep singing till we die. Let him burst."

The next day Zinni came, but he didn't hear anything, so we burst. He spoke words put into his mouth by Sharon. He talked about "the killers"—meaning me and the other wanted criminals, who should be given due punishment by Sharon. Arafat said, "We are the Authority. We sign the agreements. The Authority is in charge, not Sharon." So Zinni left and they brought in Powell. And Powell sang the same tune: "the killers" (who were us) should get their due punishment from Sharon. So Arafat said for the second time, "We are the Authority. We sign the agreements. The Authority is in charge, not Sharon." So Powell left and they brought in one of our relatives. An Arab. An Egyptian. A tough guy. So he came to us bearing chocolates. Later they said he'd brought bananas. Then it turned out it was neither chocolate nor bananas nor anything else with flavor. Mubarak sent his heartfelt condolences, and also some bottles of water. I found out later that Mubarak had actually sent mango juice, but Squad 17 drank it all and left us the bottles of water. That was what I heard. Though it wouldn't be at all strange for what I heard to be inaccurate, because I was eavesdropping, crouched behind a wall in half a building riddled with holes like a sieve. Was that why they talked about "corruption" and "a corrupt government"? I don't know. But I do know that Arafat did not even taste the mango juice or the water. He did read the message and enjoyed it very much. He left the mango juice for some of his guards to enjoy. And since I was one of his second- or third-line guards, I enjoyed one sip of water.

13

They brought the killers from the first line to court. I, unfortunately or luckily, was not taken in, because I was one of the guards in the second (or third) line. Yet at the same time I remained one of the "killers." This label was very important, because it meant I wasn't part of the deal. And the deal, even though we didn't like it much, and despite all the injustice, benefited us in two ways. On the one hand, we were doing the judging, not Sharon. And on the other hand, it managed to depressurize the cooking pot, or rather the cook—that is, Sharon—since he overlooked people like me and postponed his meeting with Arafat. In the days that followed, when I found out what happened to the killers from the first line, I felt very sorry for myself, because the killers from the first line were staying in a five-star prison equipped with water and electricity and spic-and-span bathrooms and first-class service provided by great nations with grand reputations and catchy names like George and Tony and John and Blair. We, on the other hand, had the dull, third- or fourth-class names like Abu Satour and Abu Nadour and Abu Jildeh. The guards who kept watch outside around the fences and on the rooftops and behind the windows were of a class I can't even describe, because they had neither origin nor roots nor color nor nationality to speak of. This one was from Morocco and that one from New York and that one from Ethiopia or Estonia or Rome or Romania. And other than that, everything was fine, except that the electricity was cut off, and the water and the air and the bathrooms—well, you get the idea.

Other than that everything was fine, except the water—you can't imagine—rather, yes, do that: imagine being without water or a bathroom for three weeks, three days, even for three hours. Not a drop of water comes even close to your face, or your stomach, or your back, and all those other body parts we won't mention. Can you imagine that? I imagined it. Even the president imagined it with us. For 22 days water came close only to his mouth, but as for the other body parts, well, you know. But I blame those guards who drank the mango juice and let us have the bottles of water, only to come back later and take them to use for ablution and personal hygiene. Can you believe that? I said to them, "If the president did not taste the juice or drink the water, then why worry about ablution and personal hygiene?" Word for word, they replied, "So we can fight and face the Lord with beautiful faces. After all, God is beautiful and loves beauty."

14

I am writing in my journal so I won't lose my memory and slip back into a coma.

Sharon went back to his lies. After the killers from the first line left for their first-class prison, in the best Chevrolets and Cadillacs, we stood there waving with tears in our eyes. The tears weren't for them, of course—they were for ourselves, because we were still stuck in captivity, stuck under siege, with his excellency the president and the guards from the second line, which included me. (I had been promoted and brought closer to the mango juice and bottles of water.) Despite everything, I stood waving, full of anger, just like the president who was really upset because Sharon had promised to lift the siege, and it was still underway. The guards were still on the tops of the buildings, and the heavy names were still weighing down on us inside the jail and outside the jail. In fact, there were so many more Abu Satours and Abu Nadours and Abu Jildehs now that the Americans came back to renew their demands that we maintain order and security. The president shouted, "*Allahu Akbar*! Is it possible, people, for me to establish order while I'm imprisoned and besieged? Unbelievable! And they claim they are from great nations with five stars!"

The important thing was that matters had improved. The situation was sound, and here I was, next to a journalist who was holding a cellphone that worked, because the Jews had reconnected the lines. I heard him say to his friend, "Where are you, Kamal?"

"I'm at the dispatch at al-Hamra," Kamal said.

"Watch out for the mines. Stay away from the wires."

"Don't worry—I'll walk along the tracks left by the tanks and I'll be there in a few minutes."

That's just what happened, except Kamal was not alone. They came en masse—in from what seemed like a thousand and one doors, through the holes in the walls, over the rubble, and wires and car corpses—journalists, foreigners, demonstrators, and our own people, too, including my family and my friends. I was shocked to see Laura, Suad, and my old grandmother. It was a first-class meeting of the best kind.

15

Yet relief did not come as we had expected. The situation remained exactly as it was. The president was fenced into his corner, surrounded from every direction, with snipers atop the buildings around the entire compound. And we, the wanted criminals, didn't dare move. Ramallah was surrounded, too, and cut off from every village and every city, from the whole world, in fact. There was a checkpoint at Sarda, and a checkpoint at Qalandiya, and one at Betunia and al-Baloua. Checkpoint after checkpoint, from every direction and at every entrance. The siege not only continued, but intensified, and so did the attacks and retaliations. One would fire and then the other, back and forth without end. And despite all that, I began to grow accustomed to the atmosphere—the world of the Authority and those who were a part of it. I started watching my step and the steps of politicians and leaders, calculating how to rise in the ranks. Aligning with the leader meant power, position, rank, salary. It meant becoming a cabinet director, then a cabinet minister. And the competition happened in the news and on TV. One of them would say something, another would analyze what he said, and still another would criticize him and talk down to him even though his own name was at the top of the list of people who benefited from him. They started impressing us with all sorts of technical jargon. Words like "democracy" and "fighting corruption" and "restructuring the government" and "the house of deputies" invaded the television stations and the newspapers. I found myself, consciously and unconsciously, being dragged into the heated race toward the TV stations. The whole problem started with Laura, because Laura, who was my girlfriend—or my fiancée as people believed and as she believed—interviewed me live on PBC. And as it turned out, God was good to me and I was good on television, likeable in fact. The next day she told me that the viewers really liked me, and her colleagues at Al-Jazeera and Al-Arabiyya, and Abu Dhabi TV and even in Bahrain, asked about me and wanted to know who I was. With her usual enthusiasm she told them that I was a "commander of a Tanzim of some importance." In a matter of days, I was reporting the news as a respectable TV personality. I traded in my khaki outfit for a suit, and I traded in my weapons for a pen that I waved around as I spoke and explained and said loudly and clearly things like "democracy" and "the concerns of the people" and "restructuring the government," to the point where I believed everything I was saying.

The truth was I wasn't in touch with any of it. I was under siege, in this chicken coop, surrounded by snipers and the rubble of buildings and cars, hiding from all eyes and from Israel. I had lost touch with the word on the street, with the pulse of the people. I knew nothing about my people except what I heard from Laura or on TV. In order not to sound stupid, I started reading my father's articles and calling him on my cellphone so he could explain things I didn't understand. What did he mean by this, and what did he mean by that, and then I would go back on TV and impress them with flashy reporting and analysis, things that enriched the broadcasts and made them more exciting. Overnight—or over the course of a few weeks, at any rate—I became an authority. Or rather, a TV star. Which made Laura very happy, because even her grandmother praised me and said I reminded her of him, God rest his soul. That is, of al-Washmi. That's what made me annoyed, because al-Washmi of course was known for... well, after a while, I figured al-Washmi was not ugly and not as bad as I had thought. After all, he was a product of our country, a product of the situation. Even if he was an eccentric gypsy with gypsy roots. Gypsies were part of us. If we were going to go around talking and smacking our lips and making speeches and proclaiming loudly the importance of fairness and justice and people sticking together, well, what was fair about saying the gypsies weren't part of the people, and gypsies couldn't be leaders—how could the leaders not be from the people? That's what made me wonder what they were exactly—gypsies, countrymen, or leaders? I spent days and weeks thinking about it, but then I gave up, because I was busy concentrating on the cellphone and the television. I had begun my climb to the top of the social ladder. I started dreaming of becoming a parliament minister, because the ministers weren't any better than I was. My appearing on television was a great achievement on every level. I looked decent, I spoke reasonably well, and I had experience in the art of warfare that benefited me as I rose in the ranks. And I had a father who could explain and expound upon every complication, so why not become a minister? Why shouldn't I reach for higher things if I looked acceptable and sounded reasonable? Was there any doubt? Not since my last doctor's appointment, when he told me that the fracture in my skull had healed and the concussion had finally stabilized. I was fine, perfectly normal like everyone else. Completely normal.

But Suad said the opposite. Suad said I was worse, because I was so concerned with my position and the television. She said I was just like everyone else who had been defeated and brought down with them the hopes of the people and our cause. The hopes of the people and the cause? Was there any chance for the cause? Was there any truth? Was there any justice? Did the world have a conscience? All the nations of the world sold us out and we sold them out, too. We picked up our guns and went about destroying things. People followed us and then left us. We no longer knew whom to kill. Should we kill Sharon, or would he kill us, would time kill us? Time was important, very important. Time contains all the mold and decay of history. As time passes, things wither and wilt and shrink just like a person does. A person starts out as a sweet baby who crawls and pulls himself upward. Then he becomes a naïve young man who dreams of sprouting wings and flying. Then he's an adult who is satisfied to walk slowly on his two feet. And then he's an old man who is hunched over on his crutches, and then he goes back to crawling on his belly, but downward now, toward the bottom, toward nothingness and ruin and the silence of the grave. That's how a person is, and the same goes for history and for the cause and the concerns of the people. Everything. Everything wilts and withers.

I tried to explain these thoughts to Laura and Suad. They blew up in my face like a hornet's nest, firing off thousands of stingers and bites, until I no longer knew how to fight back or hide or get out of their sight. What could I say to someone who didn't understand what it meant to face death at every second? What could I say to someone who hadn't tasted being deprived of even a drop of water? What could I say to someone who didn't know the degradation of being broken by force, by tanks, of being bled to death by the siege? Is there any doubt that a person is like history? And that history is like the cause? And that the cause, like love, starts out sweet and solid and strong, but in time wilts and dies and disappears? Time is in charge, not people. So what duty are we talking about? What time?

16

Suad stood in the square near the government complex and the presidential headquarters, where crowds came in droves—cars and reporters and foreigners and armed young men wearing khaki outfits, all amid the rubble of demolished buildings and cars. It was a very difficult time. Despite the fact that the president was locked up, politicians and ministers continued vying for TV airtime. This one would say one thing and someone else would morally condemn what the first one said until the recorder ran out of tape. "Our time is up," Laura would say apologetically. "Thank you very much. This is PBC broadcasting from the presidential headquarters in Ramallah." She stopped the recorder and the camera, and Majid followed her. Suad saw the two of them talking from a distance. They were gesticulating and shaking their heads. Then they parted, still wagging their fingers with anger and hostility.

Laura approached her. She was panting, and she immediately began yelling, "He's crazy! Crazy! I swear he's crazy!" And then she started to cry.

How often that scene was repeated! Majid wanted her all to himself. That is—he wanted to make her into one of his tools. "Interview this guy. Don't interview that guy. Listen to this guy. Don't listen to that guy. This guy has no brains, no ideas, doesn't understand. I understand. I know. I work from the inside. You are just an outside observer who doesn't know what's going on in the back alleys." At first she went along with him, until he went too far and she started getting tired of being harassed by him. She began wondering about his true feelings toward her and her true feelings toward him.

"We women," Suad said. "What do we know? As far as they're concerned, we're pretty decorations and nothing more." Suad remembered how it used to be. She remembered his eyes, his lips, his voice. The tenderness of the poetry and dearness of the cause and the flame of emotion. But now, what remained now? All she had left were memories—the image of his eyes full of understanding and kindness, and the echo of his words laden with tenderness and poetry. He was sweet. He was gentle. But only for a while—the fighter in him would return and the lover would withdraw. Months would pass without his asking about her, and then he would remember, just like that, all of a sudden. He would call her on the telephone and ask, with mild rebuke, "Where've you been?" As if she were the one responsible for his absence. Finally, when he said some things that were particularly hurtful, she declared an insurrection. The thread connecting them was severed. It reminded her of what a commander's wife had told her of her own husband: "I never see him except by chance. For a few minutes. Then I forget him and he forgets me. I'm bound and tied to a ghost of a man, I'm simply the mother of his children, the manager of his household. This is our fate as wives of the Tanzim. This is our fate!"

Not my fate, Suad vowed. And the thread was severed.

When he passed by among the leaders and the reporters, the tendons of her heart played a shortened song. She still imagined what he would say when he saw her after all these years. Three years. Four. Five. She had lost count of the years searching for a great love like Palestine. She found nothing but men who were ghosts of men. He remained in her heart, not as a lover, not as a relative, but as the example of a real man, steadfast, like a statue, untouched by falling rain or changing weather.

17

He saw her in the square surrounded by people, so he didn't go to her. He looked in her direction for a moment and then climbed the stairs between the guards and the security forces.

Her heart was pounding. He's going to look now, she thought. He's going to look now! If he doesn't look, it means he's forgotten me, and if he does look, it means he remembers.

When he reached the top step, he turned slowly to look for a brief moment, and there he saw her gazing at him, dumbstruck and bewildered. He looked away from her into the distance, took a few steps inside, and disappeared amid the guards.

She had fallen in love with the spark in his eyes and the timbre of his voice. That voice full of tenderness that flowed like a murmuring stream, calling her. She was drawn to him. He reminded her of forgotten things, of the nation divided into two halves, of the identity divided into two halves, and of the spirit dangling like a kite at the end of a string, searching for a beckoning horizon. When she saw him now, a deluge of emotions took her: sadness and longing, an overpowering childish joy, a sweet song. Was love an illusion, or was it a reality of its own? She was in the West Bank and he was far away, in exile, moving from one front to the next, one defeat to the next, battling death. It was all exile, whether it was Damascus, Beirut, Tunis, or any other capital. It was all abandonment and separation; so near and so far. He was part of the Authority and she was in the middle of the square and all the people. She waited for what never came. She waited for the solution that never came, for love that never came. She waited for the leader to wake up and tell all of them where they were, how they had gotten there, and where to go next.

He looked into the distance, leaving her alone in the middle of the square. She wanted to run after him and scream, "You're crazy just like me. You're not better than me. You searched but you didn't find me. I searched and found you and lost you, just like Palestine. Do you belong to me? Do you belong to Palestine? If you do belong to Palestine, then Amen. We'll say, 'He found himself.' We'll say, 'Palestine gave to him and he gave back to Palestine.' But if you're going to wander the world and keep your distance from me and from Palestine and keep going in circles like a bee, but a bee with no honey and no flowers, then it's a waste, a total waste!"

Laura passed by and said, "He's crazy! He's dreaming of becoming a deputy director and then a cabinet minister. Have you ever seen such leadership anywhere in the world? And he's a wanted criminal. He's besieged. He's imprisoned behind walls and snipers, dreaming of becoming a cabinet minister. Or an ambassador!"

"He's making up for things," Suad whispered.

"Making up for what?" Laura shouted. "For blowing up houses? For destroying cities? For a long list of martyrs that runs all the way to hell? Listen to this."

She played back her tape so that Suad could hear all the big talk and small talk of big men and small men. Bees without honey, without a hive, a hornet's nest.

18

"Come closer," he said, breaking the silence. The words vanished, far away from him.

Suad had thought that everything between them was gone. But suddenly here he was, rushing back to her, stirring up the air, engulfing her with doubt.

We've already lost each other, she thought. We let our love slip away. I gave you my heart. You were *the* man. The magician. The captor. But you took advantage of my feelings, so I began to resent you. How could you be the love and the chain? How could you be the liberator and the slave trader? Was I just a fling, a mere number? Was I doomed to take your blows and your insults and say, "Long live free Palestine!" while I was mired in such degradation? Yet you could only be my executioner if I allowed you. That's when I decided not to succumb to him. That's when the chain broke.

That was how she saw him now—as something broken, a vanquished country shading its eyes. She saw the warplanes and the tanks and the pulverized streets and the bunkers. A lost people. Crowds of pedestrians on the roads and at the checkpoints. The office window behind him gave a view of Ramallah and al-Bireh and the borders of Jerusalem. She looked at him. He was far away, drowning in introspection. Darkness over the West Bank and the borders of Jerusalem. Crowds of pedestrians. Long lines at the checkpoint. And he was unable to get there, unable to liberate himself and move through the checkpoint, to the forbidden.

She sat down next to him and looked out his window. She could see branches of pine trees like nativity candles. Like Easter candles. And under the pine trees, the street—what was left of that street—with its dirt and bulldozers and ditches and sewers and rubble and water pipes spewing the ruins of the war. She remembered the days of the first dizziness of love. His eyes had been like spotlights, unveiling what was under her clothes and inside her bones. Why does the heart become afflicted? Why do we moan and suffer through the melting away of passion and the loss of little things? A whisper. A word. A tune. A gesture. All those tender things had come in the midst of war. Even in the midst of the destruction of cities and the demolition of houses, love springs up like a flower. A cactus flower, from among the thorns. And then everything seemed richer and more beautiful and more painful. Why do we become like children with nothing to stop us from following our crazy whims? Why do our hearts pound and why do we confide in the winds? And what tragedy when we finally fall back to earth. What a lump in the throat. What a horrendous wound to the heart. O wound of yesterday. O wound of today. O my country.

She said, "Do you want to try again? Do you want us to see if we can revive what's left of us and our years? After the war, and the fragmented souls, and a country that survives on illusions—is there any hope? Is there any way?"

"We are the way," he said.

She looked at him and could see the lack of conviction in his eyes. Years ago, she would fall asleep and wake with the same hope of finding him. She hoped for him to come and embrace her, to light up her solitary nights. Her stored emotions were like a volcano. She was younger then. But there was always fear, social limitations. And he, too, had his own fears. He had his own limitations and struggles over the unlawful and forbidden; in short, he had a loathing of sex. Whether he knew it or not, there was doubt planted deep within his soul. On the one hand, a woman was just a fling, a fleeting emotion; on the other she was a jinn who would sap his manhood and toss him aside. A woman was fire. A woman was a shadow. A woman was a horse, and he was the horseman.

He said, "Come closer," and she was filled with fear, fear of returning to the past and what it had been—an ugly way of looking at love and sex and the female body, an ugly way of looking at his own body and his own yearnings.

Should she yearn for him? Should she embrace him? Could she control him and control his grief and confusion and the chaos of emotions and his own upbringing and what was planted in the depth of depths? She didn't know. He didn't know. That was the riddle.

19

Suad returned to Nablus. She walked those winding roads and mountain paths between the trees and the thickets of bramble. The siege on Nablus was still as intense. Nablus in particular, the birthplace of history and identity, still suffered from attacks and raids every night. Every day, in fact. Assaults and assassinations and break-ins had left horrifying traces on the buildings and on people's lives. But she had to go back, because her father had been released from prison. There had been a prisoner exchange, and they had kept in jail anyone who still had any will or youthfulness left in him. Her father had gotten old long before his time. The years in prison had eaten his life away and destroyed his body. He had intestinal ulcers, chronic asthma, joint inflammation, and innumerable hemorrhoids.

"Let him sleep," her mother told her. "Don't you dare wake him. Poor thing needed an injection to be able to sleep. Let him rest."

Suad sat in the kitchen trying to reach a decision. He had proposed to her, and she told him to be patient, let her think about it and talk it over with her parents. He said that the years were slipping away and life was passing them by. She said, "Do you want a marriage or a fling?" He looked at her with sadness and worry in his eyes, which made her feel torn inside. She wished she could stay in Ramallah and live with him and die with him and give him all she could of herself and her ability to understand. She wished she could take on the hornet's nest. The likes of Majid had gobbled up the whole place, filled the television screens and the government posts. People went in different directions, security fell apart, and the situation deteriorated. The difficulty was also within the structure and organization of the government and the various groups and people's customs. Chaos in the government, suppression at home, problems in education and distribution and justice and human rights, and on top of all that, repression and bombardment from Israel. How can you build an intelligent nation out of that? How can you fight off disease when your body is so weak and sick?

During their last meeting he had said to her, "We will be together. We will work together and fight together and rebuild what has been torn down." She looked at him and saw his powerlessness and the mountains of doubt. We were fighting Israel, after all, with America and Western science and technology on its side. People retreated into the mosques waiting for the solution to descend upon them from God. And now we were fighting those who had escaped from our world and come up with innovations that boggled the mind and annihilated what logic was left and deepened the abyss, dragging us back to the Stone Age. A million-year setback. A futile legacy. A system rotten to the core. How could we build while others were tearing things down? He said all that to her and she said, "Amen." But when she needed him for something or other, he would suddenly disappear. Vanish. She couldn't find him anywhere. He wouldn't answer his cellphone. She remembered the wife of the commander and what she had said. Could she put up with being the wife of a shadow of a man?

Her father said, "My dear girl, a woman needs a husband. You need to be taken care of. You're getting old and you need a husband and a home and children and a man to look after you and look after your life. And this man is not just any man. He's direct and honorable and has a good heart and a good future. Tell him on my behalf that it pleases me and honors me to become family with someone like him. Pick up the phone right now and tell him yes. Go ahead. Congratulations."

Her mother whispered very quietly, "Wait a little. We need to talk."

Her father heard that and said harshly, "You need to talk? With whom and about what? Umm Suad, the girl's getting old. You and I are not going to be around forever. Your sons all left and went abroad and no one asked a question. Do you want the girl to stay here and never find a husband and end up a spinster?"

Never find a husband and end up a spinster! So that's how it is. A picked-over spinster and the shadow of a man. Even her own father, who had graduated from prison with honors, was saying such things. What would everyone else say?

Her mother winked at her behind his back. She gestured secretly for Suad to follow her, and so she left her father as he said, "Bring me my medicine. Make me some tea. And shut the window. It's cold outside."

20

Umm Suad took her daughter up to the roof. Nablus was the same as always. Chimneys of bakeries, ancient cupolas and bath houses, towering minarets and arches of long-ago palaces. That past, this present, what future?

Her mother said, "Listen, dear. If you want a life with him like my life with your father, then go to him right away, today, don't wait until tomorrow. There's no avoiding marriage. Security and children and motherhood and the shadow of a man—better than the shadow of a wall. But if you want to live a life, *your* life, a life free of grief and worry, then find someone who isn't attached to anything. That man is just like your father or maybe worse because he's a commander. And don't dare tell me that you love him, because love can fool you and make you see thorns as roses and sweet basil. Watch out, I tell you. Watch out."

"Okay," she whispered. "But what about my heart?"

"Harden your heart. A weak heart can make a woman worthy of nothing but her own tears. Do you want to live with tears of fear? Do you want to live with tears of suppression? Do you want to live with your ear pressed to the door afraid of hearing soldiers and revolutionaries coming to take him away some dark night and leave you all alone with a bunch of kids and responsibilities, with a lack of means and agony and grief and jealousy, and your body swelled up from all the worries and the longing. You're young and you have feelings and emotions, and later on he'll toss you aside and wander endlessly from barracks to meetings, and when you call him he'll say he's busy, he has responsibilities. He has Palestine to worry about, and orders from the Tanzim, and he doesn't have time. Fine, but what about you? What about your heart and your body and your needs? And what about his children—who is going to look after them? And his house and his food and his needs? Let me just say it to you as plainly as possible. I think you should think it over, and be strong. Don't let your heart decide."

Bewildered and upset, Suad whispered, "Okay. But what about my mind?"

Her mother looked at her and shook her head in sorrow. She took a few steps toward the edge of the roof and stood there saying nothing.

It wasn't simply a matter of feelings and love and dreams—it was much deeper than that. To Suad it was a mixture of feelings and wisdom and thinking and emotions. And it wasn't a matter of how it had been in the past and how she had loved him when she was young. Nor was it only about the present and how she still loved him. But what kind of future would there be with any man? Could she possibly marry a man who had no interest in the cause? Could she possibly marry a man solidly on the ground with no wings and no cares for anything but himself? And what about her and who she was—her way of thinking, her upbringing, her father's history, and the kind of atmosphere she had lived in because of him. What about the reality of the mud she was mired in? All the poverty and destruction? If a man did not take action for the sake of others and for the sake of the country and the cause, was he really a man? Did he deserve her love and her life?

She walked slowly and stood in silence behind her mother. She looked out at the sunset, at the sky anointed with the blood of martyrs and victims, the blood of Nablus. Nablus is like me, she thought. I need a man, a real man who is capable of giving my life meaning and depth and hope. But then again. Then again! She remembered her father and the way he said, "You need a husband to look after you." He had forgotten that he had looked after no one. Marriage to someone like him was a burden. It meant fear and deprivation.

Just because her father had forgotten, or pretended to forget—should she? Who raised her? Who taught her everything? Who carried the whole family on her back, ran the workshop, looked after the neighbors during the incursions, worried about the soup kitchen and the Gaza boy? And even him, even this father, this prison graduate and fighter—who looked after him, who cared about his needs in prison and got him a lawyer and worried if he was sick or needed medicine, who nursed him back to health? And the same with all the sons, despite how old they got—they were men now with full-grown mustaches—they still sent her letters and requests. "Dear sweet wonderful mother, can you lend me a little money? I'll pay you back as soon as God opens the doors." The strange thing was that God's doors were always locked. And now her father was saying a woman needs a husband to look after her. Her father had forgotten. The caretaker had been his wife. And she had done it in silence, without fireworks or slogans or declarations, without medals of honor and victory torches.

21

Suad spotted Ahmad in the traffic circle getting out of the ambulance. He was wearing his white suit with the Red Cross and the Red Crescent embroidered on the front. She called to him. As he headed toward her, the shopkeepers and merchants reached out to shake his hand. "Come in for a cup of coffee," said one. "How about some tea?" said another. Still another said, "Have some *knafeh*." She watched as he greeted them in return like an adult, thanking them with the customary gesture of raising his hand to his head, and saying with seriousness, "Thank you very much. Someday soon we'll drink coffee together, on a happier occasion, God willing."

"How wonderful," she said, greeting him. "You've become quite popular!"

He nodded and said distractedly, "During the attack I treated people and got to know them."

She gave an encouraging smile. "You mean they got to know you."

He shook his head.

"Now what will you do?" she asked, concerned, because she had heard her mother worrying about him.

He didn't answer. He just kept walking in no particular direction.

His silence made her anxious, so she repeated herself. "What about your studies? What about your mother and your father?"

He still didn't answer, so she reached over and grabbed his arm. She blocked his way, glaring at him as he stared off into the distance over her shoulder.

"How is school?" she persisted. "And your mother and father?"

He didn't answer her. He continued staring over her shoulder.

"Who are you living with?" she insisted.

He stared into the distance and remained silent. She tugged on his arm and pulled him over to a long wooden bench on the sidewalk. "Sit down," she said. He kept standing there, looking around, at a loss. She pulled on him, and he fell stiffly onto the bench, still quiet and not moving.

"Listen, Ahmad," she said. "Listen, sweetheart. You're grown now."

The word "sweetheart" fell on his ears like a hammer. He glared at her. She understood and backed off.

"Okay. Okay. You're a grown-up now."

She looked at him carefully and saw that he was beyond his years in height and size and maybe even intelligence. But what about school? And his mother and father?

"What are you doing? You can't stay like this, with no education," she said, dismayed.

He turned his head, avoiding the subject. She pulled on his arm and insisted, "No education?"

He didn't answer.

"Your father is okay with that?"

He didn't answer, so she kept after him. "You want to be ignorant?"

He turned back toward her, scrutinizing her, so she said with utmost care, "Without an education you'll end up an ignoramus."

"I'm with the Red Cross," he said coldly.

"But you're still very young! How old are you?"

"What's it to you?" he grumbled.

"It's a lot to me. I'm like your sister. I'm like Majid, maybe even closer."

He shook his head several times and muttered, "Maybe even closer."

She noticed his gesture and his comment, and she remembered what she had heard about Majid having stopped asking about his parents and his family, how he was too busy with his career and the television and racing his way to the top. Feeling bad, she said, "Okay. And your father?"

He shrugged his shoulders, giving her the impression that things were not going well.

"Is your father okay with that?"

"Okay with what?"

"With things this way... you out of school and not getting an education and far from your parents and your home... and forgetting yourself!"

Coldly he replied, "No, I haven't forgotten."

"Oh yes, you have. What are you doing living like a laborer? What are you doing spending each day in a different house? What are you doing wandering around in a daze, every day in a different place, not knowing where you're headed, with no plan for the future?"

"The future?" he sneered sarcastically.

"Of course the future, sweetie. Can you possibly live without a future?"

The word "sweetie" irritated him, and so did the word "future." "What future? Don't you see the people? Go see the people."

She looked where he gestured and saw the laborers and the scores of young men, graduates and university students, grown men and young men and boys, too, little kids sitting by themselves and in groups around the traffic circle waiting for work. With no hope of finding work, just sitting, without hope.

She didn't comment.

"At least I have something to do. But those guys over there..." He fell silent and went back to thinking and looking off into the distance. Way into the distance.

"If I were there, if you and I were there, could we talk about a future?"

He stood up suddenly.

"Where are you going?"

"I have work to do," he said.

And she watched him disappear into the crowd of workers.

22

Ahmad lived among the workers. They weren't workers, really; they were day laborers. They worked in the fields in Qalqilya at first until the Wall came and snatched the daily bread from their mouths and the means of living from their hands. The wall fenced the inhabitants into a cage. Some people rebelled and some fled. Some young men joined Hamas and sought revenge. A bus was blown up and a rocket was fired on the settlement of Kiryat Shayba, so the siege was intensified. Thousands of laborers were displaced and took refuge in Nablus. Some of them lived in mosques. The lucky ones found day labor or piecework and lived temporarily in the store or the workshop or the factory where they worked. Ahmad ended up living with two students from Qalqilya who took him every Thursday afternoon to the university to attend seminars and meetings and read books and other publications. That opened things up for him, expanded his horizons, made him feel grown up, like a man. The invasion had shaken the very foundation of his existence, and he could no longer put up with being treated like a child. And there was all that fuzz growing on his chin now and on his upper lip, and he was so tall his head nearly brushed the ceiling, and his arms had grown strong from carrying heavy things like wounded people and dead bodies. He felt like a man now, a big man, a responsible man, a capable man. That's why when he went home and his father kept asking questions like "Where are you going?" and "Where were you?" he decided to go back to the Red Crescent and the Red Cross, put his white outfit back on, and let the fuzz on his chin grow into a beard. He also began stopping by the mosque and reading from the Qur'an.

The sheikh at the mosque told him that when the Prophet was asked about who the dearest people to one's heart were, he replied, "Your mother, then your mother, then your mother, and then your father." Ahmad said that the students at the meeting said, "Palestine." The sheikh said that Palestine was the mother's heart. Palestine was the mother and the mother's heart and the mother's breast and the mother's womb. Could there be a mother without Palestine? Of course not. Therefore Palestine was the mother of all mothers. And the Prophet said, "Your duty is to your mother, and then to your mother, and then to your mother, and then to your father. That is what the Prophet said. What do you say?" Ahmad said Palestine was the mother of all mothers. And so the sheikh wiped his forehead with holy water from Zamzam, and said, "You are a *mujahid*." Ahmad felt himself grow taller and the whole universe expand.

The students told him that the Wall was going to pass right through Ayn al-Mirjan. He couldn't believe it. In his mind, the wall was "over there"—in other words, on someone else's land, not on his own. The dreadful wall was something distant, something that happened to other people, like syphilis or cancer or impotence. Other people got it, but not him. That's why he, like everyone else, was late in believing it. By the time he believed it, the Wall was already sky-high and as long as the Great Wall of China. He ran as fast as he could, but when he got there the clash between the demonstrators and the armed forces had already broken up. Only a small group of peace activists remained, squatting in frustration on the hill, picking up the posters and the flyers and getting ready for a new demonstration and a new clash. Ahmad stood there looking around. He saw crowds of peasants begging for help from the foreigners and the peace activists. And he also saw priests, some die-hard leftists, the Catholic priest, and Mira.

Mira had grown. She was taller and fuller and prettier, ten times prettier than before. His heart was pounding. He hadn't seen her for two or three years or maybe more, and when he had seen her that night she had been wearing a short nightgown with a laced hem. Now she was wearing jeans and no ponytail. She had very short hair, like cat's fur, and she looked more beautiful. Was there a love that lasted forever? He could feel his heart pounding and the blood rushing to his head. He turned around and walked a few steps. Then he sat on a rock to think. Was there a love that lasted forever? And was this love or a curse? Was he allowed this love? What would the sheikh at the mosque say? Or the students in Nablus or the displaced people from Qalqilya? Then he remembered that feeling of betrayal when she deceived him and stole Amber. And everything that had ensued, from imprisonment to torture to incursions and his brother's estrangement and his father's shock. His father was never the same again, and neither was Majid. Neither was he, for that matter—so why was his heart pounding? Was this love or a curse?

His father came to him and said, "Come on, let's go to the house. Come help us." He told him that the leftists and the peace activists were planning a new attack on the bulldozers. The bulldozers? The bulldozers?! He smiled with biting sarcasm. The bulldozers? The bulldozers? He kept repeating it like an idiot… Bulldozers! His father walked ahead of him, so he followed behind. Then he turned around and saw Mira carrying a sign in Hebrew with a picture of the wall. "Is it possible?" he whispered. "Maybe. Just maybe." He truly wished it could be. "Maybe. Just maybe," because his heart was still pounding. But when he reached the house and saw his mother, he forgot Mira and the "maybe" because what he saw was much more significant. He saw his mother and some of the women from the neighborhood sitting on trunks and cardboard boxes. Boxes of glassware, boxes of books, boxes of utensils and cookware, boxes of pictures. The rooms were bare; everything had been removed from the walls except for the poster. And likewise the beds had been stripped of their covers.

His mother said the wall was going to come right through the house, and his father said the wall would have to come over his dead body.

But when it came down to it, and they came with the bulldozers and the backhoes and the army's bullets, he came out of the house, bleeding.

Ahmad found his father sitting with his buddies in the refugee camp, drinking tea with marjoram and saying in despair, "This is what it's come to! Go tell your brother." But when he went to tell his brother, Majid looked about anxiously and said, "I have a meeting. Wait for me." Ahmad stood in the square waiting for him. He saw his brother talking to the television, mentioning "the Wall," mentioning "the explosion," mentioning "suicide," but he didn't mention "the people." Because the people were in the distance now, beyond the checkpoint and the wall of the imprisoned Authority, and he was under pursuit. That was why he mentioned the Wall and forgot Ahmad, and so Ahmad withdrew, slowly at first, then quickly. He realized at that moment that his brother no longer belonged to them. His father would remain there in the refugee camp and would die there, just as thousands died there, and Mira died there.

No, Mira hadn't died; his heart had begun to die, along with his mind. That was why when Suad saw him walking aimlessly in the traffic circle area, he was muttering, "Wall, explosion, wall, suicide, tomorrow the whole thing will blow up."

23

The Catholic priest passed in front of him. He saw him standing on the hill looking toward the west, an ambulance behind him. He came closer and said in a friendly way, "Hello there, Ahmad. We've heard a lot about you."

"Good or bad?"

"Good, good, of course. You're a good fellow with a good mind and a good heart and your appearance shows the goodness in your heart. Don't let the ugliness of the world blemish your heart."

He shook his head and said hesitantly, "Yes, Father." But in his heart he felt down. He was still following her with a camera lens. A digital camera. She was done playing children's games and was grown up now. He saw her in jeans, then in shorts, then in a bathing suit like a fish with freckles on her back. When he watched her he felt afraid, then sad, then joyful when she laughed and splashed in the water. Then afraid again. He saw the young men around her like butterflies around a flower. Then there was a big bus full of peace activists he could see from the hill, and she was among them. Then the bathing suit and the freckles on her back. Then the bathing suit and her bare legs.

"Remember, Ahmad, when you were little?" the priest asked. "You used to play with my rosary beads and I would sing to you."

"I remember," he mumbled shyly, nodding his head. "I remember."

He sat down beside him on the rock and looked into the horizon over the red rooftops and the settlement fence and the borders of the separation wall. The priest said, "I am sure man is much better than his actions."

Ahmad didn't comment, but many of man's actions and

words passed through his mind. He thought of the bulldozers, and Issa, and Majid, and then Mira. Was Mira better than building settlements? Was Issa better than treason? Was Majid better than the Authority? Who could believe that?

"I came here to talk to you," the priest said.

He turned to look at him without commenting. So that was it—his coming here was not a coincidence. His father had sent him.

"My father sent you?"

The priest smiled. "You've always been able to figure things out. Of course, Ahmad, your father is worried. He's afraid for you. It's a father's right to be worried, isn't it?"

He turned toward the priest. "And are you afraid?"

The priest became confused. He didn't know how to answer. If he said he was afraid, then he would be contradicting himself and things he had spoken about and preached about. And if he said he was not afraid then it meant he was not sensitive to people's concerns, the concerns of the war and all the fear and horror of all the killing. First and foremost he was one of the people, and the monastery was just like anyone else's house. When rockets fall they don't distinguish between monasteries and houses—why shouldn't he be afraid? Of course he was afraid, but should he say so? And to whom would he be saying it? To a confused adolescent who had lost touch with reality? The fear now, as his father said, was that the boy would do something crazy.

Ahmad looked directly at the priest and asked again, "And you, Father, are you afraid, too?"

He smiled patiently. "I'm afraid for you."

"And for yourself?"

"Of course I'm afraid, just like everyone else. That's natural."

"But Christ wasn't afraid?"

"Afraid of whom?"

"Afraid of the Jews and the cross and being tortured and of speaking the truth."

"Of course he was not afraid."

He smiled wickedly and tossed a stone that had been in his hand several meters into the distance. The stone rolled all the way down to the fence at the settlement and the borders of the separation wall. The priest took note of that and said anxiously, "But Christ was not a murderer."

"Who was the murderer?"

He felt as if he'd fallen into the trap. Rather than taking on the role of the wise guide, he had fallen into the trap and found himself defending his words and Christ's reactions and deeds. Had Christ been afraid? Of course not, which is how he persisted and spurred a revolution and why people followed him. So why would he expect the opposite? And why then would he be afraid of killing? Would this child end up killing?

"Didn't you used to like drawing? Where did that go?"

"It went with the wind."

"Impossible. Other things might leave a person, but not talent and artistic sense. You're an artist. You are talented. I used to say, 'this boy is going to become an artist.' Where did the art go?"

"It went with the wind," he insisted.

"No. That's impossible. Art does not go away. It might sleep. It might doze off. It might get rusty like a knife, but with a little sharpening and patience and practice, it regains its luster. Where are you now?"

"I'm with the emergency services."

"Emergency services isn't enough. You have to go back to your studies, live at home under your parents' wings. When you grow up and become mature, then you can decide for yourself."

"I am grown up," he said coldly.

"Yes, of course, but you have to go to school. You have to study. You have to succeed and do well. And when you succeed, I'll help you get a grant to go abroad."

He smiled sarcastically. "A grant to go abroad?"

He remembered Majid and al-Washmi's promise. He remembered the grapes and the wild cucumbers. He remembered the entire scene, then Bir Zeit and the music festival and Majid's singing. Where was Majid then and where was he now! In these circumstances, in this situation, with constant bombing and fighting, we were talking about getting grants and drawing pictures?

"I am sure man is much better than his actions," the priest said. "Even the Jews, do you see the Jews? Aren't they occupiers? Aren't they colonizers? Aren't they racists and didn't they elect Sharon? But there are among them some wonderful people. See that girl standing over there?"

"You mean Mira?"

"You know Mira? Have you ever spoken with her?"

Ahmad shook his head, as he remembered the cat and everything else. He remembered Issa and he remembered her father. Then Mira in her nightgown with the lace hem. But the priest didn't notice him shaking his head, so he went on with excitement, "Even Mira, even her father the settler is much better than his actions. That's the way the world is. It's a strange world. Everyone is the same way. If you were in their place, what would you do?"

"Kill and slaughter and demolish houses."

"That's not what I mean. A person is not always responsible for his actions. I mean, when a settler lives in this reality, this horrible and messed-up reality, this mixture of hatred and horror and fear, he might start believing that attacking the other can protect him. But later he can come to his senses and he can have regrets. I am sure that a person can change his mind. If we wake him up, he can have regrets."

"And how do we wake him up?"

"By calling for peace. With love and peace we can get out of all this violence. But with killing, with military operations, we can never be saved or save anyone. There is no salvation through violence. That's what Jesus said. And even in Islam, and even in their religion, peace and love are the goals of the universe. What do you think?"

"I think we should get going before dark. The sun is setting."

"No, it's not setting yet. Soon, but not yet. It'll sink down behind those hills. See the sun and the colors of the sky at sunset, and the color of the red rooftops under the eucalyptus trees? Do you smell the soil and the fragrance of the citrus groves and the summer flowers? Smell that. Smell the grass and the soil when they water it at sunset. Smell that. Look at the world and listen to the sound of the birds before they go to sleep. It's a strange world. Incredible beauty, but human beings do not understand it. Look how closed a man's mind is, and how short his vision. He thinks the world is money and fame and power and possessions and politics, and he forgets himself. He forgets that his life is a mere journey, a journey into the universe, a short journey from his mother's womb to the earth's soil. A short journey followed by the quiet of eternity and an encounter with God. And when God encounters him, he is going to judge him and ask him, 'Did you love?' and ask him, 'Did you hate?' and ask him, 'Did you kill?' What will you take with you, human being, except your deeds and a handful of soil and the beauty of your soul? That's all that remains of our world, a handful of soil and the beauty of the soul. That's what remains. Are you listening?"

"Of course I'm listening."

"So what do you think?"

Ahmad didn't answer, because he was boiling inside. Everyone was closing in on him. All his family and friends, the whole world and everyone in it. Wasn't it enough to have been tortured by the army? Wasn't Israel's siege enough? And the checkpoint at Sarda and the checkpoint at Hawara and at Qalandiya and the hundred other checkpoints he had to pass through to get from one village to another and one city to another—weren't they enough? And if not for the ambulance, he would never be able to pass through any checkpoint or take one step outside Nablus and Ayn al-Mirjan. Now everyone was surrounding him and getting on his nerves. It was a siege on his nerves and his heart and his spirit. What were they afraid of? That he would get in trouble? How stupid they were! Then he remembered the others on the TV, young men about his age or a few years older, but in their hearts and in their souls and in terms of their courage and their audacity… he envied them!

The priest said, "When I sit at the organ and play hymns and songs to my Lord, I feel my soul taking flight. My soul leaves and flies through the ceiling and the stained glass above the altar and above the Virgin and the Cross. Do you remember the color of the glass, Ahmad? Do you remember that summer when you came to the monastery to take a painting class? Remember how beautiful your paintings were? When I asked you how you came up with those colors, you pointed to the stained glass above the altar. Remember? That was when I said to myself, this boy is going to become a great artist. Your father couldn't believe what I was telling him until he saw that painting with all the colors. Where is that painting? Where is it, Ahmad? Please don't say that you threw it away. Please don't say that."

"I won't say."

"Where is the painting? What did you do with it?"

"I suppose my mother packed it away in the box with all the other pictures."

The priest remembered suddenly about the Qassam

house. The Wall was going to pass right through their house and all the houses in that neighborhood. That sensitive painting was going to stay there in the cardboard box with all the rest of the house's artwork and pictures. He hurried to change the subject back to the organ music.

"I remember the image of the altar and the sound of the organ when I play it and the people sing. When people sing hymns it makes my heart swell and take flight. I feel like I am flying and the people are flying, too. The world turns into heaven and the people into birds. How beautiful people are when they sing! I saw you weeping once, and when I asked you why, you said 'the singing.' I stood beside you under the tree and heard the people far in the distance, and when I heard them, I was going to cry, too, because I am like you. I love music and drawing and art and the beauty of the soul and I say the world is beautiful. People are beautiful. Let's consecrate this lovely moment and go say hello to your father. Your father misses you, Ahmad."

"I saw him yesterday."

"See him today, too."

"I'll see him tomorrow."

"And then what?"

Ahmad didn't answer the question, because he didn't understand what it meant. "Then what?" Then what—what? His father was always saying, "Okay, but then what?" and Suad was always saying, "Okay, but then what?" And his mother and his brother, and now this priest. What did they want? For me to say that I plan to become a martyr? As if choosing martyrdom were that simple. How stupid they were!

"Okay, but then what will you do?"

"I'm with the emergency services."

"Other than the emergency services, what are you going to do? Who are you living with and what are you reading?"

This was clearly an investigation. He felt his spirit fluttering like a bird in a cage, but he held back his anger and said, "I don't read. I don't have time."

"No. That's impossible. You must read. You've always been a great reader. You must read. Reading helps to open your mind and refine your soul."

"I read the Qur'an."

The priest became confused and quickly said, "Yes, of course. That's understood. But you should read something else, too."

"Should I read the New Testament?" he dared.

The priest turned toward the boy and took note of his sarcasm, realizing he was starting to lose him. When the priest didn't answer, Ahmad asked, "Should I read the Torah?" T he priest didn't answer. He was trying to figure out a new strategy to get to the boy's heart, in order not to lose him. But the boy was cracking from the pressure from everyone. He jumped up, brushing off his pants. "Should I read about the Crusades? Should I read about the Holocaust and the Nazis and the gas ovens? They drive us crazy with the Nazis and the gas ovens and the Berlin Wall. 'To forgive is to be generous.' 'Forget the past.' No! We won't forget it. But the present— we forget that. You can forget or not forget all you want. I won't forget. How do you expect me to forget when I'm sinking in shit and blood? You're afraid for me? Don't be! I'm with the emergency services. Tell my father I'm with the emergency services and I don't have plans for anything else. I wish I did!"

He looked behind him and saw the priest staring at him, unable to speak. He felt ashamed and sorry at the same time. He rushed to say, "I'm sorry. Forgive me, Father. Forgive me."

And he walked away muttering, "I don't have anything else. I wish I did!"

24

Suad saw him at the traffic circle again, so she caught up with him and invited him over for lunch. "We're making something really good today."

When he didn't respond she said, "*Msakhkhan* with sheep's yogurt!"

His heart swelled because *msakhkhan* to him was a wedding celebration for the stomach and all the senses. In addition to the flavor and the aroma, the sight of the chicken on the fresh *taboun* bread, soaked in the juices and olive oil and onions and sumac and the fresh yogurt still covered with a layer of cream... oh goodness! He suddenly felt alive and as though spring had sprung in the middle of summer.

"Okay," he said shyly. "I'll come."

She stood before him, laughing. "Good," she said joyfully. "So why are you frowning?" He smiled at her, so she pinched his cheek and he went back to his gloominess.

For days he hadn't eaten anything but light, cold meals. *Za'atar*, a *labneh* sandwich, bread with cheese, chickpeas and fava beans. Now he had received an impressive invitation to a meal he loved and adored. He wandered around the marketplace trying to kill time, refusing invitations from the shopkeepers to have tea and *knafeh*, so he wouldn't spoil his appetite and he could take his time eating. But when he arrived at Suad's house, he found his father waiting for him. Had he been set up? No, it was a coincidence. His father had come to greet Suad's father, who had gotten out of prison, and also to rent a house in Nablus in place of their house in Ayn al-Mirjan, which was going to be demolished.

His father greeted him coldly, because of the way Ahmad had spoken to the priest. And he was in the middle of a conversation with Suad and her brother Saeed, who had come from Amman especially to welcome his father and to tell his mother how expensive Amman was. ("Do you have some money I can borrow? I'll pay you back later.")

Suad's brother was not a very successful lawyer. Despite having graduated from Damascus with honors and having trained under one of the best lawyers in the country, his upbringing and his father's history had turned him into a nervous type, always uptight and discussing things philosophically to the point where people kept their distance from him. That was why he lagged behind in his career and felt doubly disappointed by his professional failure and his tight finances. His failure was reflected in his personality. He tended to be pushy and tense and a know-it-all. And that, of course, irritated Suad and Umm Suad, and also their guest Fadel al-Qassam, who had proved his worth over the years as a brilliant journalist with an extensive readership. In addition to the ease with which he wrote and was able to reach out to people, he also lived and experienced the situation from the inside. That was why it was so difficult for him to listen to anyone coming from the outside and saying to the people of the West Bank, "You should do this," and "You should fix that," or to explain the secrets of the political game and the fundamentals of struggle. So when he heard Suad's brother saying, "They should keep up the military operations and not leave out a single bus or airplane or little coffee shop or restaurant!" he turned to Ahmad and asked him, "What do you think?" Ahmad immediately lost his appetite, feeling that he was going to pay for this delicious meal with his nerves and end up leaving hungry. He tried to keep chewing, as he shrugged without commenting. His father looked over at Suad's father the prison graduate and asked him his opinion. Suad's father, who was still basking in people's appreciation and flattery after spending all those years in jail far from his family and people's problems, gave an answer that resembled that of his son who lived in Amman.

"Abu Saeed," the journalist asked tactfully. "What is better for the people and the cause, to lose half or lose the whole thing?"

All excited, the lawyer shouted, "Aré you saying the homeland is a slaughtered animal that can be sold by the kilo? The precious homeland is not for sale. But our sell-out leaders are sitting around measuring and cutting it up into pieces equal to their sizes—halves and quarters and fifths. In two or three years there won't be anything left to sell!"

The journalist shook his head and said sadly, "The truth is there isn't anything left. They've already taken it all. If only we had learned how to do things right and use the right tactics, it would have been possible to take something from them."

"They have not taken it all," the lawyer shouted angrily. "We're watching their every move. As long as there is still one suckling child, we will not give up. We will not kneel down."

The journalist smiled and looked around him to see the impact of such words, which he had heard a thousand times before from poets and leaders and Friday sermons. He saw Suad smiling slyly. And Umm Suad was eyeing her son with suppressed anger. His son was staring at the food and not eating. So he said, in order to lighten things up and defuse the charged atmosphere, "How's the chicken, Ahmad? Great like the people who made it, eh?"

"Thank you so much, Umm Saeed," Ahmad complimented. "The greatest *msakhkhan* from the hands of the greatest mother."

Her husband shook his head and chimed in, "Truly. She is the greatest mother. The greatest lady. The greatest cook in the world. This is delicious, Umm Saeed. This is the moment I dreamed of for years and years. A nice group of friends and loved ones and good food from your hands. You're the best of the best."

The lawyer didn't want to change the subject and lighten things up. He kept at it, saying sharply, "People who talk about forgetting everything and accepting half are defeatists. If they were to take a careful look at history, they would see and know that oppression cannot last and that colonization will eventually disappear."

Suad whispered, "Okay, Saeed. Let's eat now."

"Abu Majid, Saeed doesn't read your articles," Suad said apologetically. *Al-Quds* doesn't reach him. If he'd read your articles, he would not have said what he said."

Saeed looked at her and scolded, "What's it to you. I'm talking to him."

The mother interfered, trying to avoid a clash between brother and sister. "Stop it, Saeed. Let's enjoy our meal. Do we really have to argue? Let's eat like normal people."

The lawyer shook his head. "I'm surprised. I'm really surprised! On television we used to see you carrying weapons and carrying out military operations day after day. But now I see that you don't really care. You're sitting here eating and complimenting each other and laughing together. And some of you are saying 'Let's settle for half,' and others, 'Let's settle for a quarter,' and we outsiders don't know who to believe. Do we believe what we see on television or the reality we see on the ground?"

"What's wrong with our reality, sir?" Suad said with restrained anger.

"It's a miserable reality," he snarled. "Defeated. Incapable of liberating us. I thought the young men, all the men—young and old—were carrying weapons and up to their ears in battle."

He looked directly at Ahmad. "The way I see it you don't give a damn. You're sitting there eating while the homeland slips out of your hands."

His mother gave him a sharp look and whispered to his

father, "Who was it that said a monkey in his mother's eyes is a gazelle?" His father the prison graduate grumbled in irritation, "There is no power and no strength save in God. Enough, Saeed. Let's eat."

While eyeing his son, who had stopped eating completely, the journalist said very calmly. "It's okay. Don't worry. Let him say what he wants and get it out of his system. Do you think, Saeed, that we're sitting here laughing and playing around? We're sitting here weighed down with worry and nobody gives a damn. The Arabs don't give a damn and neither does the UN or Europe, not even you native sons who live outside. And because we are small and weak we should have done things intelligently, not taken on a challenge we couldn't handle, not I nor you nor the Authority. The Authority made a mistake and led us to this tragedy. We carried weapons bigger than ourselves and chanted slogans greater than ourselves and carried out operations that gave the enemy a cover for all their atrocities. If we had been smart, we would have understood that carrying arms and carrying out operations in this sort of reality is not the right thing to do."

Chewing without any appetite on a small morsel of food, Ahmad asked with his head down, "Okay. Then how are we supposed to resist?"

The lawyer answered with his arrogant sarcasm, "I'm sure he'll say 'with stones.'"

"What's wrong with stones, sir?" Suad asked. "At least the whole world sympathized with us then, not like now."

"Take it easy!" he shouted, as he picked over the chicken looking for the best piece. "If you could only see what happens to us when we hear of an operation being carried out! The broadcasting stations and the satellites and the Arab street everywhere from Morocco to Lebanon, they all stand behind us and applaud and say, 'That's what heroes do. That's what struggle is all about. That's what liberation is.' And we hold our heads high and say 'That's right. We're up to the challenge. We're the ones who are defending the Arabs and giving them something to be proud of.'"

"And you, too, of course, are holding your head high," Suad said sarcastically.

He looked at her spitefully. This nasty girl's tongue and her threats deserved a million slaps on the face. Under which law or which religion can a girl be so insolent toward her brother, her older brother, and taunt him about the debts he hasn't yet paid back? She was taking advantage of his situation in order to taunt him about his debts. She was saying, "You're holding your head high," because she thought debts should make him lower his head. But she was wrong. A debt is a debt, and he was going to pay it back as soon as possible. And even if he didn't pay it back, so what? Even in religion and under the law, a debt owed to your parents is not considered a debt, just as stealing from your parents is not considered theft. She should just shut up. He turned to his father and said, "I think we should marry this girl off and be rid of her."

"Someone did propose to her," her father replied gravely.

"Well, well, well!" he burst out. "Why didn't you say so earlier? Who's the lucky guy? Who's the poor fool?"

"An official in the Authority. From Nazareth. What do you think?"

"I think we should hurry things up before he gets away."

Everyone smiled except for Suad and the journalist. "No. Let's not hurry things," the journalist said anxiously. "In my opinion you should think it over carefully, because the Authority is in bad shape."

Annoyed, Suad asked, "You mean because they've been hit hard?"

"I mean because they're corrupt and in bad shape."

"But Dad, Majid is one of them!" Ahmad said.

The father shook his head several times and commented sadly, "Majid, Majid. We've lost him."

The lawyer chimed in maliciously, "Majid al-Qassam is a superstar now. He's on television and all over the news. He's a big deal. He knows how to speak, but believe me he was a better singer. He'd be better off singing and dancing."

Suad came to his defense. "Listen, Saeed, Majid was a fighter."

He chuckled. "That was once upon a time."

Ahmad fidgeted, remembering his brother half-dead in the back of the pickup truck with the butane tanks and that trip they took. During the bombardment he had whispered in his ear, "Be strong. Be brave. Don't be afraid."

"My brother got shot," he muttered. "He was fighting and they shot him. He was paralyzed for a long time."

"What about now. Is he still paralyzed?"

His mother rebuked him as she looked over at her unfortunate guest whose two sons and house had all been damaged. "That's enough, Saeed. What's with you today?"

She looked him directly in the eye so he would get the point, but he wanted to argue, as usual. He considered arguing a kind of struggle, and struggle was something he and everyone had a right to—after all he was Palestinian down to the bone, and he had the right, the full right, to say that it was all the Authority's fault, and his parents' fault, the country's fault, everyone's fault, the whole earth and the whole world's fault. Why else had he studied law?

"I'm talking about the Authority, Mother, not Majid," he said, trying to sound nice.

"What's wrong with the Authority?" asked Suad. "Did the Authority come from some faraway place?"

The mother shook her head and tried to swallow the lump in her throat. She remembered Abu Rami and all the things he used to say. She remembered the Gaza boy's baggy pants. She remembered those days when everyone was of one heart and one body. Then there was the siege and the onslaught and the Apache helicopter missiles and the tanks and the shelling. Where was her son when all that happened? Was he really closer to her than Abu Rami and the Gaza boy?

"Mother, the Authority is corrupt and needs to go," her son said.

"Where's it supposed to go?" Suad shouted.

"It should just go. And something else should come in its place," he said stubbornly and with uncontrolled malice.

"Who should come in its place?" Suad dared. "Definitely not you."

He stared at her from behind his glasses. His face twitched and he was breathing heavily. The mother saw that her two children were about to pounce on each other. She grabbed Suad's arm in order to quiet her down. She raised her palm in her son's face and said, "Listen, Saeed. You come here from Amman all worked up, not liking anything. Look here. You listen. This man (and she pointed to Abu Majid), this man had his house demolished and his children torn away from him. And this boy (and she pointed at Ahmad), this boy lost his mind when they attacked, and since then he's been wandering about totally lost. And this man (and she pointed at her exhausted, sick husband) wasted his years and his health and his youth and his nerves, and when he came out of jail he was half a human being. And this girl (she pointed to Suad) saw death with her own eyes and did not even say 'ouch.' And I, Saeed, my son, my strength, I am your mother and her mother and everybody's mother. Frankly, I am tired because I'm ruined. Do you understand what I'm saying? I'm ruined. Don't you dare tell me that Amman is expensive. Don't you dare."

She picked up her empty plate and headed toward the kitchen. Ahmad jumped up from his chair and went out the door. They called after him trying to stop him, because his plate had barely been touched. But he ran down the stairs. Suad stood at the top of the stairs calling after him. He waved his hand at her and shouted back, "I'm done. I'm done eating."

25

On her way to Ramallah, her heart pounding, answering the call of love, Suad imagined what she was going to say and what he was going to say. She remembered his eyes, his lips, and his touch. When she was young and first fell in love with him, she felt she was a flower and he was a butterfly and the world was an eternal spring. She would get dizzy, every inch of her body melting. Instead of legs she had white wings that carried her over the trees and the hills of Jerusalem, to Tunis, then to Beirut, then to the Roman columns of Jerash. The present blended with history and the ruins and the cause and the glare of feelings. It was a strange thing, a magnificent thing, to feel the whole world summarized in one person. Is that what love is? Even more than that, he represented what a man was, what a human being was, what the cause was, what an occupied country was. From where she stood on the surface of this earth, man meant this particular man, a man who loved, a man who burned with love, a man who defended what he believed in to the death. What happened after that? Why had they separated? She had discovered in him another face, the face of anger, and a man who proclaims, "You are my harem, and I am the Sultan." He didn't say that exactly, but his behavior did. A look, a movement, a touch, a gesture, they all came together like an image in a mirror.

Now here she was doing it all over again, falling in love with him a second time or a thousandth time. If he were to die and he were resurrected she would fall in love with him a second time and a third time. And then she would leave him. She would love him and leave him again, because his image always pulled her toward him, but then when he raged and his true nature rose to the surface, she would run away. She would get scared and retreat. And now here she was going back to him.

She tried to contact him and was told that he had gone to Gaza. She tried to contact him again, and she was told he had gone to Amman. She contacted him and was told he was with Abu Ammar. She contacted him and was told he was in a meeting of cabinet ministers. Days passed, then weeks, and the glow cooled. Doubt came back to her. Love no longer lulled her. She no longer yearned to see him, to say to him that her world had meaning only when she was in love with him. She no longer heard love songs and felt that the feelings were hers and his. She became afraid and preoccupied. Where would she ever figure in his life? Was she going to be his life-long companion or a rest stop for a fighter? Was she to remain with no work except for hoping and waiting? Waiting for a man who did not belong to her, who was public property, just like the national martyr statue in the middle of the square. He was not hers. He was public property.

26

Suad left, stumbling on her way out. She knew that their relationship was over. He was not going to ask about her, and she was not going to ask about him. Their love was lost and so was the joy and the green of spring. Days returned to their former depressing severity. Nothing of what she had waited for was left. How cold the world was, how empty the universe. Nothing was important. Nothing was happy. Everything was defeated. Everything was ground to dust. The private was now mixed in with the public pain and the rubble of the war and the remnants of the shattered buildings in the president's headquarters. The president's head-quarters—where the leaders and the nest of bigwigs were—was still in tatters, just like all the promises. She had nothing left to be happy about. She had nothing left to wait for.

Majid called to her. She saw him in his fancy suit and his necktie. As he passed through the square, surrounded by all the destruction and the mess and the mountains of car remnants and rubble, he seemed to be leading a wedding procession through a massive funeral. An odd image, a dissonant tune. Everything was knocked down and broken except for the suit and the necktie! And his gait was perfectly measured like that of a first-class actor walking across a stage. Where was the rage? Where was the artist? Where was his madness? The artist was gone. The rebel was gone. What remained was someone running headlong after power. Tomorrow he would climb up to the peak, or toward the bluff, atop a blood-colored rug, while we trailed behind on his heels.

He led her into his spacious office in the middle of the destruction. His office was as wide as an auditorium, with new furniture and curtains and a huge desk and telephones and video equipment and the largest screens. What was all this affluence? Was this the right atmosphere for our defeat? Was this what Palestine had hoped for? Was this the kind of atmosphere for refugee camps and victims of a catastrophe, for a defeated people who had tasted such bitterness, and who were expelled and living like beggars, waiting expectantly for assistance and charity? A people looking for a handout wearing a necktie and a fancy suit of the most expensive sort!

He told her he was very, very busy, but he wanted a favor from her. It seemed that due to the long distance and the blockades on all the cities, he hadn't heard much from his family. Recently he heard that she had been able to get into Nablus and see his father and Ahmad. Was that true? She nodded. Was it true that his father was looking for a house in Nablus to replace his house in Ayn al-Mirjan? She nodded. And was it true that Ahmad had dropped out of school for good and was working full-time with the first aid and emergency services? She nodded. And was it true that his grandmother had died during the last raid? She said, "Yes." Suddenly he shouted, "And Majid is the last to know?"

She stared at him in disbelief. What were all the telephones and cellphones and video equipment and huge screens for, then? If all this equipment didn't do him any good, then why did he spend so much energy on it? Was it all just for display?

"You mean to say that I, the eldest son, the firstborn, am the last to know or to be consulted?"

"Did you ever ask?"

He looked at her and saw before him a frowning, sallow face on which tears had dried only minutes earlier. "What's wrong?" he asked quickly.

She shook her head and whispered, "Nothing. Nothing at all."

"Tell me what's wrong."

"I said nothing."

"Okay, fine. Then I guess that's how it is. My grandmother dies, Ahmad drops out of school, the family abandons Ayn al-Mirjan, and I don't hear about it except through other people!"

She looked at him and shook her head with sorrow and regret. What was this? Is this what power did to a promising young man? Is this what position did to the heart of an artist? She remembered him singing at the campus stadium and how all the people cheered. She remembered him when he was a fugitive and he would visit them secretly and eat supper with them under the cover of night. And she remembered him half-dead in the back of the pickup under the bales of clothing. Was this all that was left of the artist, the rebel, the son of Qassam? An office and a suit and a necktie?

"And I also heard something about marriage?" he said, in a tone closer to denial.

"It's not definite."

He smiled that wide smile. "And I'm engaged, too."

"To Laura, of course."

"No way," he laughed. "Never."

She stared at him, so he repeated, with his hand over his heart, "Laura al-Washmi? No. No way."

She stood up quickly, so he stood up, too, behind his desk and said in his own defense, "Laura is not suitable for marriage."

She didn't comment. She took a few steps toward the door.

"And neither is that guy from Nazareth suitable for you," he shouted after her.

She turned to look sharply at him.

"He's a loser, barely making it, doing everything the hard way, as if the world will ever change!"

"You've changed."

He pretended not to hear her. "You couldn't find anyone but him? That loser? Between you and me, they're all sorry sorts. Ask me, I know. I know all of them. I know every single one of them."

"And do you know yourself?"

He gazed into space, trying to digest what she meant, for she had left and shut the door behind her.

27

Ahmad picked up his camera and began taking pictures. At first he leaned against the front of the ambulance, but then he was taken in by the scene and moved closer to the events, forgetting the emergency services. Crowds of protesters and peace activists of all colors and nationalities were very calmly and quietly heading toward the Wall. It was like a funeral procession with no announcements, no provocation of tanks or members of the army, no sudden movements or chaos. It was an exemplary demonstration, and the weather was beautiful. A clear blue sky, a gentle breeze, and the fragrance of wild grass and fresh soil. Everything seemed like a dream. Milky-white rocks, silvery olive groves, and henna-red soil. Diaphanous summer days atop hills of extraordinary beauty. And the colorful shirts and sweaters were like spring flowers: red, green, yellow, blue, all against a background like a work of art.

"O Lebanon, slice of Heaven, your name upon my lips is a prayer." The song by Wadi' Safi came to him as he took pictures, so he hummed the tune and wondered if Lebanon was as beautiful as this. He had never been to Lebanon, or Syria, or even Jordan. His whole life had been lived like a prisoner in this canton. He was born here and grew up here and lived through all the events from the inside, dreaming always of getting out. His brother had told him that Amman was like the movies—palaces and bridges and nightclubs and wide streets and parks. And there were five-star hotels where Arabs from the Emirates and Saudi Arabia stayed, their robes dripping with black gold. Black gold? Oil gold, you fool. Oil gold! Oil gold and jewels and cars, just like in the movies. Villas and scantily-dressed girls, like in the movies, dancing and prancing around. And here we are in this pen like baby chicks in a chicken coop. That's what he used to say. Now he was far away. Position and power had stolen him away. The last time he saw him on TV, he had muttered to himself, "Like the movies, like Amman and oil gold and five stars. Like the movies." But here now, with the almond and olive-grove adorned hills, and the soil, and the beautiful tune wafting above, on top of this velvety painting, we were firmly on the ground.

O Palestine, slice of Heaven, your name upon my lips is a prayer. A powerful emotion befell his heart, striking chords that fear had quieted. The days of the battles and the aggression and the shrieks of the killed and wounded faded into the distance behind him. There was nothing else in that world, in his memory, except a tune that extended all the way to the horizon, like a blue summer prayer of extraordinary tenderness. Was prayer blue in color? Was blue the color of God? Was blue the color of love, or was it red? And if God were to imagine, would he imagine this, or Mecca? Mecca is a desert. Our country on the other hand was the land of olives, the land of wild herbs and fennel and thyme, the land of God. That's what the Catholic priest said. But the sheikh at the mosque said Mecca was the land of God. Who was right?

She came near. Through the lens he saw her enlarged face. Brown freckles on white skin, a tiny peanut-sized nose, and red lips the color of anemones. She was so beautiful! But she had stolen Amber.

She touched his shoulder and said, "Akhmed." He pretended not to hear her. He heard her jabbering in English with a blonde foreigner. The foreigner reached out and covered the lens with her hand and said, "Hey! Are you Akhmed?"

He looked over at them, a shy smile on his face. He didn't look directly at Mira and poured all his attention on the other girl. She was blonde with short, soft hair like Mira's. And she had freckles like Mira. And she was short and slender and petite like Mira. When he looked at her, he looked down at her from above as if he were talking to a child, which made him feel confident. He was taller than her. He was taller than Mira, too—taller than everyone. He was taller than Majid, much taller. His father had said to him joking, "You're as tall as a giant, the tallest student in your whole school!" With that he meant to remind him of school, so Ahmad had said, "I'm with the emergency services."

The young girl asked him if he understood her, so he answered her in half-decent English, "Of course I understand."

Mira asked, "Then why don't you answer?"

Without thinking he blurted, "Because you're a dirty thief."

Mira laughed and said, "I'm a thief?"

"You stole Amber," he said coldly.

The other girl turned to Mira and asked, "Who's Amber?"

With her smile still wide on her face, Mira stared at him and said, "Amber is a cat."

"Amber is a cat?"

"His cat."

She turned and asked him politely, "You have a cat?"

He didn't reply. He got the feeling she thought it was a big deal for him, an Arab, to have a cat or a dog. Weren't Arabs crude bastards? Weren't Arabs insensitive and tasteless? Weren't they terrorists like bin Laden?

"I have a Siamese cat," she said. "Do you like cats?"

He didn't reply. He felt she was getting close to him out of curiosity and nothing more. Or maybe out of concern for human rights, or some kind of teenage rebellion against her parents and the government system, or society, or Bush and Blair and the Iraq war, or globalization and Christian Aid and Catholic Relief and similar things. Charity, in other words. In other words, they're the stronger ones and we're the orphans, like America and the Native Americans, or New Zealand and the Maori. Meaning what? Meaning charity, sacks of flour, dry milk, and armies crushing us in Baghdad and the United Nations and all over the place.

She touched his arm and looked him straight in the eye, "Do you understand me?"

"I understand. I understand."

She touched his camera and said, "Wow! Nice camera!" So he pulled the camera away and spontaneously shoved her a little. The two girls laughed and exchanged looks with each other as if they were conspiring against him, which made him blush.

The foreign girl said, "Want some coffee?"

She gestured toward a little thermos like a whiskey flask, but he shook his head no. "What's wrong with him?" she asked Mira. "Is he upset? Is he upset with you? Apologize to him."

"I'm very sorry," Mira said with a mean laugh.

He looked at her and didn't respond. "Very sorry?" Was that what he got in the end? "Very sorry?" I took Amber, very sorry. I broke your heart, very sorry. They crushed what innocence you had in you, very sorry. They took everything, took his mind. Was anything left of his mind? His father had said, "Without schooling you'll end up with no mind." And Suad had said, "Without schooling you'll end up an ignoramus." But no mind was better. What was the good of having a mind in this place?

The girl said, "My name is Rachel."

She reached out to shake his hand, so he shook it, very coldly. The name Rachel sounded Hebrew to him. Like "Raheel" or "Sara," like "Jacob" or "Hagar" or "Leah." What should we do with that history? They dug up that whole history and dug us up, too. But where were we from, after all?

They were from Sarah and we were from where? And this Rachel came from where? Wasn't it London or New York? She came here in the name of history to take what was left of history and to take what was left of our minds.

"What is the meaning of 'Rachel'?" he asked.

"It means 'Raheel,'" she said. "It's an ancient name from the Torah. I don't know."

"So it's Jewish?"

The two girls looked at each other and laughed, covering their mouths with their hands.

"Stop!" he yelled indignantly, which made them laugh and giggle and squirm even more, and stomp the ground with their feet every time they looked at him or at each other, as if there was some secret between them.

"I have to go," he said angrily. The girl held onto him and pleaded, "No. No. Stay."

He gave them each a dirty look and said, "Why are you laughing? At what and at who?"

Mira's face suddenly appeared serious and she said sincerely, "Because you said 'Jewish' as if Jews were something to be afraid of."

He looked at her and shook his head in amazement. Even now, after all the killing, after all the lies and the crimes, they were saying Jews weren't something to be afraid of? Of course they were frightening—very frightening.

Rachel said, "I'm a Christian. I used to be a Christian. I mean, I have no religion."

She saw how he was staring, so she pointed to Mira to emphasize, "And Mira has no religion."

Surprised, he asked, "But what about her father?"

Mira pursed her lips and shrugged her shoulders and Rachel sneered, "What does she have to do with her father?"

He didn't reply, because ever since he got to know the priest, or rather revived his relationship with the priest and they got into all those topics, topics like science and drawing and art and playing the organ and the desert of Mecca and the land of the Old Testament and the Mount of Olives, he no longer knew which was closer, Mecca or Jerusalem.

She kept after him, "Do you have a religion or no religion?"

He answered evasively, "If I have a religion or if I don't have a religion, what does it matter to you?"

"Of course it does," she said clearly. "Young people in the West don't have a clue. They don't care about the synagogue or the church. But for you here in the Middle East, religion is important. It's a big deal. You want my opinion? Religion is history, but that's all."

Mira nodded her head and agreed, "Religion is history."

"Do I have a history or no history?"

Rachel waved her hand and said, "Religion, religion. What have we got to do with it?"

He said, "Religion is important. People without religion are like lost people."

She said slowly, to make herself clear, "Religion is logic. Religion is humanity. Human rights. Animal rights. The right to education and air and water and even the ozone. Religion is history. What's it got to do with us? Leave history to the academics and the bookshelves. Religion is humanity."

He looked at her, doubtful. The West, after eating its fill, after eating too much, had come here to preach to us about the ozone? We had no land, no sky, and no rights. We had no environment and no humanity. And she was saying religion belonged on bookshelves? If they take away religion, what will be left? The ozone?

"You have no religion? I am religious. To me religion is more important than food."

"More important than food?"

Rachel shouted, "Do you know what you are saying?"

"Religion is faith," he said. "Religion is identity and nationality and history, too. If religion goes, what would remain?"

In unison the two girls said, "The conscience."

He shook his head and smiled a doubtful smile. What was this? The Jewish girl was saying, "conscience," and the Western girl was saying, "conscience"! The satiated telling the hungry to go on a diet!

"What's your origin?"

"My origin?" she asked in surprise. "What do you mean?"

"I mean, like, what country are you from?"

"England."

"Ah." He smiled bitterly. "The origin of this whole mess, this calamity."

"I'm the origin of this calamity?"

He pointed at Mira and said sharply, "You're the ones who brought them here. The Balfour Declaration and all the rest. Go back to history."

She glared at him in disbelief and said angrily, "What have I got to do with them and Balfour and history? Or should I tell you? You're history."

He put his hand over his heart, "You're saying I'm history?"

"Yeah. You're history."

"You mean I'm backward?"

She didn't answer. Instead she turned around, walked a few steps away from him, and looked toward the demonstration in the distance. She tugged on Mira and said, "Let's go. They're way ahead of us."

The two walked off, leaving him standing there wondering to himself what she meant. What did she mean by "history" and what did she mean by "ozone" and "no religion"? After a few steps, she turned to him and shouted, "Are you coming with us?"

He shrugged his shoulders and said dryly, "I'm with the emergency services."

28

It was an exemplary demonstration, but then it broke loose, bullets flew, and he started taking pictures. He took pictures of young men scattering into the trees and down under the trees, throwing stones and bottles while the army trailed after them like hound dogs. One of them jumped over the fence and another crawled under the tires and a third one climbed up on top of a tank. Ten here and twenty there, like little devils, some of them little kids not yet out of elementary school with their backpacks still hanging on their shoulders.

A peasant woman pounded her chest and shrieked, "The olives! The olive trees! There goes your livelihood, Subhiyya!" The soldier pushed her out of the way and a bulldozer tore one of the trees out of the ground, right from its roots. Bulldozers were like dinosaurs. They had mouths as big as whales that devoured trees and rocks and stones and the depths of the earth, ripping them apart and eating everything that was disturbed and broken before dumping the rest to the side and diving deeper into the earth. The jaws plunge in while the head goes around like a mythical dragon and the tires dig monstrous tracks and crush what's left of the branches and the rocks and the beautiful stones. The beautiful stones! Like bellies of pregnant women or milk-filled breasts, harboring clusters of moss and anemones and snapdragons. The beautiful stones! So full of the most beautiful childhood days. How we remembered them in our exile and how we pondered their beauty at sunset when they were dyed the color of the sun or when they glimmered in the rain like mirrors. The beautiful stones! The whale-jaws pushed forward and chomped the stones as if they were sugar cubes, their fangs and limbs screeching as they chewed. Take a picture. Take a picture. This is history. Click. Click. The earth's grief. Click. Click. People's pain. Click. Click. While Wadi' Safi sings the praises of the beauty of the earth and of heaven and the beautiful sea breeze. And that self-satisfied British woman talks about the environment, talks about the ozone, talks about humanity. In this atmosphere there's no such thing as environment, no such thing as ozone, no such thing as humanity. There's only bulldozers trampling what is left of good health and what is left of sound mind. If the mind goes, what will be left? History?

She said religion was history. So let the British one present herself and show us the conscience of her forbears as they demolish the Baghdad Museum and human beings and the color of ozone. They say religion is merciless, that our religion shows no mercy. But, dear Rachel, what about you? Do you and your people have a religion? She said, "No religion."

He saw his father through his lens. His father had taken part in the demonstration procession and then he rushed to his house to stand by it. He sat cross-legged on the front stoop. He declared the bulldozer would not pass except over him, over his own body. That was what he had said before and then retreated. But this time, this time he carried it out. The forward rush, the cries of all the people, the tanks, the army's gunfire and the throwing of stones all strengthened and fortified him and he lost his mind. The soldier grabbed him by the neck and dragged him like a sheep as he struggled in defiance. Ahmad watched as the soldier kicked his father and he remembered that trip to Nablus in the pickup truck. Getting kicked like that is extremely painful, especially in the stomach and the guts. He saw his father vomit. He ran toward the scene but the soldiers blocked the way. He saw the Thatcherite girl running toward the house to protect his father. She opened her arms wide in the shape of a cross and started screaming, "Stop! Stop!" but the bulldozer kept going "Stop! Stop!" like an earthquake shaking the earth violently and tearing it asunder and marching forward like the legendary roc and tottering like a ghoul. She walked toward it like a cross, her arms stretched wide and her blonde hair blown about by the summer glare. The bulldozer crept and staggered forward while the driver sat up on top of its head, a head of glass shining in the sun's glare. And the driver shone, too, for he was wearing eyeglasses like a frog or a deep-sea diver. The driver didn't budge, didn't move, didn't give any indication that he understood. A piece of steel, a mechanical man, an iron man, with glasses like a frog.

They screamed, "Stop!" But he didn't stop. They pummeled him with stones, but he didn't stop. A peasant woman beat her chest with her fists and the young men cried, "*Allahu Akbar*! God is great!" but God was setting down the course of history. History marched forward like the hands of Big Ben toward a girl who dreamed of love and the human conscience. The British woman beneath the tires. Click. Click. She had no religion. Take a picture. She has become one of us. She became a saint the moment the Catholic priest pronounced her dead.

They carried the girl and put her behind him. Mira was crying and sobbing and his father was shouting, "Don't, son." He was still saying, "Don't, son!" After all the harm and the insults and the house getting crushed like an eggshell or breadcrumbs, "Don't, son!" And Mira was yelling and screaming, "Go on! Hurry up!" He saw her crying and remembered how much he cried when they arrested him after the cat incident. How he wished he could make her weep a thousand tears for each one of his own. If only he could torture her the way he was tortured. If only he could double-cross her the way she double-crossed him the night she handed him over like prey to the soldiers and the night guards. She used to cry when she was little. She cried out of fear, not for his pain. She didn't cry over him or because of him. And now she was crying because of the soldiers, her soldiers, their soldiers. You bitch! I loved you so much! Now you're crying? Alligator tears! You're beautiful. How I loved you and carried you around with me—a picture near my heart beneath my sweater—and I imagined you like a bird and apricot blossoms as I gazed at your hair on the swing as it flew and billowed on a kite, a paper kite, a spiritual kite in the distant horizon caressed by the summer breeze and the desires of an adolescent dreaming of love. Dreaming of the picture and the cat and the beautiful hair. You are beautiful, but in this atmosphere, there's no beauty, there's no humanity.

Here there are soldiers, there are tanks, and my father cries like a baby and says, "Don't," and Umm Suad says, "Don't," and the Gaza boy's mother told him, "Don't."

He sees the driver in the bulldozer staring from behind his frog glasses. The invisible man. Like a machine. Not moving and not showing any understanding or compassion, just going forward. He comes closer with his monstrous machine and the young men shout, "Go back. Back up. Back up." He looks into his side-view mirror and sees the soldiers. Five, seven, ten or more.

Mira screams, "Back up! Back! Go back!" And the bulldozer comes closer to Ahmad. Ahmad backs up, then turns and sees the soldiers facing him. They see him approaching the checkpoint. A round of bullets is fired at the ambulance. The glass shatters and flies apart. "Go. Go!" the young men shout. "Step on it! Go!" Ahmad steps on the gas pedal, muttering like a lunatic, "Sons of bitches!" Anger overpowers fear and the world becomes a blur through his tears. All he sees is his father's arms waving and Mira shouting, "Hurry up! Hurry up!" Another round of bullets and he loses his senses. He takes pictures of the events like he's making a movie. Fast forward. But it's an overexposed film. He's filming, without taking pictures, inside his mind, what mind he has left. He surges forward with all his might, like a rocket, toward the soldiers.

Five, seven, ten, or more. He can't tell. His mind has gone blank. He sways. His soul flies up like a kite, like ozone. His father cries, "My son has been martyred!"

The next day we heard what they said on the news. "Terrorism," they said. "Terrorism."

Notes

3 The Nakba (literally, disaster, catastrophe, cataclysm) refers to the plight of Palestinians during and after the 1948 war and occupation of Palestine. The Naksa (literally, setback, relapse) refers to the 1967 mass displacement and dispossession of Palestinians during and after the Six-Day War.

4 *waqf*: religious endowment in Islam, typically devoting a building or plot of land for religious or charitable purposes

6 *halawa*: Arabic for halvah, a confection made of sesame and honey

8 *Ghazl-il-Banat*: cotton candy (here, the title of a film)

12 *tanzims*: militant organizations. The Palestinian Tanzim is the name of a particular organization formed during the Intifada and associated with Fatah.
La hawla wa la quwwata illa bil-llaah: There is no power and no strength save in God (Qur'an).

13 *knafeh*: an Arabic sweet made of shredded filo dough, cheese, and sugar syrup

15 *fattoosh*: a tangy salad made with toasted Arabic bread

17 *dabke*: traditional dance, with stomping steps

30 *Achat, shtayim, shalosh, arba*, etc: Mira counts to four in Hebrew, and then Ahmad counts as well, first in Arabic, and then also in Hebrew.

36 *Haati*: Let me have it.

40 *Maayi', saayi', daayi'*: Melting, submissive, lost

43   Umm Ahmad's calling Majid "mom" is an instance of a common endearment in Arab culture and language. The practice of the mother addressing her child as "mom" and the father his child as "dad"—and uncles and aunts addressing their nieces and nephews as "uncle" and "aunt"—is used within families, as if to gently remind the child who is talking.
Shater Hasan: Egyptian boy folk-hero

44   mukhtar: a traditional village mayor in charge of helping with simple official and legal matters, such as registering a birth or a marriage.
baladiyyeh: an official governing body similar to a town hall; also called a municipality

48   al-Washmi: literally, the tattooed one

49   *muwashshah*: classical Arabic song; a strophic composition of Arabic poetry popularized in al-Andalus, Arab Spain
meze: hors d'oevres, traditionally including hummus, baba ghannouj, tabbouleh, *labneh*, various kinds of cheese, olives, various salads and vegetables, sausages, and other meats, all served in small dishes with fresh, toasted Arabic bread

50   LBC: the Lebanese Broadcasting Corporation

61   al-Washsham: the mighty, the tattooer

70   *majd*: glory
Majid: glorious

73   *mawwal*: a poem in colloquial language often sung to the accompaniment of a reed pipe; also an introductory melisma to a song, like a prelude

76   *qanun*: a flat, trapezoid, zither-like plucked instrument, which is played on the lap and has 78 strings arranged in

triplets and held by a bridge over a fish-skin patch
Mughr al-Thuwwar: literally, cave of the revolutionaries
Sheikh al-Imad: literally, Imad means the most steadfast
one

78   *mirjan*: pink coral

82   *tayyun*: Linula viscosa

117   Aziza: dear one, precious

134   *adon*: sir
hajji: a Muslim who has made the pilgrimage to Mecca;
here, Majid's grandmother

140   PBC: Palestinian Broadcasting Corporation

143   mihrab: niche for prayer in a mosque, part facing closest
to Mecca
Fatiha: the short first sura of the Qur'an, used by Muslims
as an essential element of ritual prayer

149   *Ya layl*: O night

159   Surat Yassin: The 36th chapter of the Qur'an. It has 83 ayat
(verses) and was revealed in Mecca; recited for the dying.
Ayat al-Kursi: Verse 255 of Surat al-Baqarah (the chapter
of the cow), the second chapter of the Qur'an. Called the
Qur'an's greatest verse

168   *shahada*: the Muslim profession of faith: "There is no god
but God, and Muhammad is His messenger."

174   *msakhkhan*: bread-wrapped chicken, roasted with sumac
and onions and other spices
179   *kibbeh*: a dish of ground meat, usually lamb, with bulgur
wheat and seasonings, eaten cooked or raw

180   *sambousek*: meat pies
         Umm arba'a w-arba'a een: Arabic word for centipede; literally, lady of 44 legs

183   under the Sulta: under the Palestinian Authority
         salata: salad; here, a play between the words "sulta" and "salata," which are spelled the same in Arabic, since the language uses only consonants: s-l-t.

184   *serwal*: traditional very full, baggy pants

210   *shahidan*: martyr, witness

214   Abu Satour: Mr. Machete
         Abu Nadour: Mr. Binoculars
         Abu Jildeh: Mr. Whip

240   *mujahid*: freedom fighter

251   *za'atar*: a blend of spices—thyme, sumac, and sesame
         labneh: strained yogurt, somewhat like cream cheese

276   roc: a gigantic mythological bird in the Arabian Nights

Acknowledgments

I would like to thank the women of Hosh al-Atout in old Nablus who opened their memories to me like windows through which I was able to see their experience of the events. If not for their detailed accounts and the depth of feeling they conveyed I would not have been able to capture the atmosphere or visualize the tragedy. I would also like to acknowledge with deep gratitude the work of my friend and colleague Rashid Hilal, Abu Ammar's attendant journalist. Everything described in the scenes detailing the siege of President Arafat's compound in the spring of 2002 was borrowed from (indeed, some passages are taken verbatim) or inspired by Hilal's personal account, which he published in the Kuwaiti daily *Al-Watan* that year.